I0763346

THE CROW AND THE KING

E.G. STONE

A Tarney Brae Creative Endeavours Production

Cover by Keylin Rivers

 Created with Vellum

He who does not understand your silence will not understand your words
- Elbert Hubbard

This book is for the people who understand silence

CONTENTS

CHAPTER 1

The horse was frustrated. It was bad enough that the day was hot, but to have to put up with a pain in his hoof and a fidgeting rider was too much. The boy was young and clad in silk and velvet and was feeling the heat of the sun's just as much. The horse danced along the dirt path and tossed his head in an attempt to loosen the reins. The boy, much too small for the horse, tugged on the reins. Hard.

With an outraged whinny, the horse reared backwards and tossed his rider. The boy rider slipped off the great saddle and onto the ground with a thud. Dust clouds flew and the boy spoke words no nobleman, let alone a child, should say. He got up, nursing his bruises and pride, and attempted to catch the flighty horse, blinking fiercely to keep tears from his eyes.

"If you cannot keep that seat, you should not be riding," a deep voice said, tones sharp with disdain. The speaker came closer on another horse, his clothes of a green brocade to match the ones the boy wore. His father. His deep-set features were curled in annoyance. "Get on the horse, boy, or you will walk the remainder of the way to Kyper."

The young boy glared at his horse and moved towards the saddle, grasping at the leather. A slight cough had both the boy and his father freezing.

"Actually, erm, my lord, the horse would have thrown your son no matter what he did," a third voice said. "One of the shoes is made wrong."

The nobleman whirled around to face a lean youth with short black hair and fine, fair features. The youth was of average height and skinny, obviously from the malnourished diet of the peasants that he so obviously was. The brown breeches and grey patched shirt bespoke his station and hung loosely on his frame. The youth could have been no more than sixteen years of age, and despite the worn clothes, was beautiful and could have been born of the faeries. No matter his appearance, the youth had dared to contradict a nobleman. He would be punished.

"What do you know of such things?" the man wheeled his horse around to stand next to the lad. He sneered down at the youth. "Are you a hostler, perhaps?" he hissed.

The youth took a step backwards, shaking his head. "No, I don't pretend to know anything about horses. But I am a blacksmith apprentice and I know when a shoe is made wrong." The nobleman leaned over to peer more closely at the youth. He saw green eyes shining back at him with honesty and an inner hidden wall of steel that told of strength. The youth had obviously seen more of life than most men, yet he still looked back at the nobleman with eagerness and curiosity rather than the deference and fear of most peasants.

Frankly, the nobleman wasn't sure what to do.

"If you want, I can fix it. I don't have a fire and it's not great to work on cold steel, but it should last until the nearest town," the youth said, smiling and shrugging his shoulders.

"What is your name, lad," the nobleman asked, tone softening slightly but giving no leeway to the youth. As far as he was concerned, the faerie-child could just move along and be grateful that he hadn't been punished.

"Folks call me Crow, my lord, er..." the lad replied, furrowing his brows and looking up at the man in question. The noble raised his chin slightly, acknowledging his superiority.

"Duke of Westmont. Boyd Garner, Duke of Westmont. This is my son and heir, Thomas," the man said. Crow immediately bowed low, the pack on his shoulders shifting awkwardly as he did so.

"Duke," Crow said, straightening but still keeping his head inclined slightly, as was only proper. The Duke raised his shoulders at the proper response to his title. Not all peasants were so polite or knowledgeable. Perhaps the youth really did know what he was about. Crow pointed to the horse Thomas had finally managed to still. "Would you like me to see about the shoe?" he asked.

The Duke snorted, but waved his hand in assent. Crow took the pack off and opened it, revealing a few bundles of clothes and some hammers. He pulled out a decently sized hammer and stuck it in his belt, moving to the horse. Thomas glared at Crow as the youth approached, but said nothing, eyeing his father carefully. Crow bowed slightly to the young boy, "My lord." Thomas straightened and tilted his nose upwards, looking away.

With a shrug, Crow moved to the horse, lifting up the offending hoof. He pried the metal off with his bare hands, an unexpected show of strength from the skinny youth. The baggy shirt hid much of the boy's muscle. The horse snorted in response.

Crow moved to a rock off the side of the path and started pounding the metal into shape, frowning at the cold steel. The Duke moved closer, intrigued. "Where are you from and who is your master to have taught you this?"

Crow shrugged mid-swing, an odd sight. "I lived out by Hotun and my master—" his eyes clouded for a moment before clearing, "was ol' Sythfeld. He died in the last wave of fever to pass through. The new smith didn't want an apprentice. So I set out for Barem."

The Duke started laughing, a full-bellied sound that only came at the expense of others. Crow furrowed his brow in confusion, holding the mended shoe in his hand. He put it back on the hoof and moved over to the pack, the question unspoken. The Duke stopped laughing long enough to explain. “Lad, you passed Barem twenty miles back. You’re about a mile from Kyper, the capital.”

“Oh,” Crow said, sounding surprised but not put-out. A cheerful disposition, indeed. He scratched his head. “Well, alright, then.”

The young lord huffed indignantly at being ignored in favour of this peasant youth and clambered his way back onto the horse, only making the creature snort in annoyance. Crow didn’t move to help, knowing Thomas would only take it as an affront. Thomas indicated to his father that he was prepared to move on, but the Duke was watching the youth, fascinated. He shifted in his saddle and cleared his throat.

“If you are looking for a new master, I know of one that might be in need of an apprentice,” he said. Crow brightened and beamed, his eyes suddenly greener and more intense than before.

“That would be wondrous, your Grace,” Crow grinned. The Duke chuckled and clucked to his horse, moving along and satisfied with his solution. Thomas fell in behind and Crow took his cue to fall into step a few feet behind that.

“Isn’t Crow a bird?” Thomas drawled angrily, not used to being ignored by his father, especially not in preference of a lowly blacksmith apprentice.

“Yep. Folks took to calling me that because of my black hair. It stuck and I’ve been Crow ever since,” the pale-skinned blacksmith replied, ignoring the slight. The boy huffed and kicked his heels into the side of his mount, moving away from Crow. He only shook his head and smiled, trotting along in the rear.

After a mile, the forested hills opened up into a large, flat plain and the capital city of the Garth states came into view. Crow swallowed a gasp, but stared with wide, astonished eyes at Kyper, City of Kings. The outer city was made up of a myriad of buildings, some stone and some thatched, pressed together along streets of pressed dirt. It was a glorious collection of people, colour, sounds and smells that were so different from the open land behind. The trio moved through the city, getting closer to the inner walled city. At the wall, there was an open-air market where people flocked to buy and sell an enormous amount of wares. Crow slowed his pace to try and take in the entire sight, nearly losing the Duke of Westmont in the process. He realised he was being left behind and jogged to catch up.

Much to the youth's surprise, the Duke did not stop at any of the small forges or farriers shops along the way. He just kept riding towards the far edge of the city, where Kyper Palace sat. It was surrounded by another stone wall, tall enough to keep people out but not shut them out. The closer they got, the larger the streets and houses became, and the fewer the common folk were. Crow spotted guards wearing the royal crest at the entrance to the Palace grounds. The nobleman rode straight past the guards in leather armour without anything more than a single glance. They, in return, ducked their heads deferentially and let him pass. Crow went in unremarked, possibly forgotten by the Duke.

It wouldn't be surprising, Crow thought. Nobles often forgot about peasants and didn't bother to interact unless they were demanding a service or deference. Peasants, on the other hand, never forgot about nobles.

The courtyard in which they found themselves took Crow's thoughts from politics to pure wonderment. It was large. Large enough to host the open-air market they had recently passed and still have room to manoeuvre. The ground was tightly cobbled with plants in beds along the edges of the wall and the Palace itself. There were a few buildings along the wall—kitchens, a guard's hut, a small store room and a path that led behind the Palace, presumably to the stables, barracks and training yards—before a body could even reach the Palace. And when his eye was finally drawn there, Crow couldn't help but stop and stare.

The Palace was made of beautifully hewn stone, each piece fitting perfectly in with the one before. There were two enormous wooden doors leading inside and windows everywhere. The lower windows were all done in vibrant stained glass murals, the upper clear and shining. The sheer size of the building had Crow craning his neck to look at the taller tiers.

Crow was pulled from his reverie by an amused voice, "Crow, come." He snapped to attention and ran to catch up with the Duke. The nobleman had already dismounted his horse and handed it off to a waiting servant and was watching Crow expectantly. The youth followed obediently, sneaking a glance over his shoulder at the edifice behind him. When he realised where they were going, his attention focused straight ahead, a jaunt to his step. The forge.

It was little more than yard backing the wall with a roof overhead to keep out the rain, sitting next to a stone building where the smith probably lived. It was larger than any of the other forges in Kyper and there were well-made tools set about, a fire flickering in the actual forge, its heat blazing forth. Crow practically ran to go investigate when a large, dangerous-looking man came out of the house, his face set in a permanent scowl.

He was tall and barrel chested, his body packed with immense muscle that took a lifetime to develop. His face was covered in soot and unshaven hair, which precisely matched the uneven, unruly cut on the man's head. There were numerous burns and scars on his arms and face, and he walked with purpose in his stride. Crow immediately admired the smith and did not cower from his harsh gaze.

"Yer Grace, Duke of Westmont," the smith growled, bowing slightly at the waist. He inclined his head to the boy, "Lord Thomas."

Without preamble, the Duke pushed Crow forwards, smiling broadly. "I have found you an apprentice." Crow looked at the Duke in slight astonishment and was about to mutter something polite when the smith came forwards, sticking his crooked nose into the faerie-child's face. He snorted and shook his head.

"I don' need no 'pprentice, 'specially no stick," he said, voice low and gravelly.

"Hear me out, Master Smith," the Duke said, using

the man's proper title to try and gain sympathy, his tone haughty at the slight to his find. Crow doubted the tactic would work, but you never could tell with nobles. "This boy spotted a mis-made shoe on Thomas' horse and fixed it with only his bare hands and a hammer. He is very skilled."

The smith fixed his gaze on Crow again, almost outraged. "Ye worked on cold metal?"

"It was only a temporary fix," Crow said. "Better than going without a shoe."

The man curled his nose and shook his head, moving away into the firelight of the forge. "I don' need no 'pprentice."

"Just give the lad a trial," the Duke exasperated. "Then you can judge for yourself."

The smith gave a glance of indignation to the Duke—though he quickly stifled it—before turning to Crow once more. After a moment of silence, the smith growled and stepped inside the shop to the rack of hammers. He pulled out a large one, testing its weight and eyeing Crow. He thrust the hammer and a pair of tongs out to the youth, who immediately grinned and set his pack on the ground. The smith gestured to a pile of mismatched horse shoes on a work bench.

"Make a shoe big enough fer a fair sized gelding, like them others," the man ordered. "I'll see your work when you're done."

Crow wasted no time moving into the fenced-off yard. He made sure the forge was hot enough, using the massive bellows to blow air over the coals before he heated a bar of iron and turned to the shoes. He picked through them until he found one of a size he liked. After running his hands over the metal piece, he put it back in the pile and turned to the fire. He pulled the heated metal out of the forge and onto the anvil, striking it with power in each stroke. Crow beat the metal flat before bending it into the proper shape, thrusting it back into the fire for the final touches. He punched out holes for the nails and then reheated the metal one last time, pulling it out at the perfect temperature and dousing it in a barrel of oil beside the fence for the heat treating.

When the steam and fire had abated, Crow handed the shoe to the smith, ignoring the residual heat in the metal. The smith blinked in surprise as he inspected the piece, comparing it to the others in the pile.

"Well?" the Duke asked expectantly, folding his arms over his finery.

"I'd say tha's the best work I've seen in a fair while. I'll take ye on, lad," the smith was no longer addressing the Duke, but focused his entire attention on Crow.

"Wonderful. Do you need funding for the boy? I found him, after all, and I feel rather responsible for his well-being," the Duke reached for his full coin purse. The smith scoffed and shook his head.

"His Majesty provides an allowance fer when I take a 'pprentice," the smith waved the Duke away. Seeing that his debt for fixing the shoe had been repaid in full—and then some, likely—the Duke of Westmont waved his son after him and walked away with only a friendly clap on

Crow's shoulders in farewell. Crow was too busy admiring his new master to care what the noble did.

Crow stood in the forge, hands fidgeting with the fabric of his breeches, eyes taking in every detail of the forge. He had a smile on his face and he looked almost ethereal in his joy. The smith saw this as he studied the lean frame and fair features. He was an unusual blacksmith, but there was hidden strength there, the smith decided. "What's yer name?" he asked the youth.

"Folks call me Crow," was the cheerful response, the smile turning into a grin that lit up his features. The smith grunted.

"I'm Jek. No Master. No Sir. Just Jek, got that?" the smith grumbled. He pointed to Crow's pack, "Pick that up, Crow, and we'll get you situated in the house. Yer lucky I've a spare room."

Crow did as he was told and followed the smith to the house. It wasn't terribly large, with only two rooms flanking a central area with a table and make-shift kitchen, but it was well kept. Jek led Crow to an obviously abandoned room which was full of dust, as well as a small bed and tub. "This here's yer room. Ye can get water from the well near the kitchens. Clean yerself up an' then we'll see what we can do with ye. I don' want to see hide nor hair of ye until yer clean, got that?"

"Yessir," Crow chirped easily. Jek threw him a glare, but Crow didn't waver in the slightest. Sighing, the big man left, closing the door behind him. Crow deposited the pack on his bed and did his best to clear out some of the dirt, though that would require a proper broom.

Crow wiped fervently at a small window that looked over an alcove into an overgrown garden that likely was meant to be kept by the smith. It was plain that the garden hadn't been pruned back in far too long. Crow didn't care if no one went there, though, and covered the window with a cloth.

It took three trips to the kitchen well to draw enough water for a bath, and even then it was frigid. Crow propped a lone chair against the door to prevent Jek from coming in and peeled off the grey shirt, revealing wrapped bandages. With care, Crow unwrapped the bandages, breathing deeply with each layer removed. As more and more skin was revealed from the navel upwards, so were the intricate scars running over the pale skin, twirling and dancing in a maze. But when the pile of bandages on the floor was complete, so was Crow's secret revealed. Two round breasts, barely large enough to gain notice, heaved with each breath.

For Crow was no lad. He was a she, and she meant to keep that fact quiet for as long as possible.

CHAPTER 2

The sun beat down on the courtyard of Kyper palace, heating an already hot forge further. Crow's short, black hair was slick with sweat, causing it to be plastered to her pale skin. More rivulets of sweat rolled down her back, soaking her shirt. She raised her arm high and let the hammer swing, a powerful peal ringing out as she struck the hot metal.

One week had passed since Crow's official offer of apprenticeship by the royal blacksmith. She had taken to her new life like a fish to water, working every day with an eagerness that few could match. Jek had started by testing her knowledge, having her make whatever she knew—horse shoes, tongs, plate armour, knives, blades and more—piece by piece. He would critique her work after each stage, holding nothing back and still being patient, surprised at her capabilities.

Not to say that she wasn't working hard. She was. From morning till dusk, Crow was running about, stretching her muscles to the limits. As an apprentice, Crow had many other duties to tend to. She was responsible for preparing all of hers and Jek's meals, keeping the house and forge clean, delivering finished products and messages, taking measurements, orders and anything else she was asked to do. Coupled with the exercises Crow did to strengthen her leg and stomach muscles each morning, she fell into bed at night exhausted and content.

The continuous running about had already made Crow well-known to the Palace servants and soldiers. For the first few days, people would look with wide-eyed curiosity at the faerie-child who had gotten on the good side of the ornery Jek. Heads would turn as she ran past, and she was generally a curiosity. But after a few days, people became used to her. Turn around and there was Crow, fetching water or an apple from the kitchens, in the barracks, taking a soldier's measurements or delivering a piece of armour, beating the hammer in the courtyard with precise strokes. And just as Crow was known to the people, so they were known to her. She would hardly pass someone without giving a friendly greeting, naming each person as she went. She received a smile in return. If she were going to be a fixture to the Palace, at least she was a pleasant one and fine to look at.

Crow was known to the common people of the Palace, but the nobility and royalty had been absent since her arrival. Frankly, she didn't care and got on with her work. That would soon change.

On this bright day, Crow wiped her head with her

sleeve, quietly glaring at Jek. He walked around the forge without a shirt, sweat gleaming on his flushed skin. The sun breaking through the roof made the firelight dance and shadows to leap on all contained within, making Jek look more powerful and giving Crow a headache from the heat. Her last position had been completely outside, meaning she could at least get a breeze every now and again. Crow wished, desperately, that she could walk around without a shirt, like Jek, and deal only with her bandages. She knew that even with the bandages, she looked more like a boy than a girl, and their presence was easily explained: she wanted to hide unsightly scars. It was true, but she did not want the questions, the stares. So she wiped away more sweat and kept working.

Crow had some fabric wrapped around her hands to contend with the heat of the metal. Jek had ordered leather gloves for her, but they had yet to arrive. The extra heat only made her feel warmer. She beat on the sword she was making and groaned quietly, straightening to stretch just as a commotion was starting in the courtyard.

Five horsemen were returning from what looked like a prolonged trip. Judging by the cloaks, they were all members of the Royal Guard or knights, dressed in the cool, loose clothing of hunters. They were all young and had none of the worry lines that often graced the faces of peasants. They laughed and talked with one another, excepting the man at the group's head. He was the one who sat the straightest, looked the most powerful and was eyeing the Palace with something akin to weariness.

He had flaxen hair and regal features. One of the others let out a particularly raucous laugh, and the leader looked back, his muscles tensing like a taut bow. Nobles, Crow thought with a mental shrug, and went back to work.

She pulled the metal blade out of the fire and set it on the anvil, striking it with enough force to send a ringing through the courtyard. Her mind focused on the task at hand and everything else slipped away, as it always did when she was working with metal. The sound, though, had drawn the attention of the leader of the riders. He dismounted and jogged over to the forge, just as Crow was dipping the sword into a bath of oil, steam rising from the barrel. She dipped the cooler blade next in a barrel of water and didn't notice in the slightest when the man came into the forge to talk with the smith.

"Jek," he said with a pleasant baritone. The Master Smith moved from where he was wrapping wire around the hilt of another sword that Crow had made. She was especially skilled with making blades.

"Sire," Jek bellowed back, clapping the man on the shoulder and sending him staggering into the lean back of Crow. She whirled around, blade and hammer still in hand, and found herself face to face with the stately man whose blue eyes met her guarded green ones with curiosity. "I thought ye'd be on yer huntin' trip fer another day or so."

"We had little luck but for a few rabbits and pheasants, so we came back early. Who's this?" he asked, looking over the faerie-child with a bemused smile. Crow fought the urge to bristle at the newcomer.

"This twig?" Jek laughed and took the sword from Crow, whose knuckles had grown white as she gripped the hilt. "This be my new 'pprentice. Got 'im just last week."

"Oh?" the man said, raising his eyebrows with interest. Crow studied him, taking in the sculpted features and powerful body, deciding that he probably was nineteen or twenty to her sixteen. She managed to push her distracted observances aside and decided that he seemed nice enough. "What's your name, then?"

"Folks call me Crow," she replied automatically, rubbing sweat away from her eyes with the fabric wrapped around her hands. It seemed to work for the moment, but she could feel more beads start to form. At least talking with this man allowed her some reprieve.

"Crow? Unusual name," he said, considering her. "I'm Alexander Fenryr."

Crow gasped and her pale skin, unable to flush with heat or blush, grew even more ghostly. She dropped into a low bow, quickly spouting apologies. "I'm sorry, Your Highness, I didn't realise."

She heard a grumble from the man—the Crown Prince of Iona—and straightened in confusion. She glanced at Jek to clarify, hoping that she hadn't just made some serious blunder. Instead, Alexander frowned, exchanging a grimace with the Master Smith, "This is why I don't tell people my full name. Next time, just hit me over the head, alright?"

Jek, despite the impropriety, laughed his full-bellied laugh and set Crow's blade down. "Nah, don' worry 'bout 'im, Sire. 'E's new 'round here an' not used to the way o' things."

"So I noticed," the Crown Prince muttered, and Crow found herself bristling indignantly. Just because he was some royal didn't mean that he could just—She tamped down on that line of thought and curled her fingers into fists, daring only to give a glare to His Highness.

"But 'es the best damn 'pprentice I've ever had fer, well, ever," Jek said, and Crow found herself relaxing slightly before tensing at the unexpected compliment. Not that it wasn't nice to hear the gruff man say that, but still. She preferred to just get about her work. Compliments made her uncomfortable. "'E made all o' these here swords," Jek said, waving his hand over the wall where a selection of blades hung. She had, briefly, shown off her skill when Jek asked if she knew how to make swords and she replied with, what kind. He grumbled and told her to make whatever sort she wanted. She had come up with the five blades she knew. Including the Scheren.

Alexander looked over the swords with interest. He saw the thin, triangular blade favoured by the warriors of the Eastern Lands and gasped. "Is this—" he asked Jek softly.

"Aye, lad," Jek nodded gravely with a smile dancing on his lips. Crow watched in silence, waiting, as she had been taught. "Scheren. I don' know a single smith outside o' those in the Eastern Lands tha' even knows how to use one, let alone make one. An' Crow did this in half-a-day. Ne'er seen a finer crafted one o' these."

"I'd love to try it out," Alexander said, turning to look at Crow. She blinked and then realised he was asking her permission. As if he, of all people, needed to ask. She was gratified with the request, though.

"Go ahead," Crow shrugged. The Prince grabbed the sword from its rack and grinned at Jek before jogging off to the practise yards behind the Palace. Crow followed without a second thought, intrigued. Jek made to do so as well then shook his head and went back to wire wrapping the hilt. It would do for the Prince to make a friend and Crow was a good lad. Better than most of those Lords' sons that the Prince was normally forced to spend time with.

Crow trotted past the knights that the Prince had arrived with and emerged onto the training ground. She took up a stance where Alexander had discarded his cloak. He moved a few feet off and took up position with the blade. As he settled into his pose, Crow laughed. She tried to disguise her laugher by swallowing it down and failed. Stung, Alexander straightened and turned towards the blacksmith, brows drawn.

"What is so funny?" he snapped and Crow straightened, forcing herself to put on her most serious expression.

"You're holding it wrong," she said, quietly enough that Alexander alone could hear. He looked at her incredulously and stalked over to her, thrusting the blade into her hands.

"Then show me," he growled and stepped back, folding his arms. Crow hesitated, but shook her head and did as she was told. She moved off a bit and settled into a slight crouch, the sword gripped non-standardly in her hand. Anyone who worked with a broadsword or long sword would have balked at the unusual grip and stance, but she held it expertly. Crow straightened and handed the Scheren back to Alexander, who had grown silent. He tried to mimic Crow's stance, watching her reaction. This time, she managed to keep down the laughter that had been bubbling, but amusement still showed in her eyes. The Prince, for all that he was probably very capable with a blade, was standing like any buffoon with the Scheren in hand.

Alexander noticed Crow's look and stopped, drawing himself up to his full, imposing height. He threw the sword at Crow, who caught it deftly, and drew his own long sword. He cut it through the air in a couple of quick slices, showing his prowess.

"If you're so good at this, then you can fight me," he snarled. Crow looked from the blade in her hand to the Prince, whose wounded pride showed clearly in his eyes. She could have fought. She could have proven herself to be a worthy adversary, but instead, she shook her head and kept the Scheren pointed down at her side.

"Nah," Crow drawled. "I don't want to fight you."

"Oh?" Alexander snapped. "Are you a coward?" Had he been a mean-spirited person, his words would have been followed by a sneer. Crow only saw a stung ego and desperation in his face. She knew that look and pitied the man. He was not used to being criticised by his teachers and companions, no matter that they were meant to do just that. He had become a good swordsman merely by practising, not fighting. All who pitted themselves against him were afraid of offending the heir to the throne and praised and coddled where criticism would have better served.

"No," Crow chose her words carefully, making sure to keep a bland and somewhat interested look on her face. Now was not the time to start a fight. "But I'm not a swordsman. I'm a blacksmith. I'll leave the fighting to you."

Alexander relaxed at her words and sheathed his blade. He was met with no challenge to his skills as a swordsman from the pale blacksmith, and that alone caused him to trust the quietly cheerful Crow. With each master in their own domain, it was easier for Alexander to casually put his hands in his pockets and walk alongside Crow back to the forge. Crow hung the Scheren back on its rack and turned to Jek.

"Did ye figure it out?" Jek asked, gravelly voice booming over the fire. Alexander shook his head, an easy smile on his face as he glanced at Crow.

"No. I'll leave the Scheren up to the East Landers and folks like Crow, here," he said. Crow blinked at the subtle compliment, saying nothing. She hadn't needed to fight to prove to Alexander that she had skill with the sword.

"Wise lad, ye are," Jek said and thrust a small piece of metal at Crow. "Kayn wants a new set of shoes for his gelding. See to it."

Just like that, Crow was back in her now-normal walk of life, with only one difference: Alexander was included.

There was an unspoken acknowledgement between the two of their alliance and friendship. Crow grabbed a knotted string and dashed out of the forge to the stables without a second glance. Alexander followed, interested.

Crow ran through the doors and saw the scrawny hostler standing at the head of a shining black gelding, eyes bright and wild. At the sight of the Crown Prince, the hostler blushed scarlet and bowed as much as he could while still holding onto the lead of the horse. "Sire," he muttered reverently.

Crow shot a slightly amused look at a scowling Alexander. As the hostler straightened, Alexander's scowl vanished and blue eyes met green in shared amusement. "Kayn," Alexander muttered in response to the awed hostler, shifting awkwardly. Crow took the opportunity to relieve the frustrated Prince of his formal obligations and hold up her string with a grin.

"I've got orders to measure this beauty for some new shoes," Crow danced forwards, looking the horse in the eye and patting his neck before bending down and measuring with the string. She held up the string in a variety of different ways, taking mental notes and drawing a picture in her mind's eye. She repeated the process with the other hooves and then emerged from behind the horse, smiling.

"Just watching that's a treat," Kayn said. Crow scratched her hair self-consciously and waved off the compliment.

"You're welcome to come by the forge anytime," she said. The hostler shook his head.

"My place is here. Besides, it's too dratted hot. Don't know how you stand the heat," he said, patting the gelding's flank.

"I was born to it, I suppose," Crow said, thinking of her sweat-soaked shirt and the fact that she hadn't yet adjusted to having a slightly enclosed forge. She nodded to Kayn and was off again, darting out of the stables as quickly as she had come. She skidded into the forge and started working immediately. Alexander took a position on the other side of the fence, just outside of most of the heat. As Crow got warmer and warmer, the Prince stayed nice and comfortable. She glared at him as sweat started to form on her brow, then started beating the shoes into shape.

Alexander watched, fascinated, for a few minutes before growing tired of the silence. "Do you like hunting?" he asked. Crow shrugged mid-swing, still managing to hit the metal with a clang.

"I like it some. There was never much to catch where I was from, so I didn't bother. But occasionally, I would catch a nice, fat rabbit." She bent the hot metal over the anvil's horn and put holes in it with a chisel.

"No, I mean real deer hunting," Alexander said. Crow shook her head before dousing the metal.

"Never done it," she replied. "Catching deer's not allowed for people of my status, not without special permissions. Especially when deer were as scarce as they were." A flash of memory brought the taste of venison to her mouth. Crow swallowed, the memory gone in an instant, back into the iron vault where she kept it.

"What?" Alexander asked, outraged. "Where do you come from that you can't hunt deer?"

Crow shot him a look of true annoyance and the Prince recoiled slightly from the shock and joy at the honest emotion given to him. "I'm from Hotun. The nobles there were particularly protective of their herds, but hunting deer is illegal for peasants everywhere that I know of."

Properly cowed, Alexander hunched his shoulders slightly in apology. "Oh," he murmured. "I forgot."

Crow snorted as she finished up the last shoe, the sound of metal on metal covering the sound of her indignation. "I bet you did."

"What's that supposed to mean?" Alexander snapped, standing and following Crow across the courtyard to the stables. She slipped inside, Alexander waiting outside, determined to get an answer from the blacksmith. When Crow emerged again, he folded his arms impatiently. "Well?" he demanded.

"Some temper you've got on you," Crow raised her eyebrows and ran back to the forge. Alexander caught up, breathing heavy with anger rather than exercise. "Relax. I just meant it would make sense that you would forget, 'cause you just got back from hunting and do it frequently."

"Oh," Alexander said, lowering his arms and sighing. Crow laughed outright at the image and got back to work.

For the remainder of the day and well into the evening, Alexander hung around the forge, talking with

Crow about the various tools, about the construction of Kyper Palace, about anything, really, and occasionally starting another bicker. It was immediately apparent to Jek and anyone looking on that the two would become great friends. Crow didn't mind such an honour, pleased to think that the entertaining person that was the Crown Prince would even want to be her friend when he could spend time with people of his own relative status. Alexander was pleased to simply have someone to talk with that didn't care a jot about his position and would give an honest answer. Only once, when the light of the fire and the dying sun caught his hair did Crow even allow herself to acknowledge that he was handsome. She quickly stifled the thought.

When Alexander was called by one of the guards, he stood from his perch on a barrel and stretched, his muscles creaking from having sat and watched Crow work at the fire for so long. Watching that, he thought, was like watching magic. An art that had been all but forgotten and survived only in the myths spread at a storyteller's hearth. Firelight danced over her pale skin and dark hair and Alexander wondered if the blacksmith were not really a faerie-child. He shook his head and bid Crow and Jek farewell.

Crow finished her last project—hammering flat a piece of metal that would become plate armour—and set down her hammer, putting a cover over the fire so that it would slowly die down until it was nothing more than a few brightly glowing coals. From these coals, the flames could easily be revived the next morning. Jek watched with mild interest, seeing, as Alexander did, an artist at work.

"See if ye can beg supper from the kitchens," Jek said. "Ye look tired enough that I don' want ye burnin' the food."

Crow smiled at the thinly veiled excuse for a break from work and ran to do as she was told. She always ran places, it seemed, stretching her legs before her to burst into a place with little warning, a smile on her face and an eagerness about her that all attached to. This night was no different. Crow materialised in the kitchens and startled a kitchen maid into giving up a loaf of bread, some cheese and meat left over from the midday meal. With a quick and sincere thanks, Crow vanished as quickly as she had come, bounding back to the house and somehow managing not to spill the food.

That night, Crow lay on her cot, her belly full and her body tired. Her mind, though, spun circles, keeping her thinking. She couldn't sleep. An image of the Crown Prince ran through her head, as did every word of their conversations. The question about hunting appeared in her mind over and over, dredging up the taste of venison and all of the other memories associated with that vault where she kept her memories. That was where the ones she wished she could forget lived. Those were the ones that haunted her as she finally managed to slip into sleep.

She woke in a cold sweat, her breathing heavy and uncontrolled, a burning fear and anger in her stomach. Wildly, Crow looked about and grabbed the dagger she kept under the cot. She pointed it at the shadows in her room, spinning as if facing multiple opponents. Or just one who was hiding. Crow took a deep breath and forced herself to lower her hands and put the dagger down. She lay back on the cot, her heart still racing in her ears. She forced herself to remember where she was and why she didn't need that dangerous, wonderful anger that threatened to boil over.

"Gone," she murmured. "He's gone, Crow." She relaxed enough to lay her head on her pillow and ran a hand through her hair. Crow turned on her side, repeating, "He's gone" over and over until she fell asleep.

The shadow outside her window turned and frowned. Jek brushed off the garden's dirt from his hands and let the overgrown alcove in peace. He lumbered back around the house and into his own room. Worry filled his thoughts. Worry for the apprentice that he had taken under his wing. Who was this brave-faced lad that had so suddenly filled a void in his life? And why was he jumping at shadows in the dark?

CHAPTER 3

"You two had better get out of here!" the head cook roared, brandishing a wooden spoon at the fleeing forms of Alexander and Crow. Despite the plump woman's yell, there was amusement and relief in her eyes. Finally, it seemed, Prince Alexander had a friend that was more than a kowtowing, obsequious knight. And here the two were, stealing cakes like little boys.

Crow dodged out of the way of the cook's spoon, but Alexander was not so lucky. He got a good thwack to his shoulder and Crow laughed raucously. The cook ran closer and Crow danced back, her eyes gleaming. "Alright," she said around her laughter, "we're leaving." She turned and snatched another cake off the table before dashing through the door, too swift to catch. Again, Alexander was not quite as lucky—he missed getting another hit by a hairsbreadth.

"And I'd better not see the two of you for at least

three days," the cook hollered after them. Crow spun on her heel and gave a friendly wave before turning and running into the forge where Jek was stoking the fire, stopping just in time to keep from crashing into an anvil. Alexander skidded to a halt a few feet away, managing to gain his composure before leaning on the fence.

"Would you like a cake, Jek?" Alexander asked innocently, holding one out to the smith.

"Was that what all the ruckus was 'bout? Ye got to learn to be more careful when stealin' from the kitchens," Jek took the cake and stuffed it whole into his mouth, ignoring the crumbs that slipped from between his lips. Crow laughed and took a bite of her own cake.

"Did you see her face?" she beamed, around her mouthful. Alexander just chuckled and settled on his usual barrel-seat to eat his stolen fare.

"Ye lads are more trouble than yer worth," Jek said, grumbling and turning back to the fire. Alexander exchanged a look with Crow and the two started laughing again. Eventually, the Prince settled down and shook his head, gold hair falling into his eyes.

"My father would kill me if he found out that I had been stealing cakes from the kitchens," Alexander said. Crow licked the last of the sweetness from her fingers.

"Why? Is it undignified for someone who is meant to be spending his time on important matters of state and running the country?" she asked. Alexander scoffed.

"Running the country? Not likely. He wants me to spend my time learning how to fight and hunt better than any of the nobles out there. The only state craft I do is being polite to diplomats and other nobles," he said. "Apparently, I'm not worthy enough to handle the important matters of state until I come of age."

"That's silly," Crow said. She opened her mouth to say more when Jek cut in.

"Tha's one lesson ye'd better learn, lad," he growled to Crow in a low voice. "Don' criticise how things is done. Now tha's enough trouble fer one day. Time to get back to work. Take this completed armour to Sir Gavin. Go an' make sure it fits proper a'right?"

Cowed, Crow nodded her head in a polite bob. What was she thinking, going about commenting on things like statecraft? She was a blacksmith. She took the parcel of armour from Jek and cast an apologetic at Alexander, who had turned silent. Without another word, she was off to the Palace, the armour clunking in her arms as she ran. Alexander was close at her heels, the incident of moments ago forgotten.

She ran around the back entrance and up a couple flights of stairs to the hallway where the knights were quartered. Alexander followed at a brisk jog, thinking that he had never run so much in his life before meeting Crow—training included. She slowed at the top of the stairs and he was quietly pleased to see that she was panting slightly. Granted, she was carrying heavy armour, but still. Crow walked down the hallway to a wooden door and knocked.

"Enter," a growling voice said and Crow struggled to keep her easy smile. She did not particularly like Sir Gavin. She hadn't interacted with him except for measuring him for the armour, yet every time she saw him, an uneasy feeling flickered in her stomach. She pushed the door open and walked in, setting the armour on the as-yet unmade bed. By the looks of the flustered maid, she hadn't quite gotten around to cleaning the man's chambers, yet. Alexander stood just inside the door, out of the way so as not to be noticed. Sir Gavin didn't even give him a glance.

"I brought your armour," Crow announced, spreading the pieces out on the bed. "You'll need to try them on for a proper fit."

Sir Gavin, long hair unruly and a sly smirk on his lips, stretched out his arms lazily, looking at Crow with expectation. She swallowed a sigh and set about putting the various pieces of armour on, doing the work of a squire or page, not a blacksmith. There was nothing for it to get working, though, as Jek probably had more tasks for her. She stared at the floor as she dutifully strapped on the breastplate, greaves, leg guards and the remainder of the pieces. She stepped back to let the burly knight test out his new gear.

He turned at the waist a couple of times and flexed for the benefit of the maid who looked pointedly away. "It's a little loose in the chest," he purred, keeping his eyes on the cleaning girl.

"You'll want it that way," Crow commented, folding her hands behind her back and watching as the knight moved about as if fighting, though the moves were greatly exaggerated, all for the maid who had finally started her work. "That way when you get struck, your chest won't get crushed when the metal bends. And any tighter and you would have a hard time breathing."

"And the bracers are off," he said, turning his forearms towards Crow to show the bracers that were precisely the right length for wielding a broadsword, Sir Gavin's favoured weapon.

"When you're using a sword, you won't want those bracers in any other spot," Crow said, growing increasingly frustrated with the bothersome knight. He didn't even seem to hear what it was that she was saying.

"Oh, and you're the expert fighter now?" he snapped, moving the bracers around as if he could reposition them and they would be fine. All he managed to do was stretch the leather that held them on.

"No," Crow said flatly, any cheer she might have evoked gone. She forgot about Alexander standing by the door or Jek back at the forge, all of that falling away with the rise of her temper. Carefully, she suppressed her anger until she knew it was safe and wouldn't boil over. "But I do know about armour."

"Aren't you supposed to make it to my specifications?" Sir Gavin asked, his voice sickly sweet. He hadn't forgotten about the maid in the room and was still trying to make a good impression, but it was plain his own temper was rising.

"I'm supposed to make it to your measurements and needs based on how you fight and what you fight with, not your specifications," Crow replied, struggling to keep her voice flat rather than the fire she wished to spew.

"I don't think so, peasant. See, I'm the one paying

your pitiful master for the armour and therefore I'm the one who gets to have it made any way I wish," Sir Gavin said, walking up to Crow and attempting to look down his nose at her. It didn't work as he was only an inch taller than her.

Crow straightened and looked directly into the knight's eyes, green eyes blazing with hidden anger, "What did you say about Jek?"

"Who?" Sir Gavin asked, moving away slightly, the only visible sign that he was intimidated. He knew perfectly well who she meant but enjoyed getting a reaction out of the lean apprentice.

"My master," Crow said through clenched teeth, the hands behind her back clenched into fists.

"Him? Oh, yes. Rather pathetic, isn't he? Uneducated brute, who knows how he got to be the royal smith. He certainly doesn't know his place when speaking to people who are far above his class," the knight said with an elevated tone.

Crow felt her control snap. She stepped forwards, getting in Sir Gavin's face, lips curled ferally. "I don't care what you say about me, but don't you ever, ever, talk about my master that way."

"Oh? And what are you going to do about it, peasant?" Sir Gavin sneered. "Fight me? Or are you a coward, like your master?"

The words, so similar to the ones Alexander had spoken upon their first meeting, caused Crow to straighten, her muscles relaxing as if preparing for a fight. Coward said with fear and desperation was in no way the same as coward said with a sneer. It was with that thought in mind that Crow murmured, barely loud enough to hear yet heard by all, "You want to test your new armour?"

Sir Gavin stared, eyes widening in disbelief. Arrogant amusement spread over his features and he laughed, the sound filling the room. "As if you could even hope to take on a knight, boy," he spat at the bold creature who dared challenge him.

Crow simply watched him with her otherworldly looks, the green eyes, pale skin and black hair. "I will fight your for my master's honour. The practise yards. Swords. Twenty minutes."

"You are a fool," Sir Gavin leered, storming out of his room with his nose in the air, a dangerous gleam in his eyes. He brushed past Alexander without seeing him. Crow waited a beat to let the tension dissipate before turning to Alexander, letting out a breath of annoyance.

"I wonder when he'll realise that these are his rooms he just left," she said, cracking a smile at Alexander who just stared open-mouthed at her.

He blinked and then nearly bit her head off, "Are you crazy?" Crow shrugged and started walking—not running—back to the forge, a far-off expression on her face. She turned her head to Alexander, eyes full of grief.

"I couldn't let him attack Jek like that," she whispered. Alexander put his hands to his head to keep from taking her by the shoulders and shaking her.

"Crow, no matter how annoying and idiotic Sir Gavin may be, he is a nobleman. Not only that, but he is a knight of this realm, sworn to uphold the peace and defend this land against any threat. He is used to dealing with respect and has obviously misused his standing. Does he deserve to be taken down a notch, sure. But he has wielded a weapon just about every day since childhood. He will skin you alive," Alexander insisted, wanting nothing more than to knock sense into his friend's head.

Crow shook her head at Alexander as she walked across the courtyard, "I'll be alright."

"No," Alexander countered, temper flaring. "Crow, you're going to get yourself hurt and this whole fight will have been for nothing. You'll have proved nothing. I could take Sir Gavin in a fight, but that's because I've been training for years, longer and harder than him. You have no chance!"

"No chance o' what?" Jek asked as the two neared the forge, basking in the heat of the flames. He set aside his current project and folded his arms across his barrel chest, looking at his apprentice expectantly.

Crow didn't say anything, just ducked into the house and emerged moments later with strips of fabric that she proceeded to wrap around her hands. She didn't meet Jek's questioning gaze. Alexander growled, "Crow challenged Sir Gavin to a fight to defend your honour."

"My honour?" Jek asked, incredulous. A smile built at the edge of his mouth and promptly vanished when Crow looked at him, perfectly serious. Jek frowned and put a hand on Crow's shoulder. "Lad, what happened?"

"He called you pathetic," Crow murmured, "and said that you needed to be taught your place."

Jek let out a long breath and rubbed his face, soot smearing over his skin. He shook his head, "Ye cannae go 'round challengin' knights a'cause o' things they said 'bout me. I've had worse an' I don' care 'bout no bully like Sir Gavin."

Crow looked at Jek from beneath her brow, looking for all the world like an injured pup. "But I care," she said desperately. Jek nearly staggered back by the force of the emotion held in the eyes of the child standing before him. He hadn't known Crow for very long, but the lad held wisdom and experience beyond his years. Jek often forgot that Crow was a mere sixteen years old. Capable, yes. Yet still young. When Crow looked up at Jek in that moment, he saw that the lad was still young and trying to find a foothold in the world. Seized by a strange impulse, Jek wrapped his arms around Crow and sighed.

"An' I thank ye fer it," Jek said. "I can take care o' myself, though, lad. An' words is just words. Leave them bullies be, a'right?"

Crow nodded, pulling back from the hug with a lopsided smile that didn't quite reach those green eyes. Jek shook his head and ruffled the short hair into unruliness.

"That's all well and good," Alexander interrupted, suppressing the burst of jealousy he felt at the relationship between the two, "but Crow's already challenged Sir Gavin. To back out now would be..."

Crow broke out in a grin that had both Alexander and Jek standing back. "Oh, don't worry about me."

"I've told you," Alexander snarled, exasperated, "Sir

Gavin's stronger and more powerful. You don't stand a chance, especially not with a sw—" Alexander broke off as he saw the weapon Crow pulled from the wall of the forge. It was that strange, thin triangular blade that had brought the two of them together to begin with. The Scheren. Crow smiled mischievously, holding the blade as she would an extension of her arm. It was obviously an old friend.

"I'll be fine," Crow reassured the Prince.

With that, she dashed out of the forge again, running to the practise yards. Alexander exchanged a glance with Jek before running after his friend. Jek hesitated a heartbeat before shaking his head and lumbering after the two. They came upon the grassy practise yards to find Sir Gavin already there, a crowd of people forming. Rumour of the challenge had already spread to the soldiers and guards and a few of the servants. The knight adjusted his armour—he wore the bracers and breastplate but did not bother with a helm or the rest of the gear—and ignored Crow as she waited for him to finish his preparations. After a minute, he turned around to face Crow, an arrogant smirk plastered on his face.

"You wear no armour, boy? You'll need it," he chuckled loudly to the waiting ears around the field. The audience murmured amongst themselves and pointed at Crow. She just tightened the fabric around her hands and lifted the Scheren.

"Armour will just slow me down," she replied. Sir Gavin laughed boisterously and shook his head, drawing his broadsword and taking up a fighting stance.

"Ready, boy?" he barked, brandishing the sword with a flourish in an attempt to impress his audience and intimidate his opponent. It didn't work, at least where Crow was concerned. She simply stood, calm and waiting, giving a nod to acknowledge her readiness. The two bowed as formality dictated and then the fight began.

Crow slid into the proper stance for fighting with the Scheren so that she could utilise each deadly point of the blade. Sir Gavin began circling her like prey, a petty smirk continuously present as he waved his sword through the air in various acrobatics. Crow didn't move, just followed him with her head, waiting for the right moment. She saw, out of the corner of her eye, a terrified look on Alexander's face and wondered why her stomach clenched at the sight.

The knight chose that moment to attack. He lunged forwards with a speed that his size would not have indicated. Crow was faster, though, being both smaller and not weighed down by armour. She sidestepped the swipe and lifted the Scheren with a flick of her wrist. Gavin flicked his right wrist to assess any damage and the leather ties on his bracer slipped apart, the metal falling to the ground. There were a few shocked murmurs from the crowd and Jek had the gall to chuckle. Sir Gavin's smirk turned into a snarl of anger and he began to attack in earnest.

He lunged again, this time using his considerable skill to push Crow into making a mistake. The broadsword was longer than her Scheren and he had a greater reach. But his fighting style wasn't taking into account the differences of hers. And no one had trained the knight against someone of the Eastern Lands. Crow sidestepped again, but Sir Gavin had learned one lesson. His sword followed her, getting close enough to nick her shoulder, slicing through the shirt deep enough to draw blood and ache with a subtle, throbbing pain. Frustrated, Crow straightened and shifted her Scheren in her hand.

"Had enough, boy?" Gavin hissed. "Too much pain for you to handle? Tsk. That master of yours should have taught you better. I always knew he wasn't worth what the King is paying for his keep."

Crow attacked, fury burning just below the surface of her calm, threatening to take over. She pushed forwards relentlessly, startling Gavin into taking a step backwards. It was enough for her to take advantage and she pressed in farther. And then, she began to dance.

The art of mastering the Scheren was a complicated one that involved many difficult techniques and a way of moving that did not come naturally to the body at first, straining the muscles and stretching one's balance to the limit. Though most Easterners had a basic knowledge of fighting with the Scheren, few took the time to truly master the intricate and strenuous fighting style. Crow, it quickly became apparent, had taken the time.

The odd style of attack and furious offensive caused the knight to stumble more than once, struggling to keep his sword up in the face of the swift, weaving Crow. When he managed to lunge, Crow darted in, snicking her blade through the leather ties on the other bracer before darting back, turning with a flurry that caused Gavin to move backwards in shock. Roaring in anger, he tried to attack again, rushing at Crow while waving his broadsword through the air.

Crow ran around him, using her speed to catch him unawares as she cut the ties holding his breastplate into place. When that fell to the ground, Gavin leaped clear in a practised move and faced Crow with a snarl on his face. He crouched slightly, holding his sword out protectively. He watched Crow with wary eyes, having learned that the blacksmith apprentice was a worthy adversary. Crow stood still on the field, her Scheren held calmly at her side, returning the favour to Gavin, green eyes meeting infuriated brown. Without a sound, Crow stepped forwards in a movement too quick for the broadsword to follow. She barely missed another nick on her leg but managed to get past the protective barrier, putting the tip of the Scheren at Sir Gavin's neck. The knight stiffened and dropped his sword to the ground, admitting defeat. Crow lowered her own sword and stepped back.

"Please don't talk about Jek like that ever again," she murmured. She turned and walked back to where her master stood with Alexander. Both stared at her, completely stunned. Crow just stood in silence, feeling the weariness that came after fighting crawl into her bones. She let her shoulders slump as she reached Jek and dragged her feet away from the practise yards to the forge where she hung the Scheren up and started unwinding the fabric on her hands. Crow slunk into the small house and sat on her cot, muscles aching in weariness.

"I'm going to have to practise that more," she muttered, rubbing her stiff legs.

"Why?" Alexander strode into the room as if he owned the place. "That looked pretty in practise to me. That was amazing, Crow. I didn't know you could do that."

Crow gave a half-smile, a remnant of her usual cheerfulness. "That's because you've never seen me do that. Remember, I backed down from a fight with you."

Alexander sat on the bed and saw the red beginning to stain Crow's shoulder. He poked the wound and Crow winced. "You should get that seen to. I'm sure Matharus would be happy to wrap that up for you," Alexander said, referring to the Palace physician. Crow nodded and stood, groaning at her sore muscles. "I thought you backed down because you weren't a swordsman."

"I'm not," Crow said, trudging through the house to go find the physician. She saw Jek approaching, Matharus already at her side and slumped against the fence enclosing the forge.

"That sure looked like swordsmanship to me," Alexander commented, folding his arms and surveying Crow with raised eyebrows.

Crow shook her head, "Fighting with the Scheren, no matter what it may look like, is not swordsmanship. It's a technique called Mak'tal. Translates as Dance of Knives. Completely different."

The Crown Prince frowned, glaring at Crow with

mock anger. "You still could have beaten me to a pulp. Why didn't you?"

Crow shrugged, wincing as her shoulder stretched. She tried to ignore it, telling herself silently that she had dealt with much worse, but it was a constant pressure and quite annoying. So she focused on Alexander instead. "Because you didn't need to be beaten to a pulp. You didn't want a fight any more than I did. Besides, what would have been the point of fighting you?"

Alexander considered her words as Jek and Matharus approached. The palace physician, an old, hunched man with stringy white hair, rolled up Crow's sleeve and clucked his tongue in disapproval. He prodded the wound and Crow attempted to pull away, but the man's grasp was surprisingly strong. Matharus pulled out a salve and smeared it on the wound, not even bothering to bandage it as he let the sleeve fall again.

"That should teach you not to fight fully fledged knights with seven years on you. You're lucky this is all you got from this stupidity. Anything less than a formal challenge would have had you imprisoned, boy," he sniffed, stalking away after a quiet thanks from Crow.

Jek stared at his apprentice for a moment before folding his arms and huffing, "A'right, lad. Tha's enough fun fer today. Back to work with ye."

Crow broke the moment of tension by grinning and practically skipping into the forge as if she wasn't injured or tired in the slightest. She picked up her newest project and thrust it into the fire, pulling on the bellows string to stoke the fire up. It was as if nothing had happened.

Alexander and Jek looked at one another before shaking their heads and going about their duties, Jek to the forge and Alexander back to the palace.

Crow's words fresh in his mind, Alexander walked through the doors and through the maze-like corridors of the Palace to his quarters. His manservant waited with a hot cup of tea and Alexander slumped at his desk, looking over the papers. These papers, the records of kings long past, were all the statecraft his father allowed him until he was of age. It wasn't much, but he would do the best he could until he was able to take over the running of the kingdom. That didn't stop him from thinking over Crow's words and looking out the window to see if he could spot the forge in the courtyard below. A bright glow, obviously from the fire, met his eyes and he smiled, shaking his head again.

Crow, while the Prince read over historical records, covered the fire and went about preparing the evening meal. She set it before Jek a short time later and set to, eating like a starving child, Jek looking on with amusement. As Crow was cleaning up, Jek watched her, beginning to feel something like a father's affection for the lad.

"Crow?" he asked after a few minutes.

"Yes?" she put the remainder of the bread under a cover for the morning meal before turning to her master.

"What do you think about silversmithing?" Jek asked. Crow's eyes lit up and she replied with a wide grin.

CHAPTER 4

Crow took to silversmithing like breathing. The techniques involved were often intricate, delicate and time consuming. She loved it, working to master each task set to her and producing fine results. As she worked, first days passed, then weeks and finally months. The routine that she had settled into became normal and her friendship with Alexander grew.

The first few days of their acquaintance, it had been slightly shocking to see the Crown Prince with the blacksmith apprentice. After months, it was as normal as having to draw water from the well. The two spent hours together. Alexander sat on a barrel and watched Crow work or she spent time in the practise yards, wire-wrapping some hilt or sharpening a blade while the Prince trained. They talked constantly, about whatever topics piqued their interest, sharing opinions and ideas or even —on rare occasions—enjoying each other's company in silence. They fought, too, as good friends are wont to do.

The bickers never resulted in anything more than flared tempers and an evening of sulking on both sides. By the next morning, all was forgiven and forgotten and the normal routine reestablished.

One morning, when the weather was foggy and cool enough that Crow was glad for the heat of the forge, she carefully heated up an ingot of silver, shaping the metal with tools smaller and finer than those she would have used for blacksmithing. She was about to link the silver strands into a delicate chain when a hulking, stalking figure emerging from the fog caught her eye.

"You look particularly happy today," Crow noted as Alexander glared his way into the forge. The Prince huffed and crossed his arms over his silk shirt. Jek raised his brows in question at Crow and she shrugged. There hadn't been an altercation between the two for a couple weeks and the last thing that she had said to him the night before had to do with making food for supper. Whatever it was that was wrong with him, it wasn't her fault. She thought.

Alexander said nothing, just glaring at the fire as if it were fuelling some sort of rage. His blonde hair was curling even more with the humidity and Crow found herself noting that he looked like a vengeful god in the fog and fire. She pushed the thought aside and went back to working on the chain, reheating the metal at the edge of the fire so as not to ruin the temper. Crow worked in silence for a time, putting links in the chain one by one. She put the last link into place when Alexander grumbled something under his breath.

"What?" Crow asked, setting the chain on a workbench.

"Do you want to go on a hunting trip?" Alexander half-snarled, kicking the dirt floor with the toe of his boot. Spite was rich in his voice, making Crow even more confused. Since when was a hunting trip something to be annoyed with?

"Why?" Crow ventured tentatively, watching her friend carefully. He leaned against the fence and glowered at the floor.

"There's a party of important nobility coming and my father," Alexander fairly spat the word, "thinks it would be a good idea if we could feed them venison caught by my own hand. Since hunting and training is about all that I'm good for, apparently."

"I take it you don't think this is a good idea," Crow said drily, picking up some of her tools and wiping them down with a bit of oil and a rag. Her skin fairly glowed orange in the firelight and for a moment, Alexander was drawn from his grey mood and allowed himself to be fascinated by the sight. It didn't last and he went back to kicking at the floor in annoyance.

"No," he grumbled. Crow set aside her tools and ran a hand through her hair, making it stick up at odd angles.

"I don't know if I'd be able to go—" she started at last, casting a pleading look at Jek. The smith was already far ahead of her.

"Go ahead, lad," he said, waving a hand with a hammer in it at Crow, who ducked with the practise of someone who had done so many times before. Jek saw his blunder and mumbled something before bringing the hammer down on a horseshoe with a resounding clang.

"Are you certain?" Crow asked, "I mean I've still got the house to clean and there's lunch to be prepared and..." She was already dancing towards the house, a hopeful look in her eye. Jek shook his head in mock annoyance and waved her away.

"I've managed fer years a'fore ye came, lad. I can manage fer a couple days," he growled good naturedly. Crow flashed him a brilliant grin before darting into the house. She emerged a few minutes later, hurriedly stuffing the tail end of a cloak into the top of her pack. Jek rolled his eyes and went back to work, barking a 'have fun' to the already-vanishing apprentice. Alexander led the way to the stables and Crow wandered along beside, smiling eagerly. She turned back to the forge a moment later at a quick run. Alexander turned and saw her sprinting back towards him, the Scheren in its specially designed sheath in one hand. Crow shrugged at his look.

There were two horses ready and waiting in the stables, as if Alexander had anticipated her acceptance. Crow was tempted to give him a good thwack on his head for that, but shook her head instead. He was the Crown Prince. He could do whatever he wanted. Alexander took the larger of the two horses—a dark stallion—and swung his weight expertly into the saddle. He tied his pack behind a quiver with bow and arrows and looked expectantly at Crow.

She eyed the smaller sorrel horse with apprehension. "Alrighty," she muttered to the creature. "Don't kill me.

Please." With a half-prayer and the skill of control over her body, Crow grabbed onto the pommel of the saddle and swung onto the horse. She managed to make it in one try, slightly surprised at herself. She hadn't ridden a horse in years. Once Alexander was certain that Crow wasn't going to lose her seat, he dug his heels into the side of his horse and set off at a canter into the fog. Crow sighed and clucked her tongue. The sorrel flicked his ears and jolted off, startling Crow into wakefulness.

The two horses and riders raced through the Palace grounds until they came upon a break in the wall—the back gate—and Alexander surged through that as if it weren't there at all. Crow, for her part, spared backwards glance at the walled city and wondered what she was getting herself into. After a few minutes of hard riding, Alexander slowed his horse to a walk along a game trail barely wide enough for Crow to ride alongside. She was already beginning to feel the years of not being in the saddle and hoped that they wouldn't be doing much running that trip.

"So," she said once it became perfectly clear that Alexander wasn't going to be hunting. He just glowered into the fog-hidden trees, saying nothing, his grip on the reins tight enough to make his knuckles white. "You want to tell me about this party of temperamental nobles? Or should we start with your father?"

Alexander said nothing, continuing to ride in silence. Crow let it fester for a minute, listening with pleasure to the sounds of the forest coming alive. There were birds and crickets, wind in the plants and so many other things. It was more than just beautiful—it was alive. Her pleasure in the sight was marred by the bad mood of her friend, so Crow tried again.

"Alright, let me guess," she threw him a glance, noting in the quiet part of her mind that the fog was condensing on his shirt and making it plaster to his skin. A flattering look. Crow shook herself and looked ahead, determined to cheer him up and push such thoughts from her mind. "These people are led by a distant cousin of yours who is a complete slob. He manages to eat nearly everything on the table and gets most of it on his tunic, talking with his mouth full. Or maybe, these people are a bunch of snobby prats who, despite that this is Kyper Palace we're talking about, think that nothing is good enough and demand the finest that can possibly be acquired. They are impossible to please and really quite expensive to maintain. Perhaps it's an ugly old aunt with a lazy eye and hunched back who is determined that you are her sweetums and she won't let you out of her sight. The only way you can escape is to go run errands for her, like fetching an apple or sweet cake or having another gown brought up. But what is your only escape is really your bane because she then thinks that you are devoted to her and everything gets worse. Maybe it's—"

"Enough! I get the point," Alexander interrupted, barely able to control the laughter that simmered within. He shot a frustrated glare at Crow who just straightened herself in her saddle and smiled her best, most innocent smile.

"So, which is it? Cause I can keep doing this for

hours," she said. Alexander groaned in mock pain and all thoughts of the hunt were suspended. Now, it was nothing more than two friends out for a ride and a good gripe about life. Right then, Alexander needed a friend, and if that took the form of a hunting trip, so be it.

"It's much worse than all of those," the Prince said with a shudder. Crow winced and raised her eyebrows in question. "The man that is coming is an old friend of my father's. Lord Vincent Tyber of Halfpeak. He's not so much of a problem, unless you consider that every time he shows up, both he and my father get roaring drunk. No, the problem is his daughter Yvonne. A real monster. She's a year younger than I am. For as long as I can remember, it has been speculated that the two of us would marry. There has been no official agreement, as my father—at least he can do one thing right—is determined that I choose my own bride from amongst the nobles in our court or that of a neighbouring land. That hasn't stopped Yvonne from attaching to the idea. She thinks that she can make me fall desperately in love with her. Not to mention she's insanely annoying."

"Ah," Crow said, affecting an accent and superior airs. "Say no more. The evil and obsessed woman. You have my greatest sympathy."

"Stuff it," Alexander grumbled. "This is serious. She's attractive enough, but not in a way that interests me. She uses her assets like... well, like a common whore and it's disgusting, the way she throws herself at me. For example, last year, she pretended to sleepwalk in next to nothing and somehow ended up in my locked quarters."

Crow winced and frowned. "Alright, so... problematic. They're coming and your father is throwing this banquet in Lord Tyber's honour, right?" Alexander nodded and Crow considered. "And you have to provide the main course?" Again, Alexander nodded. "So what happens if you don't come back with anything? Oops, sorry, can't eat, guess the whole thing's off, might as well go home?"

"No," Alexander huffed. "If I don't come back with a catch, then we'll have beef and I'll be seen as incompetent, embarrass my father and prove to him that I am unable to do anything, especially when it comes to statecraft or running the country. It's like he doesn't trust me at all!"

"Well, then you'll just have to prove him wrong," Crow said. "It can't be that hard to catch a deer, right?" Alexander shot her a withering look and Crow lapsed into silence, feeling sorry for the man riding beside her. Having to deal with this Yvonne Tyber sounded bad enough, but to throw a bad relationship with his father on top of it, well, amounted to a very bad mood.

The two rode in silence for a while, not really keeping an eye out for game but also not purposefully ignoring their task. The fog burned off by mid-morning, but the air remained cool and crisp. Once, they managed to stumble across a brace of pheasants and brought two of the stupid birds down. Alexander was convinced that his arrow killed one, but Crow rather thought that the birds just died of fright. It didn't matter, though. Game was game and so they kept on. The day progressed with no more luck. The two rode deeper and deeper into the forest, venturing on game trails that looked as though they might belong to a deer or to nobody. Alexander insisted they eat their lunch of dried meat and bread in the saddle—which Crow was becoming ever weary of—and became more snappish as the day went on.

Crow was about to suggest they stop for the night and set up camp when Alexander roared, "This is hopeless!" A few feet away, invisible until it moved, a large buck with an impressive rack leaped from cover at Alexander's words. Long, slender legs carried it swiftly through the forest and Alexander sat on his horse, too startled to move. In a heartbeat, drawing on instincts she hadn't used for years, Crow lifted her bow and nocked an arrow, letting it fly after the buck. She saw it strike the rump of the fleeing deer and the animal gave a cry of pain. Crow urged her sorrel forwards, Alexander not far behind.

With a slight shout, Alexander took the lead, leaning over his horse with the practise of someone who had trained for it. Before Crow could nock another arrow, he had already loosed. His arrow caught the animal in the exposed chest as it leaped and it fell to the ground, dead. Crow lowered her bow and eased her horse into a walk, adrenaline pounding through her ears. She spotted Alexander kneeling by the buck and dismounted, going to assess the damage.

"Nice shot," he said to her, pulling her arrow out of the creature's flank. She took the weapon and stared at the beast.

"Oh," she said, not sure what else to say in such a

situation. Alexander recovered his own weapon and straightened, admiring the prize. He looked over his shoulder at Crow and saw her obvious confusion. Not discomfort, just confusion at the situation presented her.

"I didn't know you could shoot so quickly," he said, trying to draw her out. Crow blinked and looked up at him and for a brief moment, Alexander thought he saw wariness in her eyes. Then, the moment was gone and Crow merely shrugged.

"Neither did I," she said, hoping that he would leave it be. For one, it wouldn't do to go prying into her skills with weapons. For two, having Alexander praise her was making her stomach flutter with emotions she couldn't even begin to understand. She was glad her skin wouldn't let her blush, because that would have taken some explaining. Her shrug, hopefully, passed her actions off as a fluke, an accident, something never to be repeated.

The two set about getting to work, lifting the deer carcass and draping it across the testy sorrel. The horse snorted in annoyance as they tied the creature to it with ropes. After they walked a ways to the nearby stream, Alexander called a halt, and they set up camp. Crow worked on getting the deer off the ground, hanging it from a tree while Alexander set about starting a fire. Or, he tried to. The fog from that morning had seeped its moisture into the wood and the Prince snarled at the damp wood.

Crow laughed at his struggles and crouched by the fire. "Perhaps you should let someone who works with fire every day deal with the campfire," she said, snatching the flint and steel from Alexander. He threw up his hands and watched. Crow set the twigs up in a cone and put larger pieces along the outside. In the middle, she set a few drier pieces that she scrounged up from inside a hole beneath a tree. Then, she flicked her wrist and the flint created sparks, catching almost immediately. After a few coaxing breaths, Crow had the fire going at a decent blaze.

Alexander grumbled with annoyance and grabbed a few supplies, stalking off. Crow shook her head at her ornery friend and started plucking one of the pheasants they caught. By the time she had it cleaned, skewered for roasting and sitting above the fire cooking merrily, Crow was beginning to slump from the day. Her legs were sore, her body protesting at the odd exercise demanded of it. She dazed, staring at the fire and enjoying the smell of roasting meat. That is, until Alexander walked back to the campsite, directly into Crow's line of vision.

She coughed and averted her gaze to the fire as she realised that the Crown Prince wore not a stitch of clothing. The feelings that had surfaced earlier under his praise reared up again, this time louder by far. Attraction, she thought, realisation dawning on her. She had been masquerading as a boy for so long that she had forgotten that one simple fact. Attraction. Lust. And, as Alexander stuffed his legs into trousers and a shirt over his well-defined chest, there was no doubt that she had a lot of it.

Crow turned the spit, trying her best to shove those thoughts aside. It wasn't doing any good, though. The more Alexander moved, arranging his bedroll or running his fingers through his wet hair, the more Crow couldn't deny it. She felt her stomach clench and her breasts tighten under the bandages. She closed her eyes for a moment and swallowed. *Deal with it, Crow,* she scolded herself. *Push it aside and say nothing, or you'll deserve what's coming to you.*

Crow's eyes flew open as Alexander snatched the spit from her and cut off a bit of pheasant, handing some to her and keeping some. She bit into the bird with a vengeance, the only way to do something about what brewed beneath the surface.

"You're in a mood," Alexander said, taking a piece of bird off his belt knife with his teeth.

"I'm sore," Crow said truthfully. "I haven't ridden a horse in years."

"Really?" Alexander asked around a mouthful of pheasant. He swallowed and coughed slightly. "Then how did you get to Kyper?"

"I walked," Crow sniffed with borrowed airs. Alexander burst out laughing. Indignant, Crow bristled in silence, tearing into her supper vehemently. After a moment, the Prince stopped laughing to stare at Crow as if she were crazy.

"You're serious?" he asked. She nodded, her own mouth full. "Oh," Alexander said, looking down at the fire. Crow ignored him for the remainder of the meal. There was too much going on in her head for light banter, especially with Alexander. She disposed of the remains of the bird a ways from the camp to keep away any unwanted predators and then returned to settle into her bedroll. Crow stared at the dying fire and yawned, turning her back to the warmth.

"Hey, Crow?" Alexander asked from his own bedroll.

"Hmmm?" she replied, already half asleep despite the whirling of her thoughts.

"Thanks," he said. Crow murmured a goodnight and a few moments later, she was asleep. A few moments following that, so was Alexander.

The next two days of the hunting trip were no less successful than the first. By the time the two hunters returned to the Palace, both horses were laden down with a deer and Alexander carried a brace of pheasants, Crow one of rabbits. They were both bone tired and weary from walking back to Kyper, the horses no less so. Both smelled of horse sweat, dirt and hard work and the conversation had lagged for weariness. Crow, for her part, had managed to sequester the feelings for Alexander in a quiet part of her mind and things were as they ever were between them. Finally, it seemed, they arrived back in the courtyard and delivered their prizes to the kitchens. Alexander, with a murmured thanks, walked into the Palace to bathe while Crow trudged to the forge, greeting Jek with a slight shout.

"Crow, lad," Jek said as the apprentice entered the forge, looking smug despite her weariness. "How was the hunt?"

"I shot a deer," she said happily. Jek laughed and slapped Crow on the shoulder, sending her staggering. Jek shook his head at her in fondness then froze. He sniffed the air once, twice, then recoiled.

"Lad, ye smell somethin' awful. Go bathe. Now," Jek said flatly. Crow shook her head and stretched, depositing her pack in the house before going off at the fastest walk she could manage to fetch water. Three trips later, she stepped into the frigid water and set to scrubbing. It felt good to be clean, but Crow wished she had a bath of steaming water to relieve her sore muscles. She looked at the chair propped against the door and the window to the garden, which she had left uncovered. It was a bitter reminder of all that she had to hide, especially since her discovery regarding her feelings for Alexander. Her thoughts wandered and by the time Crow came to, she was shivering, her skin almost grey from cold.

"Lad!" Jek called. Crow froze for a moment in horror then lunged for her bandages and wrapped them around her chest with the quick, practised motions of someone who had done so for years. She tugged her breeches on and was grabbing a shirt when Jek burst into her room as if the chair had never been there. He stared at her chest for a moment and frowned. "Lad, why are ye wearin' those?"

"I have scars..." Crow said quickly, eyes wide. "I don't like to show them."

Jek shrugged his large shoulders at the folly of vain apprentices. He spoke, the words rumbling in his barrel chest, "Lad, I'd get out to the yard right quick. The Prince is a'waitin' and said somethin' 'bout some party comin' now."

Crow blinked, then, "Oh." She threw the shirt over

her head and darted past the big smith, running into the yard. Alexander was standing on the steps to the Palace, having already bathed and dressed in royal regalia. A retinue of knights stood nearby and even some of the servants were standing nearby in their best clothes as they awaited the guests. Alexander caught Crow's eye as she started to cross the yard and shook his head subtly. She fell back, hurt. Their months of friendship had softened the barrier between their classes and to be reminded when all she wanted to do was support him, stung.

Trying not to show the hurt on her face, she retreated to the forge and prepared to stand watch until the company arrived. A small gleam of silver caught Crow's eye and, growling, she grabbed the sliver, thrusting it onto the rack that sat above the fire for slower heatings. As the metal began to heat, Crow pulled out the bones of an intricate necklace that she had been working on, determined to be productive while she waited. If nothing else, it distracted her from thoughts of Alexander.

Over the last few weeks, Crow's renown as a decent silversmith had spread and she had been getting orders from wealthy families for jewellery, buckles, candlesticks and even cutlery. As an apprentice, they weren't required to pay her nearly as much as they would Jek, so Crow found herself quite busy. She didn't mind the work, happy to practise her craft as much as she could. But just then, she wasn't working on a commission. She was working on something for herself, for the day when she would no longer have to hide behind bandages and masculine mannerisms, when she could be herself. It was a necklace of beautiful design with a few glass beads Crow had haggled from the merchant's market.

So busy was Crow with her work that she didn't notice the group of people that came into the courtyard, riding fine horses and looking like a grand procession. The leader was older, his silver hair and beard trimmed in the latest fashions that made him only look more regal. He wore silks and velvet in a stunning purple and his horse was decked in similar finery. He was closely followed by a grey, delicate pony whose rider was a girl who wore only the latest fashions, also in a deep purple. She was slenderly figured and had curling blonde hair so fine as to be almost white. She looked upon the world as if she owned it and there would be few who would question her. The Lord Tyber and his daughter Yvonne, then. Following them was a collection of servants and soldiers, all bearing the Tyber sigil.

Alexander waited in annoyance as his father, a tall, proud man who wore his weight in muscle rather than fat, face cleanly shaven and silver-brown peppered hair combed back under a circlet of gold and silver, stood beside him. He shot a glance at Crow who seemed to be oblivious to the goings-on in the yard, envying the blacksmith. Then, he had to focus on the people in front of him as they dismounted and handed over their steed to the palace stable hands. The girl smoothed her dress and shot Alexander a flirtatious smile, the man walking up the steps to the King, his hands held out in greeting.

"Byron, you old fool, it's good to see you," Lord

Vincent Tyber said, clapping the King familiarly on the shoulder. Despite the fact that he left out the usual Your Majesties and bowing, the King didn't seem to mind. He embraced Lord Vincent like a brother and the newcomer turned to greet Alexander. He held his hand out to be shaken by the Prince, smiling cheerfully, "Alexander. Every time I see you, you seem to get bigger."

Alexander took the man's hand, "It's only been a year. I haven't grown, Lord Vincent."

He put on a false smile as Vincent examined him and then stifled a groan as the man clapped him on the shoulder affectionately. The woman started walking up the steps, having finally gotten her dress resettled from riding. Alexander barely managed to hide the pained smile as he bowed slightly to Lady Yvonne. She curtsied and cast a sly look his way, extending her hand to be kissed.

"My lady," Alexander grumbled, taking her hand and nodding his head, purposefully not kissing the exposed flesh. Yvonne ignored the slight and blushed, turning her head so as to show off her slender neck and the best angle of her face, fair strands of hair falling slightly forwards, serving to emphasise her beauty.

"Prince Alexander," she replied, falsely demur. Alexander said nothing further and handed her off to his father.

"Lady Yvonne," the king said, brushing his lips against her hand and smiling. "You grow more beautiful by the day. I'm amazed your father manages to keep you at his side."

“You are too kind, Your Majesty,” Yvonne purred. Lord Vincent laughed and that was the end of it. The formal greetings were done and the people, both nobles and servants, could go into the Palace and get about their work. Over his shoulder, Alexander shot a desperate look to Crow who raised her head just in time to be startled by Alexander’s look and the people that were now streaming into the palace.

"Did I miss it?" she asked Jek who just shook his head and chuckled.

"Aye, lad, ye did," he said. "Though I wouldn' be too worried. That lady there is a mean one, ye can be sure o' that. An' I dare say Alexander will be out here right quick. He ne'er took a shine to Lady Yvonne. But she'll foller 'im out here, I'd stake my forge."

Crow winced in sympathy for the Prince and shook her head, making her short hair more mussed. Somehow, the look suited her. She returned to her work and was just setting a deep blue glass bead in the centre of her necklace when Alexander did indeed come to the forge, eyes wide with fear.

"Hide me," he begged and looked over his shoulder, giving a strangled cry when he saw the beautiful lady following him. She had spotted him and there was no chance of his escape, so Crow simply shoved him to the other side of the forge and picked up a large hammer, heating a long piece of iron and stoking the flames higher. She put her necklace aside and hoped that the heat and flying flakes of metal would be enough to deter the lady. It was the least she could do for her friend.

"Alexander," Yvonne said, voice high and slightly whiney. She stopped just on the other side of the fence, hesitating on silk slippers as though she were deciding whether she should actually enter the forge. To Crow's relief, she decided to stay outside. It was crowded enough with three people. Four would have been impossible. Not to mention Alexander's panic became almost palpable. "Why did you come here? It's so hot."

Crow shot her a glance and at once, understood why Alexander didn't like the woman. She raised her hammer and struck the iron, once, twice, making the tip into a point and then dipping it back into the fire. Noise and dirty work were the best way she knew of to get rid of prissy nobles. Most of the men didn't even bother getting too close. Alexander was a pleasant relief.

"I came here because I happen to like it," Alexander replied flatly, all pretence of flattery gone with his father no longer present. He stayed on the opposite side of the forge and Yvonne didn't seem willing to cross the sooty stone and get in the way of the powerful Crow or the flying sparks from the fire. "And these are my friends."

"Well," the lady dripped sweetly, eyeing Crow with a calculated look in her eye. "Then you'll have to introduce me."

Crow furrowed her brows in confusion and tried to catch Alexander's eye, to make the lady go away. But Alexander was watching Lady Yvonne and seemed to see her plan. He glanced at Crow and understanding dawned on his face. Relief swam through the Prince and pity for what he was about to do to his friend, but Crow would understand his desperation. He hoped. He would make it up to Crow later.

"This is Crow, the apprentice smith to Jek," Alexander said smoothly. "He's probably the best smith, discounting Jek, of course, in the kingdom. And he's fairly skilled in silversmithing as well." The Prince gestured to the half-completed necklace and Yvonne gasped, burning desire in her eyes. She was as drawn to the jewellery as she was to men and, braving the fire and dirt, stepped into the forge, making Jek back up to properly accommodate the woman. Yvonne didn't even seem to notice the tight quarters and stepped straight up to Crow, grasping the blacksmith's arm in a move to seem willing and interested.

"Oh, Crow, is it? What an unusual name. I'm Yvonne Tyber of Halfpeak," she purred, pleased at the muscle she felt beneath Crow's shirt. Awkwardly, with a hammer in one hand and the lady holding the other arm, Crow managed to bow slightly. She shot a look at Jek and he snatched the hammer from his apprentice, allowing some freedom of movement. Crow straightened and shifted to look at the noble.

"My lady," she said formally and Yvonne beamed, tossing her hair over one shoulder. Without regard to the other people present or the fact that she was getting dangerously close to the fire or the metal being heated there, Yvonne pushed her way to the workbench, staring at the silver piece.

"I do so love that necklace you're making there. Allow me to buy it," she pouted and Crow straightened in alarm, flicking her green eyes to the necklace. It wasn't finished and hardly polished, and it was hers.

"That one's already spoken for, my lady," Crow started in desperation.

"Then let me commission one from you," Yvonne stated, pressing herself against Crow's chest. The smith stepped back and frowned. There was nowhere to go. "Please," the noble added, willing a blush to her cheeks as she examined Crow through narrow eyes.

"I suppose. You'll have to let me know what sort you want," Crow said hesitantly and immediately, Yvonne squealed in delight, causing Crow to wince. The smith, to hide her discomfort, pulled the iron from the fire and picked up another hammer, beating the metal into submission much to the amusement of Alexander and Jek.

"We can get to that later," Yvonne said, trilling as she stepped away from the furious blows of the apprentice, gazing apprehensively at the fire. "At the banquet, perhaps?"

"I'm not going," Crow stated, voice flat. Her patience was beginning to wear thin and, noble or not, if Yvonne kept pushing her, Crow was going to snap.

"Oh, but you must," Yvonne pouted, shooting an arrogant look at Alexander. He simply watched with a smile daring to come to the corners of his mouth. Crow shook her head and Yvonne put her hand on the fair smith's broad shoulders, stopping her in the middle of putting the iron back into the fire.

"I'm not invited," Crow tried to protest, attempting

to shake off the woman as politely as possible. Yvonne was not deterred.

"Then you'll come as my personal guest. I like you, Crow, and I want to dance with you," she stated and then turned away as if Crow had already agreed. "I'll see you there," she called, striding across the courtyard, brushing away imagined dirt from her dress. Crow watched her retreating form, bewildered.

"What just happened?" she asked Alexander who came to stand next to his friend. Jek chuckled and folded his arms, waiting for the Prince to explain.

"You just became the key for me to escape Lady Yvonne Tyber of Halfpeak," Alexander said. "She thinks that she'll make me jealous by flirting with my friend rather than me, but she's wrong."

"No, no," Crow snapped, wide-eyed. She held up her hands in desperation, shaking her head. “I won’t do it.”

Alexander blinked as if the option of Crow refusing had never occurred to him. "Please?" he begged, blue eyes meeting green ones. Crow felt her insides melt as he stared at her with pleading eyes and she sighed, putting the hammer on the workbench. She hunched her shoulders and looked up at him pitifully. Alexander just repeated his plea.

"Fine," she agreed with an exasperated sigh. "But you owe me."

"Thank you," the Prince grinned, relief dancing across his handsome visage. Crow sighed and grumbled.

"If it were anyone else," she muttered to herself and then turned fully to the Prince, crossing her arms. "I hope you realise that I don't have clothes for this banquet, am not good at dancing and have never been to so much as a feast in my entire life. In a room full of nobles, I'm going to stand out like a sore thumb."

"Don't worry," Alexander replied, gripping her shoulder assuredly. "I'll get everything sorted."

CHAPTER 5

"I haven't danced in ages," Crow said desperately as Alexander led her through the palace to his quarters, a pleased look on his face and a slight pep to his walk as he realised he was free, for the time being, from Yvonne. There was a brief moment of guilt for putting Crow through that, but it soon passed. He did his best to reassure Crow, but the blacksmith was determined. Not that Alexander could really blame Crow.

"I can help you brush up. Besides, if you step on her toes a bit, I'm sure it wouldn't be a problem," he replied easily, pushing the heavy wooden door to his room open. "Actually, make sure that you do step on her toes. That would be good." Alexander's manservant, Geoff, straightened where he sat polishing a pair of boots and Crow tried to plead silently with him. Geoff just widened his eyes as he realised what was going on and left, taking the boots with him. Crow was left to plead with Alexander, who was not listening to her or to reason, it seemed.

"I'm no noble. I don't know how to act at one of these things," was her next argument and Alexander scoffed openly as he threw open his wardrobe and rifled through the clothing contained within.

"Just follow the lead of others around you. Everyone will be too busy drinking the wine provided by my father to care whether you're a noble. Besides, you'll be dressed like one. You're smart, you'll catch on quickly," he said, pulling out a fine grey shirt and deep blue tunic. Under normal circumstances, Crow would have been pleased with the back-handed compliment. Now, she just wished that he thought less of her intelligence. Alexander threw the shirt and tunic at Crow who caught the beautiful clothing deftly and stared at it in confusion and despair. Alexander looked at her and sighed, "Put them on. We haven't got all day, Crow."

She glared at him and moved away to the changing screen as the Prince attempted to find a pair of breeches that would fit. Clutching the fabric in her hands, Crow hesitated, closing her eyes. She then used the only argument remaining to her, her voice barely more than a whisper, "But I don't like her."

At that, Alexander stopped his search and turned around, gaze pitying and somewhat guilty. "Crow, please," he said, voice thrumming quietly and Crow clenched her stomach muscles involuntarily. "We talked about this. You're my only hope for getting Yvonne to stay off my back. I wouldn't ask you to do this if I weren't desperate. Please," he begged, blue eyes searching her face. Crow sighed, defeated, and remembered the exact same conversation they had gone through in the forge, not half an hour ago. She had foolishly thought him to be joking. Now, she was trapped, bound by her word and the attraction to him that ensured she would do anything he asked.

"Alright," she acquiesced. "But like I said earlier, you owe me. Big time." Crow spun on her heel and darted behind the changing screen, peeling off her shirt and dropping it on the floor, taking a moment to run the fine fabric of the grey shirt through her hand. She remembered the feel of such fabric on her skin like a dream, half-forgotten but present, nonetheless. She resisted the temptation to bring the fabric to her nose and smell it, but Alexander's scent whirled around her in any case. Torn, Crow didn't hear Alexander approach from behind.

"Crow," Alexander said warily, snapping the fair youth back to reality. She turned and looked at the Prince and realised, belatedly and with fear, that he was looking at her bandaged torso with confusion. "Why are you wearing bandages?"

"I have scars," she said lamely, using the same true excuse she had told Jek. It was the truth, but with Alexander, it sounded more pathetic than otherwise. "They're ugly and I don't want to see them."

"Scars?" Alexander questioned, interest piqued. "From what?"

"A long time ago," she said flatly, her tone giving no doubt that this conversation was over. Alexander, as with most things, didn't do as he was told.

"I'll get you to tell me," the Crown Prince said confidently and Crow shook her head, gaze hard as she pulled

Alexander's shirt over her head, broad shoulders flexing with powerful muscle. "I just have to get enough wine in you," he scoffed and Crow said nothing, glaring at him, none of her usual cheerful personality showing. She pulled on the tunic and folded her arms across her chest.

"I'll get you some breeches," Alexander said, suddenly nervous at the harsh gaze of his friend.

"They won't fit me," Crow said, emerging from behind the changing screen. "You're taller than me by a good three inches and I'm skinnier."

"Let's see," was the muffled reply and Crow looked around to see Alexander sorting through a trunk in a shadowy corner. He pulled out a pair of blue breeches, almost the same exact colour of the tunic Crow wore. "These were too small for me anyways." He threw the fabric at the black-haired Crow and she held them up to her. They looked like they might fit, but they would certainly be too big around the waist.

"You can wear a belt," Alexander said, waving away Crow's incredulous look. She went behind the changing screen again and pulled on the Prince's clothes, realising that they were, indeed, a good fit but for the waist. The fabric hugged her strong legs and it was loose enough near her loins so as to be fairly comfortable. The waist, as predicted, was too large and Crow reacted out of instinct when Alexander threw a belt of leather at her. She wrapped it around the pants and cinched it as tight as it would go then pulled the shirt and tunic over the top.

"Well?" she asked, standing in the middle of the room and holding out her arms. The Prince regarded her with a careful eye, wondering why he found her angry look so fascinating, intriguing. Perhaps it was the faerie-looks that Crow sported, both beautiful and dangerous. Shaking himself mentally, he walked in a circle around the smith and then nodded.

"You look like a proper noble," he said finally and Crow stiffened, her expression hardening. She grumbled and waited while Alexander pulled out his own finery for the evening. He was obviously less modest than she, for he simply stripped then and there, drawing Crow's gaze to his powerful abdomen, defined chest and shoulders. She swallowed back a blush when he pulled his breeches off, standing in his loincloth alone. She turned and pretended to look around at the furniture and decorations while he changed.

"When is this banquet supposed to start?" Crow asked to hide her increasing discomfort, fighting back the image of her walking forwards and stroking his muscles, he peeling back the shirt and tunic and slowly, sensuously, unwrapping her bandages until she stood there, all secrets out in the open, for him to see. She imagined running her fingers through his hair until he leaned forwards, mouth open and ready for hers-

"Oh, about an hour from now," Alexander said, ruining Crow's thoughts as he pulled on a pair of silk, black breeches and a red shirt. He wore no tunic, instead tucking in the shirt and putting a wide belt around his narrow hips.

"And I still don't know how to dance," she stated, shifting uncomfortably after stifling completely the train of thought in her mind. She had never dealt with such desires before and she knew, beyond a doubt, that the direction her mind was going was dangerous. She was Alexander's friend and he could never know her secret. The only way to be safe was to keep silent and banish all such thoughts from her mind. Crow forced her thoughts to the situation at hand. "I mean, I haven't done it in so long," she amended, but Alexander ignored her statement and held up his hands.

"Alright, I'm Yvonne," he said and Crow made a face at him and backed away swiftly. Alexander sighed and tried not to laugh at his friend's reaction. "Fine. I'm your partner and you have to lead."

Crow grumbled and stepped forwards, awkwardly taking Alexander's hand and putting her hand on his waist. She tingled where her hand met his skin and wished that he wore no shirt so she could feel him there, too. Crow forced her thoughts to dancing, wondering hopelessly why she couldn't keep such thoughts regarding Alexander contained.

"A waltz," Alexander said and started humming out some music. Crow stepped through the dance in half-remembered movements, trying to lead where she had been following the tall man that had been her father so many years before. She tried to keep any debilitating images out of her head and keep her mind focused. Only years of practise allowed her to do as well as she did in terms of focusing her thoughts and managed to make it through a dance, a short one, without much mishap.

"That was fine," the Prince said carefully and Crow scowled.

"It wasn't and you know it," she snapped and balled her hands into fists at her side. "This is going to be a disaster and I'm going to be humiliated in front of the entire court while you get to sit happily on the sidelines and watch."

"Come on, Crow," Alexander pleaded. "It wasn't that bad. You're just stiff is all. Maybe it'll be easier when you have actual music." Crow snorted and shook her head just as Geoff came to fetch them. "It'll be fine, Crow. It really wasn't that bad," Alexander tried to assure his friend, but Crow just turned away towards the window, arms folded.

"It is time to take your place, Highness," Geoff said and bowed slightly to Alexander. The Prince led the way and Crow felt her dread growing as they neared the banquet hall and the music grew louder. Alexander straightened his shoulders and shot a guilty look at Crow as the doors opened to reveal the waiting people. Too late to turn back, now. There were musicians in a corner playing gently and nobles of all sorts stood in the hall, dancing or talking. The tables were set up in a horseshoe along the walls so there would be enough room to move about while dancing and the finery that people wore glittered in the light. Crow was pleased to see that many noble ladies were wearing jewellery of her make and that there were a few silver buckles she could claim as well.

Stately and regal looking, Alexander strode into the

room, nodding graciously to the people that murmured respectful greetings to him. Crow stepped into the room and instinct bred into her caused her to straighten her shoulders and step lightly, moving through the people with a noble's grace. She acknowledged the people she passed and, wearing her borrowed finery, fit into her new role like hand in glove. Her transformation from desperate, lowly apprentice blacksmith, no matter how beautiful, to noble of high birth and exquisite looks was dramatic and when Alexander turned his head to check on his friend, he recoiled in literal shock at the change. Crow, it seemed to him, had been hiding before and was just now coming into the light.

The two approached the head table and Alexander nodded his head to acknowledge his father while Crow bowed deeply to the King, as was proper. She bowed, less deeply to Lord Vincent and nodded her head to Lady Yvonne, who had saved a chair for the guest she had commandeered. The blonde was pleased with Crow's transformation and looked over the smith with appreciation in her eyes.

"My lady," Crow said, moving around to take the open seat next to Yvonne while she wished that she could have sat next to Alexander. The noblewoman wore a low cut dress of a glimmering yellow, the waist cinched tightly and the hem decorated with gold beads. Her hair was piled on her head and she wore paint on her eyelids which had been narrowed to send a flirting glance to Crow. Yvonne was beautiful and she knew it. She would use her beauty to get what she wanted, and what she wanted then was Alexander. But getting to him would be difficult and so she would use his fair friend, a not unappealing prospect, to meet her needs. How could any peasant, no matter how well they cleaned up, refuse?

"Crow," she said, remembering the smith's name. "You look so handsome in that shirt and tunic."

"Thank you," Crow replied stiffly, looking around to see what others were doing. She began to put food on her plate as Alexander was doing and got stopped by Yvonne grasping onto her arm.

"I bet you're a wonderful dancer," Yvonne purred, wide eyes taking in Crow's features. "Dance with me."

Crow opened her mouth to protest and knew, rightly, that she could not refuse without offending Yvonne, who would then complain to her father, who would speak to the King, who would ask Alexander what she was doing there, which would, in turn, embarrass the Prince. So instead, Crow dipped her head in acquiescence and stood, offering her hand to the Lady as she bowed slightly.

Yvonne giggled, causing Crow to flinch inwardly and took the offered hand, standing with as much grace and flirtatiousness as she could muster, a cunning smile directed at Crow. With straight posture, Crow led Yvonne to the open floor for dancing, just as the musicians struck up a slow and sensual waltz. Just as instinct had taken over when Crow entered the banquet hall, instinct took over for the dance. Despite having always followed before, Crow took to the leading role with an ease that surprised her and pleased Yvonne. It was like fighting with the Scheren in Mak'tal. A dance of knives was no less a dance than what she led Yvonne through. It was only a different adaptation. Crow, as a skilled fighter, found the dance as smooth and easy as sparring. She rather thought that her current partner was a far more dangerous adversary than a sword.

Alexander, Crow thought, was right about the music. She led Yvonne along in the dance, her expression flat and pointedly not meeting the blue eyes that desperately tried to draw the attention of their partner. "You dance so well," Yvonne giggled, "for a smith."

"I've had practise," Crow replied smoothly, thinking of the brief lesson Alexander had given her. She didn't think that Yvonne would like to know that Crow thought of this as sparring or fighting.

"Oh, really," Lady Yvonne purred, purposefully rubbing her hand on Crow's shoulder. Crow gave no response but held the Lady properly with her hand just below her shoulder blade. "Speaking of smithing, I've been thinking of that necklace that I want you to make."

Crow raised her eyebrows, wondering how much more she would have to play the pet of Lady Yvonne. If it would help Alexander, Crow knew she would do it. No matter how unpleasant. The blonde Lady smiled unabashedly and nodded, "Oh, yes. I want it to be large and grand, with lots of whirls like the one you were making. I want topaz, to match my eyes, and I want a little butterfly to be on either side of the centre stone."

Crow visibly winced and chose her words carefully, disliking the woman more and more by the minute, "A necklace like that will cost you at least twenty gold pieces and finding the right stones requires me to go to the Merchant's Market. I'll need a special pass for that, which is another two gold pieces. Not to mention that it will take most of three weeks to make something like that, with all the other projects I have to finish."

Yvonne pouted, fluttering her eyelashes, "Price is no cost. Daddy only wants the best for me and," she dropped her voice to a whisper, stepping closer to Crow even as the music slowed and deepened, "you are the best." The woman didn't move when Crow did and the smith found herself uncomfortably pressed up to the noble with the low-cut dress giving Crow a glimpse of breasts she did not want to see. Crow's thighs were being rubbed against Yvonne's and the fair smith stepped back, bowing to her partner as the music stopped. Yvonne looked put out for a moment and then curtseyed in response.

Crow held out her arm to escort the woman back to the head table and Yvonne grasped it, trying to get in close, something which Crow did not allow. "As to your other projects, you'll just have to put them aside for my necklace," Yvonne said, taking up the previous thread of conversation.

"I cannot," Crow replied coldly. The Lady waved a hand and scoffed.

"I'll pay you whatever fees will arise for putting aside the other projects. I want that necklace to wear for the King before I leave," Yvonne said. Crow sighed and held the chair out for the Lady as she sat, straightening up.

"That will not be cheap," Crow muttered to the

woman who only simpered and shrugged. She was obviously willing to give away her father's money and Crow really couldn't refuse such a good price. Grudgingly, Crow nodded. "I will have it done by next Tuesday," she said and Yvonne beamed.

"Young man," a voice called and Crow snapped to attention as someone touched her shoulder. A woman at least three times her age, wearing a matronly maroon dress with glittering jewels stitched into the bodice faced Crow with a harsh look in her eye.

"My lady?" Crow asked, bowing slightly to the woman, confused. She desperately wanted to sit and eat, as she had not done so since returning from the hunting trip that morning. The venison on the table was giving off such a pleasant aroma and Crow was really quite hungry and rather tired.

"I saw you dancing with the Lady Yvonne. You seem like you know what you are doing. You would be honoured if you would ask me to dance," the woman said, staring down her nose at Crow, a feat since Crow was taller by at least a foot. Trying to hide her wince, Crow bowed and offered her hand. The woman grinned and shot a look at a group of other noblewomen. The group chattered and shot glances at Crow and the smith immediately knew she was in for a long night.

Indeed, the banquet lasted well until the morning and Crow was on her feet for the majority of the time, entertaining the countless noblewomen who were anxious for a dance with the beautiful apprentice smith. She was exotic and an oddity amongst the nobles and that made her desirable. Crow danced three times more with Yvonne and glared at Alexander repeatedly. The Prince, to his credit, did dance with Yvonne once, but it was clear that her attention was riveted on Crow who had thus far refused her repeated advances. That made the black-haired, pale skinned, lovely youth a challenge and a challenge was something Yvonne could not pass up. Her attention became more determined.

Crow managed to sit in her chair once, for a whole of five minutes, before being whisked away by another inebriated noble. The King and Lord Tyber, true to Alexander's word, got roaring drunk and by the time the other nobles had wandered off to bed or dark corners for whispered liaisons, the two were laughing and giggling at the head table, their words all but incoherent. Yvonne had slipped off to bed, finally giving up her ploys for the evening and annoyed at both Alexander and Crow, and the Prince hadn't stayed long after that, only stopping long enough to clap Crow on the shoulder encouragingly. At least someone was pleased with how the night had progressed.

The end of the banquet found Crow standing on nearly trembling legs, supporting the weight of an old woman who had drunk far too much wine and was swaying back and forth despite the fact that the music stopped. Carefully, Crow led the woman to the table and set her on a chair then left through the doors to the banquet hall before anyone else could get her attention. She dragged her feet as she wound through the palace and into the frigid air that filled the courtyard. She saw that the fire in the forge had been doused for the evening and Jek did not awaken when Crow pushed open the door to the house and slunk past his room to her own. She realised, belatedly, that she was still wearing Alexander's clothes.

"Well, tough luck," she growled angrily, her resentment of the easy time that Alexander had experienced growing. Crow simply stripped out of the tunic and shirt and breeches and pulled on her own loose pair that served as her sleeping pants. She closed the door and collapsed onto her bed, pulling the covers around her and slipping easily into a deep sleep.

The night passed both slowly and quickly and Crow's exhaustion lowered the walls that she kept up in her mind. For the first time in a while, Crow dreamt of her past, amplified into raging nightmares. Everything was shadows and blood, her heart pounding in her ears. Adrenaline overrode the tang of fear and instinct had Crow attempting to fight. She felt something, a hand far too large to wield the delicate tools that it normally held, wrapping around her torso. Scrambling desperately at the appendage, Crow tried to loosen its grasp. The hand released her, its owner letting out an earth-shaking howl. Crow ran, feeling the numerous wounds she had dancing and snaking across her skin bleed afresh.

The scenery around her was dead and black, trees appearing out of a dense fog, their roots causing Crow to stumble as she bled. She screamed as a jackal jumped out at her, long fangs ripping into her arm. She fell to the ground as the jackal started to feast on her flesh and when the pain became almost unbearable, she awoke, panting and feeling a scream dying in her throat.

The door to her room slammed open and Crow sat up, seeing the ghostly form of Jek come into the room, illuminated by a single candle. His eyes were wild and afraid and Crow imagined she did not look any better.

"Lad," Jek said gruffly, taking in Crow's face and keeping his gaze there. "I heard ye screamin'. It's just a nightmare. Lad?"

Crow stared blankly at the smith, shivering at the cold air that filtered into her room from the little garden. She felt her breasts shiver from the cold under her bandages which had been loosened in her nightmare-induced desperation. Taking a shuddering breath to calm her nerves, the bandages slipped from their precarious position on her chest. Crow froze in fear. She stared wide-eyed at Jek who stared back, a stunned expression on his face.

"Oh," Jek breathed as he took in Crow's bare chest, his heart a mix of emotions, his face betraying only shock. "Not a lad."

Crow shook her head, fighting back tears. She pulled the covers of her bed up to cover her shame.

"Ye lied to me," Jek whispered and Crow gasped at the sudden pain that his words brought about. She shook her head again, tears falling freely now.

"No, I-" she started and Jek held up a hand, cutting her off.

"Did ye lie to me 'bout anythin' else, Crow? Is there anythin' else that I should know?" Jek hissed, disappointment plain. Crow let out a sob and clutched the blanket closer, knowing her fate. She had let her master down, the man who had been so kind and good to her, who had been like a father to her. She would burn forevermore with that guilt and, far worse, she would have to leave him behind. Leave this wonderful life she had created behind. Leave Alexander behind. What other options were there?

Crow stared through watery eyes at the burly man, biting her lip. He turned away from her, as if in disgust and Crow moaned in pain of guilt. Jek moved out the door and Crow watched as he started to close the door.

"I'm sorry," she called out and Jek froze for a moment, his back turned to Crow. He shook his head and closed the door behind him then leaned against it, the full realisation of what Crow was hitting him.

"Not as sorry as I," he whispered.

CHAPTER 6

Despite everything, Crow tried to sleep. Exhaustion plagued her body and she knew she would need rest before setting out in the morning. Yet, she could not sleep. Her mind kept her awake, filled with shame for being what she was, what she could not prevent and guilt for having to lie to Jek. When she could bear the thoughts in her head no longer, Crow rose and began to pack her belongings, not bothering to fit everything neatly into her pack. She opened the door slowly and crept through the small house, attempting to leave before Jek awoke. She could spare him anymore pain, Crow thought. She failed.

"Where do ye think yer goin'?" Jek asked softly and Crow turned, staring at the bulky form of her former-smith master sitting at the table in the main room of the house. He looked at her with sadness and wariness, like she was a favourite dog that had bitten its master. That look hurt Crow violently and she averted her gaze, staring at the floor.

"I thought it best," she started, voice trailing off as she gestured to her pack. Jek said nothing for a moment and openly stared at the guilty look on Crow's face, assessing her true intent.

"Thought it best that ye leave wi'out givin' me an explanation? Is that right?" Jek accused and Crow fidgeted uncomfortably, not meeting the gaze of the smith. "Ye owe me to at least explain things."

"You're right," Crow whispered and backed up against a wall, sliding to the floor next to her pack. Jek watched with a solemnity that caused Crow to shudder. She closed her eyes and began her tale.

"At the age of ten, I found it necessary to masquerade as a boy. I won't explain why but to say that it was either that or be sold to slavers. I had been fascinated with smithing since I was a little girl and I spent more time in the forge with old Sythfeld than most boys of the village. I learned more, too. When my parents—" Crow swallowed, trying to figure out how to phrase her words. "When my parents died," she said carefully, "Sythfeld took me in. It was right about then that I started my charade. A boy in a forge is not unusual, but a girl is something to be ogled. Besides, most people don't think girls can do smithing. Not to mention it's not really even allowed.

"Anyways, I learned under the tutelage of Sythfeld what it meant to be a smith and what it meant to be a boy. I was never questioned about being a boy so long as

I was secretive about any feminine needs I might have. When Sythfeld died, the new smith came and, thinking he would be the same as my old master, told him my secret. He kicked me out and I came here."

Jek blinked at Crow's unremarkable rendition of her life. He knew that there was much more she wasn't telling him, like how she learned the art of the Scheren, who her parents were, but he could see that what she had told him was the truth.

"Why did ye lie to me?" he asked softly and Crow snapped her eyes open, a slight anger burning there along with the guilt.

"I never directly lied," she replied. "You assumed, like everyone else, that I was a boy. If you had asked, I would have told you. I... I didn't want to be pushed away, again."

Jek frowned and considered, "What about the bandages? Ye said they were fer scars."

At this, Crow seemed to shrink into herself, and her eyes clouded over with dreadful memory. In a hoarse voice, she replied, "That was the truth."

Silence filled the room, a pervasive silence that was pregnant with the reality of Crow's guilt and the thoughtful musings of Jek. Crow managed, "I'm sorry, Jek. I never meant to hurt you. I did it for the smithing."

"Crow," Jek said quietly. "I cannae pretend that what ye did isn't wrong. And what makes it worse is that ye were right. Bein' a boy saved yer hide in this world, 'specially when it comes to smithin'. But ye shoulda trusted me," he snapped, voice rising, fist clenched on the table.

Crow turned her head to hide the tears that threatened to fall.

"I made a mistake, alright?" she replied, voice colder and harsher than she had intended. Standing, Crow grabbed her pack. "Now, if the explanation is over with, can I leave?"

Jek recoiled then, as if he had been hit. He stared at Crow and she wished that she could shrink into the wall and vanish like a ghost. "Is that what ye want?"

Crow let out a strangled cry, shaking her head madly, "No. But what other alternative do I have?"

Silence came again and this time, Jek bored into her with his harsh gaze, considering, coming to terms, creating plans. Crow was about to turn and leave the house when Jek spoke, "I had begun to think of ye like a son, Crow. Sons cause hurtin' every now and again. So do daughters."

For a moment, Jek's words didn't register with the fair featured girl hunched over as if in pain, guilt swimming in her deep green eyes. Then, they sunk in and she gaped in disbelief at Jek who was beginning to look at her with more affection in his eyes. The hurt was still present, but so was forgiveness. Crow dropped her pack and lunged forwards, wrapping her arms around the smith and letting her tears flow fully. Jek awkwardly patted the girl on her back. How was he supposed to act around a girl?

"Now don't go getting all feminine on me, lass. Ye still have to keep up yer ploy for the rest o' the world," he said and immediately, Crow pulled back, wiping the salty water away. She grinned and nodded. "An' we're gonna have to come up with some rules. No bargin' in unannounced. No comin' to me 'bout girl problems. Can ye handle that?"

"Yessir," she barked out, standing at attention.

"Now what have I told ye 'bout the sirrin," Jek grumbled, a smile teasing across his features despite his efforts otherwise.

"Not to call you that, sir," Crow bantered and picked up her pack, putting it back in her room and running out to the forge before Jek could respond.

"Trouble, that's what that kid is. Pure trouble," he muttered, feeling happy in spite of himself. When he got out to the forge, Crow had already begun to stoke the fires, reorganising everything. It was barely past sunrise, but Crow felt as though she had slept for days. A weight had been lifted from her shoulders and joy sang in her veins. All exhaustion she had felt at the banquet was gone and she practically bounced around the forge, doing whatever tasks Jek threw her way.

The sun was well on its journey through the sky when Alexander trudged out to the forge, a scowl on his face. He wore comfortable, every day clothing and his hair mussed, as if he hadn't felt like getting out of bed. He stalked over to the forge, eyeing the extraordinarily cheerful Crow with disdain.

"Did you sleep at all?" Crow asked brightly. "Because you look terrible."

"Gee, you're awfully nice this morning? Did you kill Yvonne? Or maybe you fancy yourself in love with her," Alexander replied, voice brittle. Crow made a face and beat out some arrowheads, shaking her head at his incredulous suggestion. Jek looked at Crow blankly for a second then started laughing loudly, making Alexander flinch. Crow rolled her eyes at her master then turned her attention to Alexander, concerned.

"What's wrong?" she asked, looking at his drawn and pale features, so unlike the handsome man that was her friend. Alexander shook his head and rubbed his temples.

"I had too much wine," he mumbled. "My only consolation is that my father is worse off than I am."

Crow winced in sympathy and gestured for him to sit on his usual barrel. Alexander did so, grabbing onto the railing to keep himself steady. He looked at the cheerful blacksmith, in a much better mood than the day before, and found himself grumbling in jealousy.

"How are you so cheerful? I thought you had a terrible time last night," the Prince muttered, glaring holes into the back of Crow as she worked. Laughing, Crow shrugged and shaped the arrowhead.

"I did have a terrible time," she said frankly. "I got to sit for five minutes and was dancing with women who were all over me for the remainder of the time. Yvonne threw herself at me quite visibly and I didn't eat at all. I was tired and cranky, but I'm much better now."

"I hate you," Alexander said, burying his head in his hands at Crow's cheerful tone.

"I'm sure you do," she petted, grinning in spite of her efforts to remain at least partly serious for Alexander's sake. She worked for another hour, talking to Alexander as he nursed a headache. Carefully, she drew him out of his shell of pain and even got him to eat an apple. Then, Crow's day, made much better by Jek who would look at her and smile every now and again, each time making Crow beam, got worse.

Yvonne, dressed in a simple blue frock that had been decorated to noble standards with silver thread, strode across the courtyard. Crow felt her cheery mood slipping away as the blonde approached, a seductive smile on her face and a bag in her hands. Yvonne did not, unlike Alexander, have a hangover. And she was on the hunt.

"Crow," she trilled, causing Alexander to wince and put his hand to his head. "I brought the money you need for my necklace!" With a flick of her wrist, Yvonne threw the bag at Crow who caught it deftly, only out of instinct. Carefully, the girl counted each piece of gold and then nodded in satisfaction despite the frown on her face.

"I should have it done by Tuesday, Wednesday at the latest," Crow murmured and Yvonne grinned, showing off her white teeth. She stepped closer to Crow, attention riveted by the one who had resisted her. All thoughts of Alexander were temporarily displaced and Crow was now the sole focus of her attentions. So, when she rubbed herself suggestively on Crow, she expected her ploy to work. Instead, the blacksmith turned away and started stoking the fire, drawing the flames up even more.

Huffing in annoyance, Yvonne spun on her heel and stalked back to the Palace, Crow feeling relief at the woman's exit, Alexander glad of the silence and Jek chuckling obviously. Finally, the Prince looked out of narrowed eyes at the smith and mumbled, "What are you laughing at?"

"That Yvonne woman is wastin' 'er time on Crow," Jek responded and Crow found herself shaking her head. Of all the things to draw from her situation, Jek found the fact that Yvonne was throwing herself at a fellow woman the most entertaining. No wonder Crow wasn't thrilled with her advances.

"I knew that," Alexander replied. "That's why I picked Crow to help me out." Jek just shook his head and Crow frowned over the money.

"I was really hoping that she wouldn't get the money. A project like this could take all my time," Crow complained quietly, putting the money into two separate bags and tying the smaller one to her belt.

"Yvonne's necklace, you mean?" Alexander asked and Crow nodded.

"She wants it to be really quite complicated. That alone could take a while, but she also wants topaz and that means a trip to the Merchant's Market," Crow grumbled. "I hate going down there. They're all so... pushy."

"The Merchant's Market?" the Prince asked, foul mood slowly dissipating as he sensed an adventure. "I've never been," he said, trying to be sly.

"You want to go, don't you?" Crow sighed. Alexander grinned sheepishly and nodded. Groaning, the blacksmith apprentice nodded and gestured for Alexander to follow. So much for her good mood.

"Now, I know that these pants won't fit you, so you'll

have to wear what you have, but this shirt should do fine," Crow instructed after leading Alexander to her room and rifling through her pack. She threw a woollen shirt of a deep grey at Alexander who stared at the garment as if it were a wriggling babe.

"Why do I need to dress differently?" he asked, holding up the shirt to examine it. There were no patches on it and Crow was rather fond of the shirt, but the way that Alexander looked at it, it was vermin. Yet another blow that Crow felt acutely.

"Because the Merchant's Market is crawling with thieves and assassins and bounty hunters, not to mention merchants. One sniff of wealth and power and you are going to end up in a side street, beaten, naked and without a cent. Dressing and acting like an awe filled peasant is much safer. Just follow my lead and try not to say anything," Crow instructed and Alexander hurried to put on the shirt, reaching up to straighten his hair. Crow shook her head and the Prince grumbled, looking down at the shirt in disgust. Privately, Crow thought that the simple clothing suited him better than much of the finery that nobles wore, but she said nothing.

The journey to the Merchant's Market was on foot and the pair wove their way through Kyper to the River Docks, where the Market was usually held. Crow grudgingly paid the entrance fee and gestured for Alexander to follow her. As they entered the Market, Crow affected the visage of an amazed person, not used to seeing such splendour. Alexander didn't have to act much, though the splendour was not unusual for him. The sight of the brightly clad people of all walks of life, the stalls with their numerous items, the sounds, the smells, overwhelmed him and he fairly gaped as he followed Crow.

Crow stopped once or twice to look at a gem merchant's stall, but the stones she saw were not up to her standards. She reached a stall that was covered by a purple cloth awning and stepped forwards, examining the gems. The merchant, a wiry old man with a keen eye and neatly trimmed beard, watched with interest as Crow picked through the stones, taking out a few pieces of topaz.

"How much?" she barked, startling the merchant. He stared at her and the gems she had in a pile.

"Ten gold pieces," he replied, folding his arms. Crow gaped at him incredulously and then launched into the haggling with a vengeance. Alexander, unrecognised by the people that walked around him, watched Crow with a sort of quiet pride. His fascination with the smith caused him to shake his head and he tried to follow what Crow did.

The fair-featured girl managed to get it down to five gold pieces and walked away happy, the Prince trailing along behind her. They passed a few well dressed merchants who paraded through the vendors with hands on dress swords. They had daggers strapped on their belts and Crow was sure that these people were displaying wealth because they could protect it. As they passed the Prince and smith, one of them clipped Crow's shoulder and rammed full on into an unsuspecting Alexander.

Crow ignored the slight, only checking to make sure her money and jewels were still there, but Alexander, unprepared and unused to such an attack, fell to the ground in a huff, throwing up dust as he did so. Crow froze as she watched the Prince's face grow angry and one of the merchants laughed nasally.

"That'll teach you to keep out of our way, peasant," he chortled and crossed his arms, eyeing Alexander with obvious disdain. Alexander stood and brushed the dirt off of himself, temper flaring.

"Maybe that wouldn't happen," Alexander snarled, "if you looked where you were going."

Crow flinched at the effect that the Prince's words had and leaped in front of her friend, holding out her powerful arms to protect him. The merchant hissed and drew his sword, placing the finely honed tip on Crow's chest, applying pressure that she barely felt through the bandages.

"Get out of my way, fool. I have a score to settle," the merchant growled and the other two finely clad people stepped up, hands already drawing swords. Crow resolutely did not move, knowing the odds were against her should an actual fight break out. She had no weapons on her and fighting without one against three well-trained fighters would mean serious injury. Not just for her, either.

"'E don' know what 'e's doin'," she drawled loudly, feeling Alexander's burning fury at her back. "My brofer finks 'e's special, what wif Mum tellin' 'im 'e'd be a great soldier some day." Crow's lie seemed to make the merchants falter but the one with the sword on her chest pushed harder, expecting to see blood. When he did not, his eyes narrowed. The point of the sword pushed deeper into the bandages around Crow's torso but did not break through the thick fabric.

"I don't care how special your brother is, boy," the merchant sneered. "He has slighted us and will pay the price."

Crow lowered her hands and fumbled desperately with the pouch at her waist, three gold coins remaining after her bargaining. She held out the purse to the merchant whose companion snapped it up and opened it. "The money's good. Probably all the boy has on him. These peasants never carry much."

The leader of the group eyed Crow and lowered his blade, letting the tip linger near Crow's loins. "If I ever see you again, boy, you will be finding yourself doomed to die," he hissed and stalked away, pocketing Crow's money. When the threat was gone, Crow let out a shuddering breath and rounded on the Prince who was still seething with anger but had at least been wise enough not to say anything.

"Are you insane?" she demanded, grabbing a fistful of the Prince's shirt and pulling his face down to stare him straight in the eye. "They would have killed you had I not been there. Peasants never, ever, get in the way of those who have money. Do I make myself clear?" she snarled, her lips drawn back in a wolfish snarl. Alexander stared into her green depths and shuddered at the amount of power and roiling anger he saw there.

Only a small portion was directed at him, but he was still afraid.

"I don't like bullies," he said softly and Crow let him loose, running her hands through her short hair. She shook her head and started walking. "And besides, they walked into me! Yet you paid them off like we were the ones at fault."

"Whether you like it or not," Crow said as they neared the exit to the Market. "Bullies exist. Most of them in the form of nobles who are determined that they live solely to put peasants in their place. They could have taken much more than my money and would still be hardly reprimanded for doing so. That is the law."

Alexander said nothing, the reality of the rules under which he lived starting to sink in. "The law?" he finally managed to choke out. Crow nodded.

"When a peasant hurts another of equal rank, the same hurt or a fair amount of compensation is taken out on him. When a peasant hurts a noble, he can be killed, depending on how severe the offence is. When a noble hurts a peasant, the world sees it as though the noble was well within his rights to put the peasant in his place," Crow replied, feeling the inner turmoil that her words were causing in Alexander. She looked at him and frowned, seeing the shock on his face. "You didn't know?" she asked.

"No," he said. "I've never had to enact punishments. I just report to Father and he sends someone to do that for me. He says that when I am King, I will do the same, but I didn't know. How could I not know? This is just...

wrong and I didn't even know about it. Some King I'm going to make." Alexander blinked furiously against tears of shame, turning his head so Crow wouldn't see.

Crow was tempted to brush away the strand of golden hair that had curled into the Prince's face. She knew that others, when he was dressed like a peasant, saw him only as one of lower rank. But she doubted, sincerely doubted, that she could ever think of him as something so simple as a peasant. He was noble and regal, proud and handsome. He would be King someday and Crow believed he could become a great one. Though, looking at the sadness etched onto his face, she wished for nothing more than the chance to make him feel better, to hold him in her arms until his fears and guilt vanished. She wanted to grow to love him, but for her sake as well as his, she knew she could not.

The thought almost broke her heart.

CHAPTER 7

Crow was hardly seen at all by Alexander for the next week, as she was slaving away over the extravagant piece of jewellery for the spoiled Lady Yvonne. Every waking hour not spent scarfing a few morsels of food and cooking for Jek were spent in front of the flickering fire, heating silver and delicately shaping it for a chain, decorations, even the little butterflies the woman wanted. The few times Alexander did stop by the forge in the hopes of dragging Crow along to some picnic he was being forced to take with a group of nobles, or show off his prowess in the practise yards, the finely featured smith barely acknowledged his existence. Instead, she muttered instructions to herself and started building the settings for the topaz.

Jek, who was busy with forging arrowheads for the nobles' pleasure or new shoes for horses, was able only to watch the Prince try desperately to see his friend and then move away in disappointment. One evening, Jek was sitting down to eat and Crow had wolfed down some bread before heading out to the forge, when Alexander walked up.

"Crow?" he asked, watching as she shaped one delicate butterfly wing with a finely pointed chisel. She did not respond or even notice his presence. Her work consumed her every thought and she was desperate to finish it. Sighing, the Prince moved around Crow and walked into the house where Jek was eating in silence.

The burly smith looked up and frowned at the expression on Alexander's face. "What's got yer face all scrinched up like that?" he asked, gesturing to the seat across from him. Alexander shrugged, unable to explain the feelings that tightened his chest. Quietly, Jek watched and then shook his head, standing. "Foller me, a'right? I think I know somethin' that'll help."

Alexander rose and followed the lumbering smith out of the house and past the engrossed Crow, to the kitchens. As Jek entered, the head cook immediately raised her spoon and glared.

"Now, I told you, Jek, that if you ever came in here uninvited again, I'd whollop you," she warned, eyeing his bulk uncertainly. Jek grumbled and stepped aside, revealing the Prince, who just looked confused and somewhat out of place.

"I ain't here fer me, Mayra. Alexander here needs somethin' to do while Crow works on Lady Yvonne's necklace," Jek growled, folding his arms. Stunned, Alexander looked at the smith.

"That's not what I—" he tried to protest. Jek set one

eye on the man and glared, causing him to fall into silence and fidget uncomfortably.

"Oh," Mayra said, lowering the spoon and looking at the Prince with unveiled interest. She saw the look in his eye and sighed, fisting her hands on her rounded hips. "Come on, Sire. You can help me with the baking for tomorrow."

With a slight push towards the cook by Jek, Alexander stumbled slightly through the kitchen and found an apron thrust into his hands. "Unless you want to get your clothes dirty," Mayra explained. Alarmed, he looked around for the smith, but Jek had vanished back to his dinner. Alexander stared down at the apron in his hands and thought of Crow in the forge, working away for Yvonne. Alexander put on the apron and held out his hands for something to do, resigned.

"Here," Mayra said, handing him a bowl of flour. "Spread this on the counter and start rolling out the dough, adding more flour when it gets sticky. We want it nice and flat, okay?" She watched for a few moments while he awkwardly did as he was asked, putting a liberal amount of the white flour onto the counter and then adding some more for good measure. He spread it out over the counter and then, looking at his floury hands in distaste, put the dough onto the counter. Mayra hid a laugh behind a cough and set to helping Alexander.

Baking, as it turned out, was not something that the Crown Prince was particularly adept at. But he had fun and, later in the evening, when he had followed Mayra's instructions on putting the candied fruits and nuts in the dough and rolling it, the talking began. "So, what's Crow up to these days? I hardly see one of you without the other, but here you are, making sweet rolls with that pretty little smith nowhere to be found," the cook said, knowing exactly what Crow was up to and also knowing exactly what Alexander needed. She kept his hands busy so his mind was less able to censor what he thought.

"Crow," said the Crown Prince, unaware of the ploy to hear his woes, "is slaving away on Lady Yvonne's necklace. She wants it before she leaves and paid quite a sum of money to get it. But Crow spends all of his time on the stupid thing. He doesn't even notice me when I'm standing right next to him."

"Son," Mayra soothed, "Crow's a hardworking lad. He's got to earn his living somehow, and if it means that he is focused entirely on a silver necklace for a woman that doesn't deserve anything made by him, then so be it. You have to understand that."

"Understand what?" Alexander complained quietly. "That Crow doesn't have time for me because he's catering to the wishes of that witch?"

"Now that's unfair," Mayra said, thwacking the Prince on the shoulder with a strong hand. Alexander winced and looked at the cook in shock while rolling up the dough and candied bits. Mayra handed him a dull knife and he set about slicing the rolls down to size. "Crow doesn't have a choice in where he gets his money, just like I don't. We come from a different walk of life than you do, Alexander, and we have to take what work we can get. You're lucky that Jek lets him spend so much time with you in the first place. Most masters wouldn't be near so kind."

"I don't know," Alexander retorted, exasperated, "it just seems so unfair that Crow has to spend all his time working for people he doesn't even like. But even when I went to the forge before, he could always talk while he worked. Now, he doesn't even notice me."

"He's just trying to get this work done, so he can have more time again. The sooner he gets that necklace done, the sooner he can spend time with you. Be patient and understand the necessity of work for people like us," Mayra said, sliding the rolls onto a baking tray and putting them in the brick oven to cook.

"I do," Alexander replied forcefully, earning a harsh stare from the cook. "I do," he said more quietly, "but Crow is one of my friends..."

"Son," Mayra said softly, "I don't mean to be rude or blunt when I say this, but I think Crow is your only friend."

Alexander said nothing at her comment and, sensing his trepidation, Mayra simply shooed him out of the kitchens, claiming that she could keep watch over a few hapless sticky rolls. With nothing left to do to keep his mind from his loneliness, the Prince wandered over to the forge, expecting to see Crow working despite the late hour. To his surprise, the pale smith was nowhere to be seen. Feeling a sudden sense of ecstasy, Alexander practically ran into the forge and looked around for Crow. He saw her on the ground, slumped against the wall by the door of the house.

"Crow?" Alexander asked, alarmed, running over to shake her arm. Groaning in annoyance, Crow cracked open an eye and murmured something. "What? Are you okay?"

"Mmmfine," she slurred, exhausted. "Jus' tired." She shifted and pushed herself up off the floor of the forge, hopelessly wiping away some of the ashes and soot that had stuck to her. Alexander frowned, his hope of Crow being done and able to spend time with him dashed. He helped Crow through the small house and to her bed where she collapsed, clothes, ashes and all and sighed contentedly.

"Go to sleep, Crow," Alexander said, disappointment lacing his voice. Crow mumbled an affirmative and then turned her head to look at Alexander out of one sleepy eye. She took in his blonde curls which were speckled with white flour, his lonely look, his powerful and handsome build and mumbled something. "What?" Alexander leaned closer to hear her words.

"I finished the necklace," she said, only slightly louder. "We can go hunting or riding or something tomorrow."

"Yeah," the Prince said, elated. It was only Monday and Crow was done. No more waiting to see his friend, no more long days of absorbing politics from books and deadly boring conversation because he had no desire to be with Yvonne and Crow was busy, leaving only the Court to bide his time. No more pretending that he was fine, just fine, without Crow to brighten his days. No more trying to get his knights to understand him in a way that Crow seemed to find natural. "See you tomorrow, Crow." But the beautiful smith was already asleep.

Morning came and Crow slept well past sunrise, waking only when Jek lumbered into her room and threatened to dump her on the floor if she didn't get up. She did so and bathed away the soot from the day before. She was dressed and packing up the necklace she had made in a box to deliver to Yvonne when Alexander came strolling into the forge. There was more energy that morning than had been in the forge for a very long time, both Crow and Alexander practically humming.

"You finished," the Prince grinned. Crow nodded and held out the necklace. It was really a fine piece of work, with minuscule details and a design that seemed to flow throughout the entire piece. The topaz added wealth and extravagance to its look and it was likely worth more than the money Yvonne paid for it. But Crow didn't care; she had spent less than she earned on materials and only wanted it to be done.

"I've got to deliver it," she said, scowling and putting it into the box.

"Get a runner or servant to do that," the Prince said with a wave of his hand. He moved out of the forge, expecting Crow to follow. She didn't, though.

"I can't do that," Crow replied, moving off to the palace to deliver the necklace. She was halfway up the steps to the great doors when the Alexander caught up to her, the sun shining on his hair and making it look like wrought gold.

"Why not? They're happy to deliver messages and

things for me all the time," he said, barring Crow's way into the palace. "I mean, sure, you're an apprentice, but I could put in a word and—"

"It's a matter of pride. I made it, I deliver it, it's that simple," Crow retorted, feeling snappish and upset, mostly with herself. Why couldn't she control her emotions? The fact that Alexander had come to see her as soon as she was awake had boosted her ego. The fact that she could do nothing about it had shot her self-esteem right back down. Now, she was torn with wanting to do as Alexander asked and just send someone else to do it, so long as she could spend time with him.

"But I thought you didn't like Yvonne," came the logical response. Crow frowned and shook her head.

"I don't. But I won't send someone else to do my job," she said, pushing past Alexander and beginning the climb up the servants' stairs to the guest wing of the palace.

"Come on, Crow. That's what they do. Why waste the time when you have someone else, who is supposed to do these things, to do it for you? That's just how things work," The Prince said, satisfied with his sound logic. Crow froze, all thoughts of her inappropriate emotions pushed aside. She stared at the Prince with cold, harsh eyes.

"Is that what you think the world is like?" she snarled, voice suddenly deadly quiet. Alexander stepped back and down a step, and wondered why he felt like he should run away. "I thought you were better than that. Getting someone else to do something that is your responsibility, no matter how trivial, is how nobles work. People with less status, less money, people like me, we have no choice but to rely on our own two hands to do what we can to survive. If that means taking pride in what we have done enough to deliver it ourselves, then so be it. If that means that we have no choice but to do the small things so that we can have a decent standard of living, so that we can honestly say that we made our own way, then so be it. Nobles," Crow spat the word, her voice like a razor, "rely on others to do what is their responsibility because they think they are better than us. They can get away with that because they have more money, more opportunity to train with weapons so we cannot always defend ourselves. They have armies at their sides and, besides, why worry about a dead peasant. There are always more where those came from.

"If you think that I will agree to use a servant or runner to do my duty, to do something that I will do because I take pride in my work and understand what it is to see a job through to the end, no matter to whom I am delivering the necklace, then you are gravely mistaken. I thought that you were better than that. I didn't realise that you were so much like those other nobles, Your Highness." Crow finished her speech and turned, racing up the stairs much faster than Alexander could have followed. He remained frozen on the stairway, eyes wide and afraid. He was completely stunned and, to his surprise, felt the reality of Crow's words. The farther Crow ran, the more hollow and lonely Alexander felt. It was worse than when Crow had been simply working.

Then, Crow had been busy and not standing apart from Alexander. Then, Crow had been his best friend. Now, Alexander was unsure if that fact remained. Now, Alexander had driven Crow away.

Crow reached guest wing and slowed her hasty pace, her emotions kept under a tight, iron control. She used her indignant fury to keep herself in check and the only evidence of her feelings was the flaming rage in her eyes. She was not as much angry at Alexander, though some of her rage was directed towards him, but at herself for not seeing it sooner. And for wanting desperately for her to have been wrong—or worse, ignore the fact altogether—so that things could go back to the way they had been.

Outwardly calm, Crow kept her face stoic and knocked three times on Lady Yvonne's door. A skinny, pale maid opened the door and Crow inclined her head slightly. "A delivery for Lady Yvonne. Her necklace is done," Crow intoned and the maid nodded, turning to deliver the message to her Lady. An excited squeal broke out and the maid was pushed aside as Lady Yvonne, wearing a rusty red dress with plunging neckline and cinched waist, ran to the door, her hair half styled. She took in Crow and grinned.

"You finished it?" she purred, opening the door wider and inviting Crow in. The blacksmith did not move, instead holding out the box and bowing slightly at the waist.

"As you requested, my lady," Crow said, putting a subtle bite into the words. Yvonne either ignored the jab or was ignorant, and she snatched the box from Crow's deft hands, tearing into it and gasping visibly when she beheld the necklace.

"Oh, it's beautiful," she cried, holding it up and letting some sunlight from a nearby window catch the metal. "Put it on me," she ordered Crow, thrusting the necklace at her and then turning. Dutifully, Crow put the necklace on, making sure her hands did not touch Lady Yvonne's skin. The beautiful blonde turned and grinned at Crow and then dashed back into her room to find a mirror.

Crow did not follow as Yvonne intended, but turned and walked out of the guest wing, racing back down the servants' stairs, half hoping she would find Alexander still there, waiting for her, an apology on the tip of his tongue just as it was on hers. But he was not there and she did not look for him. It was too late for that. Crow wandered back to the forge and, just like the past few days, engrossed herself in her work, using her anger to focus her energies.

Two days passed until Lord Vincent and Lady Yvonne left with their train of servants and trunks, their departure marked by looks of relief on the faces of servants, soldiers and lesser nobles living within the Palace. Each day, Alexander came out to the forge, expecting to pick up easily with Crow, as had been the case with their previous spats. But, despite the words that Crow desperately wanted to speak, wanted to shout, she felt she could not without the Prince apologising first. She had to make him see her reasoning. And Alexander did. He thought on her words and recognised the truth within them, vowing to do better. But his own pride could not make him bow to Crow and apologise first. So Crow kept working, ignoring the presence of the one person she wanted to talk with most. Alexander did the same.

"Lass," Jek said after Yvonne was gone, giving wide smiles to Crow all the while and showing off her necklace which glistened in the sunlight. "Are ye goin' to tell me what this altercation is 'bout? Ye've been stormin' 'bout this place like a madwoman an' Alexander seems sorry 'bout wha'ever it were. He came by twice already an' 'e's been hangin' 'round like a lost pup. Jus' forgive 'im, a'right?"

"Jek," Crow said, frowning, "I have forgiven him. But I can't just let this be. He must apologise first or this will have been for nothing. He has to understand." She turned and went back to her work, beginning the first few links in a vest of chain-mail, closing each loop with lightning speed as she worked.

"Oh, lass," Jek said, shaking his head, "Ye both are too prideful fer yer own good."

Crow did not hear him, engaged as she was in the chain-mail, and the remainder of the day passed in silence between master and apprentice, with Alexander coming by once, then twice, hoping that things could fall in as normal with Yvonne gone. But Crow did not let her point pass and, as Jek had said, both were too stubborn to apologise.

The next sunrise found Alexander hanging around the forge, looking for all the world like a lost dog. Jek emerged into the new sunlight before Crow, a rare event since Crow was usually up early to cook the morning meal. "Jek," the Prince pleaded, stepping forwards. He shoved his hands in his pockets and hunched his shoulders, golden hair falling into his eyes limply. The image was pathetic, almost as bad as Crow's trudging around the forge, sulking.

"Aye? Is this 'bout wha'ever it is that's got between ye two?" Jek said warily, feeling surly and not in the mood for any emotional talk. To his annoyance, Alexander nodded sheepishly. Sighing, Jek ran a hand over his scraggly hair and shook his head.

"I just want things to go back to normal," Alexander said quietly.

"Lad, to do that, yer goin' to have to apologise," Jek said. "Crow's determined an' I don' want to see this friendship that ye two have go to waste, a'right?"

"I can't," Alexander pleaded. "I can't apologise. Crow has to do it first."

"Why not?" Jek asked.

"Because... it wouldn't be right for me to concede to someone of—" Alexander said, spouting off the first thing that came to his mind. He stopped, realising too late what it was that he had started to say. Jek narrowed his eyes and shook his head, stoking up the fire for the day.

"If ye were goin' to say ye cannae do it a'cause yer the Prince and Crow's common, then consider again. That's what got ye inter this, if'n I'm right," Jek said. Alexander frowned, knowing he was right and looked pleadingly at the master smith. Jek gave nothing and just watched the Prince with a knowing and hard eye.

"I've never had to apologise before," Alexander said softly and Jek shook his head. "Just to Father and that didn't really count."

"Then go practise," Jek urged. "Crow's the best thing that happened to ye and yer likely the best thing that's happened to Crow. I don' want to see this turn out badly."

"Neither do I," the Prince admitted and turned away slightly. "Practise. I can do this. I just want everything to be back to normal. I was wrong, Jek. When this thing first started, I was wrong."

"That weren't so hard, right? That's the basis fer yer apology. Crow'll forgive ye. I promise," Jek said softly as Alexander smiled gratefully and trotted back to the palace.

Crow emerged from the house a few minutes later and went to the kitchens to fetch food for their morning meal, ignoring the pitying look that Jek threw at her back. She said nothing to Jek upon her return and the two went about their work as if nothing was wrong. The silence stewed for hours, Jek's gruff conversation a poor replacement for Alexander's banter. The master smith kept watching for the Prince, hoping that this nonsense would end. By the time the day was nearly half-over, Alexander had not yet emerged to present his apology. Jek wondered if his pride were really that strong and admired the effort that the Prince was going through while acknowledging the necessity of the lesson. If only

Crow would do the same, then both could feel good about any mending.

Crow was thinking none of these things, but was focused on the finishing touches of her chain-mail, when the sound of a lone horse's hooves on the cobbled courtyard caught her attention. At that point, any distraction from her dark thoughts was welcome, so she stopped and looked. It was not unusual to have horses in and out of the courtyard, what with the knights riding nearly every day, hunting parties, nobles and their servants coming in, but a lone horse was odd. Crow looked up and saw that a tall and delicately built horse of a beautiful sable had been ridden into the courtyard by a man wearing leather armour and an easy smile on his face.

He had longer brown hair that hung around his chin in a rugged style, granting the bold featured man a heroic look. His skin was a dusty brown and he carried a longsword at his side. The man dismounted and looked around. His eye caught on Crow, who was watching with unashamed interest, and he led his horse over to the forge.

"Hello," he said in a pleasant baritone, the sound catching Crow's attention in a manner similar to what Alexander did. It was nowhere near as intense a feeling, but her stomach muscles still clenched involuntarily. She forced the emotions away, a thing now impossible with Alexander, and nodded her head to the stranger. "I'm looking to try for a place as a knight. Do you know whom I should speak with?" he asked, leaning on the fence to the forge.

"You'll want to talk to the Captain of the Guard. He's over in the barracks or out on the practise yards which are that way," Crow said, pointing out the path which led around the palace to the yards. "You can put your horse with Kayn over in the stables."

"Right, thanks. I suppose you're the smith?" the man asked, intrigued with Crow. She wiped away some of the soot from her hand and held it out in greeting.

"Apprentice smith. Folks call me Crow," she said, smiling slightly.

"Crow," the man said. "Unusual name. I'm Leon."

CHAPTER 8

Curious, Crow followed the newcomer—Leon—to the practise yards and watched him walk unabashedly up to one of the training soldiers and ask his questions. The man directed him to the Captain of the Guard and Leon turned to give Crow an encouraging smile before loping off to test his skill. Crow determined to wait, as she liked Leon and wanted to see how he would fare. Most sons of nobility trained as knights for years, though it was possible to try for a knighthood later in life. He was probably a younger son. She looked about idly and saw, to her surprise, Alexander with a dulled practise longsword hacking his way through a straw dummy.

The look of pure emotion on his face drew Crow in, her pride forgotten and emotions that were uncontrollable swirling through her head. She approached cautiously, phrasing the apology in her mind and hoping that it wasn't too late. Jek was right. They were both too stubborn for their own good. Alexander did not see her approach, focused as he was on his task. Or rather, focused on what his task was distracting him from.

As Crow drew nearer, she heard the words that he was speaking. "I'm sorry for being an unbearable noble. Sorry for pushing my opinions on you, sorry for not really thinking about my opinions and just accepting drivel from the stupid people that I was raised with. Sorry for highlighting the distinction between our classes. Sorry for being an ass. Sorry for being the damn Crown Prince!" At that, Alexander thrust the tip of the blade into the dummy with sheer strength, the metal going in to the hilt. Crow blinked, impressed with his display. The dummies were made to be as like humans as possible, and that meant that driving a sword through one was no mean feat.

"Apology accepted," she said clearly and with firm humility, knowing that his anger was directed at himself rather than her. Startled, Alexander whirled around, his fine shirt soaked with sweat and emphasising his powerful build. Crow fought against the fluttering feeling in her stomach and looked at him. "And I'm sorry as well, for flying off the handle for something you couldn't understand—not to say that you can't be enlightened, that is. I was wrong for judging too quickly. We were both... too proud. And wrong," she murmured, lowering her head slightly.

The tension that the Prince had been holding in his shoulders released and he lowered the blade to the ground, breathing heavily. Crow shielded her eyes from the sun and looked at him. He looked exhausted and not just from training. "How long have you been out here?" she asked, taking in the sweat soaked clothing and hair and the way he slumped slightly.

"Since early morning. I was practising my apology," he replied, grinning sheepishly. Crow shook her head, smiling and waved her hand for him to follow.

"Come on, we'll go bother the kitchen maids with your sweaty smell and see if we can't beg some food off of them for two starving people," she said, thoughts of Leon vanishing in the face of her renewed friendship with Alexander. She did spare a glance over her shoulder and saw the man in conversation with the Captain of the Guard. Satisfied, Crow let herself fall into her old habits with the Prince and the pair started walking down the path to the kitchens, all issues mended between them for the time being. They entered the kitchen like two sly foxes intent on chickens and immediately were spotted by Mayra.

"You boys had better not be here to steal my food," she grumbled, making a couple of the kitchen maids giggle and blush as Alexander looked at them with mild interest.

"No," Crow assured the cook, unaware of the looks she drew from the maids almost as frequently as Alexander did. "Not steal but beg," she said, grinning mischievously. The cook grumbled and gestured to a bowl of fruit and a loaf of bread.

"Take that outside and eat it," she said. "I don't want my workers distracted by the likes of you two." Crow beamed and snatched up the proffered food, darting past Alexander and out the door.

Crow settled on a rain barrel and tore into the bread, handing half to the Prince. She stuffed some into her mouth and rubbed an apple on her shirt to clean it. "What did she mean? I'm not that distracting, am I? I can be quiet and unobtrusive," Crow said after her first few mouthfuls.

Alexander looked at his friend and saw the innocence in her green eyes then laughed loudly, nearly falling off his own rain barrel. Crow furrowed her brows, feeling indignant. They had just gotten over one argument. Was he trying to start another? "You really don't get it?" the Prince asked after a moment and Crow shook her head. She had never needed to deal with emotions regarding the opposite sex until she met Alexander and as for people feeling that way about her, she didn't even consider it. Just then, the thought that she could be appealing to the kitchen maids didn't even cross her mind.

"I've lived an exciting life in many regards," she said carefully, taking a bite of apple, "and I'm certainly not naïve about a lot of things, but I really don't get it. Is it because I'm dirty with soot? Or that I talk too much? Explain to a poor soul?" She took another bite, the juices dribbling down her chin. Crow wiped it away with her sleeve and looked at Alexander. He sat there, so proud and sure, on the rain barrel like it was made for him. He didn't posture unnecessarily and always seemed to sit in such a way as to catch the light. Crow found herself wishing she could stroke his bare skin and make him tremble for her touch, just as she wished he would make her wish for his.

"Do you understand the concept of sex and love?" Alexander asked, more amused at his friend's innocence than embarrassed for talking about such things.

Crow nearly choked on her apple, thinking he had guessed the direction of her thoughts. She swallowed and looked at him. Satisfied that he had not guessed her secret, she huffed, "Of course I do. I've hung around with some interesting characters before I came here. People are attracted to each other, that's all." Alexander shot her a significant look and raised his eyebrows. Crow stared blankly at him and he shifted his gaze to the kitchens and back. Sudden realisation dawned upon Crow and she laughed heartily.

"What's so funny?" Alexander asked mildly. "I've had such problems since before I was your age. Then again, that might have had something to do with the fact that I'm a Prince..."

"Hey," Crow protested. "You're not that much older than me. I'm laughing because the idea of those kitchen maids being attracted to me is...more than absurd." She chuckled quietly as she finished the apple and then threw the core with a practised hand to the compost pile beside the kitchens. Alexander did the same and then looked at Crow.

"Are you that blind to your appeal? I just don't get it," he admitted. "Why is that so funny? I mean you're pretty fun to be around and I know plenty of girls who would say that you're handsome or beautiful or whatever." Alexander considered Crow who shrugged and frowned, "You're not... Not that it would be a bad thing, per say. I mean, there are more than a few noble houses where the marriage is a sham so that the husband can go off with younger men, or the wife, I suppose. It's just that I never took you for that sort of... you know."

Crow blinked and then shook her head frantically, "No, no. Definitely not. It's just, I don't know. I've never thought about people thinking about me that way. Being attracted to me. It just seems weird." The Prince shrugged, smiling wryly.

"You'll get used to it. Just you wait," he replied and Crow shook her head, thinking of one person who she thought about with such emotions consistently. The one person who could never know.

"Get used to what?" a new voice asked and Crow jumped, startled. She looked around and saw Leon approaching with a strut, his eye alight with joy. Crow grinned and Alexander shrugged.

"Crow's not used to girls thinking about him," he said casually and Crow elbowed him. Leon paused, eyeing Crow with confusion and interest then shook his head and came closer.

"I'm Leon," the man said, holding out his hand to Alexander. Crow smiled and Alexander returned the handshake.

"Alexander Fenyr," he said. Leon blinked, startled and bowed slightly.

"Sire," the man said. Alexander waved away the

formalities with a frustrated frown at Crow's silent amusement. Leon turned to Crow.

"The Captain of the Guard said that he would be happy to test me. I have to fight one of his people, like the rest of the knights, he said, but if I do well enough, I'm in! I thought that my family wasn't high born enough for me to get in, but apparently, it's alright. One test match and I'm a knight," Leon proclaimed emphatically, his excitement almost palpable. Crow grinned and exchanged a sly look with Alexander. The Prince, being the best swordsman on palace grounds, was always the final match before any man could be knighted. He was also the final say. Determining which men were loyal to the Crown and would defend it and its code with their lives was one thing that the King seemed to think he could trust his son with. Alexander took the responsibility seriously.

"Crow," Alexander said casually, standing from the rain barrel and starting across the courtyard. "You know Leon?"

"Only met him an hour ago," she shrugged, following him. "Come on, Leon, we'll get you all set to do your match. You get ready and I'll fetch the Captain." Eagerly, the man nodded and did as he was told, running off to the practise yards to prepare. Alexander waited until he was out of sight and did the same, energy high despite the exercise he had put himself through earlier in the morning. Crow strolled across the yards to a circle of knights and soldiers who were being yelled at by the Captain, a rough looking man with scars running across his shoulders and an unshaven face.

"If you think you're good enough for this," he barked at the men, "then think again. I can name easily five mistakes that any one of you made. Would you like me to begin?" He turned and glared openly at each of the knights who stood before him and spotted Crow standing in the background, hands in pockets and a cheerful look on her face.

"Crow!" the Captain shouted. "Name for me the first rule of fighting that all these idiots seem to have forgotten!"

Crow shrugged and looked the Captain in the eye, "Don't die." There was sporadic chuckling from the group and the Captain sighed dramatically.

"I ought to whoop you into submission, boy," he grumbled. Crow grinned. "But I can see that I'm not going to get anything done until you get what you want. What do you want?"

"There's a man claiming that he's ready to fight Alexander to prove he's worthy of knighthood," she said calmly. Excited looks appeared on the faces of the knights and they shifted eagerly.

"Ah," the Captain said. "Is the Prince ready?"

"Yep," Crow said. "And the first rule of fighting is to be aware of your surroundings. Too narrow a focus and you could find yourself tripping over a tree root and losing your head." The Captain shook his head at the apprentice smith and started across the fields to where Leon was waiting in obvious excitement. Alexander was nowhere to be seen. The rakish man was wearing his leather armour and had his longsword gleaming and properly sharpened. Crow was admiring the make of the blade as she and the Captain approached.

The Captain raised his hands and the knights and other people using the field started closing around Leon in a wide circle. Crow stood about six feet within the boundary and held a relaxed position, smiling. The Captain stood next to her, also relaxed but continuously on his guard. "Leon of Narul, are you ready for the challenge which has been placed before you on your journey to become a knight of the realm?"

"I am," Leon called back, all fidgeting over, his gaze steady.

"Then I present to you your opponent, Crown Prince Alexander Fenyr," the Captain roared and the circle parted briefly, revealing Alexander holding a thinner version of Leon's sword, a mix between a rapier and a long sword. He wore only his breeches, his chest bare despite the cold bite in the air, and Crow could not help the feelings that coursed through her. As her body clenched in quiet lust, she wasn't sure that she wanted that control.

Leon's eyes widened as he took in Alexander and bowed slightly. The Prince inclined his head and Crow stepped forwards to stand between the two. She bade them come closer and when both were standing within three foot of each other, she nodded. "Alrighty now. We can get your tendency to fight each other out of the way early. Rules are whoever draws first blood gets the match.

Try not to maim or seriously injure or kill each other. That would be annoying and unfortunate."

"That's all?" Leon snorted and Crow shrugged.

"I'm just the blacksmith," she said and walked away. The two faced each other and waited for the signal. Alexander stood with a practised ease and Leon faced him with obvious trepidation but a well versed stance.

"Let the match begin!" the Captain bellowed and in a flash of speed, Leon struck and jumped away, a drop of blood on his sword. Alexander moved, almost as quickly, and then froze, stunned. On his shoulder was a small cut, bleeding slightly. Leon hadn't used fanatic skill with a sword or strength or much of anything but wit and speed. While Alexander had been waiting for the Captain's call to end, Leon had lunged, drawing blood in a shallow cut and thus winning the match.

There were cries of foul and anger at the outcome and most onlookers were grumbling that Leon hadn't allowed a proper test. Alexander, though, simply drove his sword into the earth and smiled widely, hands on his hips. "Any man that can move with such foresight and speed deserves a knighthood. Leon of Narul, I commend you. I would be glad to welcome you as a knight of the realm. We shall hold the ceremony this evening."

There was a spattering of applause and the onlookers walked away unsatisfied. It was always a treat to see the Prince in battle and they had been hoping for something drawn out and full of deft skill. The Captain simply barked out a single laugh and walked away, a hint of a smile on his scarred and rough face. Crow stood quietly, hands in her pockets, a smug look on her face.

Alexander and Leon walked over to her and the Prince clapped his new knight on the shoulder. "That was well done," he commended and Leon smiled, showing his teeth.

"Thanks. Next time, we'll have to really spar and I can show you what I can do," Leon replied. Crow watched and chuckled then turned and started walking across the practise yards and back to the forge. "What's with Crow? I thought.. he'd be pleased," Leon asked, confused. Alexander frowned in sympathy and picked his sword out of the ground.

"Crow's pleased. That was some skill you displayed and you impressed him. He's not easily impressed," the Prince said, moving towards the palace for a bath and his duties for the evening. Leon stood awkwardly, unsure of where to go.

"But..." the new knight prompted, sensing the inevitable. Crow, especially to someone who had only just met her, was an enigma that was not easily solved. If you didn't know any better, you'd think she liked it that way.

"But you'll have to be faster if you want to beat him in a fight," Alexander replied and started jogging away to the palace. Leon blinked and then paled and stared at the retreating figure of Crow. He considered and then sighed and turned to find the Captain of the Guard.

The ceremony took place at sunset, in the centre of the courtyard. Crow stood, leaning against the wooden post outside the forge, arms folded and a pleased look on her face. Alexander wore his finery and red cloak, next to his father who wore a more extravagant version of what his son did and had a circlet of gold on his silver hair. Leon wore full armour but for the helm, and a cloak depicting the symbol of the knights of the realm. He knelt on the cobbled stones before the King and a hush settled over the yard.

"I, Byron Fenyr, King of this glorious realm, do bestow my duty upon this man. Leon of Narul, do you swear to uphold the honour and principles of this kingdom, even at the stake of your life? Do you swear to uphold justice, to defend truth, to display a noble spirit, to do what is right, no matter the effects upon your person? Do you swear to protect this land and the people here though the odds may seem hopeless?"

"I do," Leon said, his voice falling over the still crowd, tone sure and strong. Crow smiled softly, watching with a sense of pride for the man. He could go far, she thought, and hoped that she would have the chance to really befriend the man.

"Then, before these witnesses, I do dub thee Sir Leon, knight of the realm. Rise and take your place," the King said, touching the gleaming sword on Leon's shoulders and helping the knight to his feet. Cheers broke out among the onlookers; a knighting ceremony was always popular with the people, and Alexander smiled at the new knight. Leon couldn't stop grinning, even if he had wanted, his face flushed with pleasure. He looked to Crow and she inclined her head in congratulations.

Once the cheering was over, the crowd dissipated and

Alexander waved to Crow, an indication that he would see her on the next day. Usually, such a wave mean that he had things to attend to which Crow was not privy to or that Crow had to work and Alexander couldn't escape his duty. Crow turned to the forge and helped Jek with a final set of shoes for Kayn, mulling in her head what she would cook for evening meal. It seemed such a let down after the events of the day, but part of her was glad for the simple routine. It gave her a purpose, something to both fall back on and look forwards to at the end of the day.

"Crow," Leon called, causing her to look up in surprise. He had changed out of the armour and cloak and wore simple breeches and a shirt, a look which suited him no less than the one he had worn at the ceremony. His simple confidence made him able to adapt to his new situation, a trait which Crow could not help admiring. She managed to push away the odd flutterings that Leon brought on and smiled in greeting.

"I thought you'd be with the other knights getting raging drunk. That's what they usually do after a knighting, or a particularly good patrol, or hunting trip, or just about anything," Crow said. "They'll be especially rowdy tonight since one of their parties is moving out to be stationed at the Northern Border with a garrison of soldiers for the next few months."

Leon shrugged, "I'm not really into the whole party and drink thing. I usually just sit in the corner and watch with my goblet of water."

Crow raised her hands in surrender and dipped the

glowing horseshoe into a vat of water, letting steam rise into the air. Once the metal was cool, she put the shoe on a pile and wiped her hands on her breeches. "So, what can I do for you?" she asked, feeling suddenly self-conscious under the knight's appraising gaze. He watched her intensely and blinked as her words startled him back to reality.

"Oh," Leon said. "Uh, you're a blacksmith?"

"We've already established thi—" Crow started when Jek came up behind her and clapped her on the shoulder with a massive hand. He waved a hammer at Leon who took a protective step backwards.

"This here's the best damn 'pprentice I've ever had and don't ye forget it," Jek grumbled. Leon nodded hastily and Crow sighed.

"You want something to eat?" Crow asked. "If this lummox will let me go for the evening, I know a good place in town that should work." Jek waved his hand dismissively and Crow leaped at the chance, dashing into the house and returning with a few coins in her hand. She ran to the gates at the courtyard and waited for Leon to catch up.

"Do you run everywhere?" he growled and Crow gave him a cheeky grin.

"Yep!" she proclaimed and started jogging through the gate to the streets beyond. When the two reached a quiet street, Leon lunged on the unsuspecting Crow, pushing her back against a wall with his arm across her throat. Crow's eyes darkened and memories of fighting and desperation to survive flooded her mind. She staved them off but did not manage to contain the rage that nearly consumed her. She was a heartbeat away from fighting back, pushing the knight away with a few expert strikes when she paused. He did not further the attack, just held her still. Leon gazed into her eyes with curiosity and Crow ascertained he did not mean her harm, but merely wanted her immobilised. Why, though?

"What are you playing at?" Leon asked softly, tone gentle and coaxing. He released his grip on her throat and Crow relaxed, looking around. The soothing baritone of his voice caused more odd sensations to stir in her stomach and her loins and she saw a strange emotion flickering in Leon's eyes. But he meant her no harm, of that she was sure. Of what his attentions were, she was less sure.

"I don't know what you mean," Crow said quietly, involuntarily narrowing her eyes in anticipation of something she could not identify. Leon moved closer, pulling her farther into the shadows and touched her cheek lightly, an electric pulse seeming to run through their joined skin.

"Oh," Leon murmured, "I think you do, madame Crow."

CHAPTER 9

Crow was immediately on alert and jerked away from Leon with the speed of a viper. She backed away from him further into the shadows, position indicating her readiness for a fight, eyes wide and focused rather than fearful. "How did you know?" she hissed, showing her teeth like a wild cat. Leon stood calmly where he had before, startled only by Crow's speed and apparent ease with the defensive position.

"I looked," was his reply. Crow furrowed her brows and Leon shrugged, "I saw small, telltale things. Your stance, your neck, your smile, just tiny things that were off enough to give me clues. But it was the way Jek looked at you that confirmed it. He looks at you like a father does a daughter; like something precious that could be stolen away at any moment."

Crow was startled and somehow pleased with what Leon had told her of Jek but she did not straighten out of her defensive pose, eyes still betraying her readiness for a fight. She looked at Leon, the dusty skinned, brown-haired knight, and saw calmness in his depths. "So you know," she said cautiously, slowly.

"I don't mean you any harm," the new knight assured, raising his hands. Only after Crow had studied him and ascertained that he meant his words did she straighten and move back in with the knight, allowing their stroll to continue as it had before the interruption. The memory of the shock between their touching skin came to the forefront of Crow's mind and she nearly gasped with the strength of the memory.

"Then what do you want?" she asked quietly. Leon looked at her, brown eyes questioning. Crow, feeling suddenly shy, looked away.

"Who says I have to want anything?" the knight replied and Crow fell back into her normal personality, all thoughts of shyness gone. She barked out laughter and Leon looked at her blankly. "What?" he asked, tone betraying his slight frustration.

"People don't tend to jump me and demand to know what I'm doing if they want nothing," Crow said. "Also, I don't know of anyone who wants for nothing. So, Sir Leon, what do you want?"

Leon sighed, giving in. "Fine. If you must know, I'm just confused as to why someone like you—obviously capable, I mean—is going around hiding your true identity rather than showing the world what you can do. I like you, Crow. I've liked you since I first met you, which wasn't all that long ago... so I've liked you for this whole afternoon and evening. You're fascinating. I just want to get to know you. Understand you. Is that weird?" he said, kicking at a rock in the street.

"I don't see why it would be," Crow said, unsure of what Leon was trying to do. "But I have no problem with being your friend. I mean, I'm friends with Alexander, right? You can just come talk with us. As long as you keep quiet about the whole me being a girl thing. Please, don't tell."

Leon looked at the fair featured girl with a strange emotion in his eyes. Crow would have guessed pain, but she didn't understand why he would be pained. She hadn't said anything odd. "I don't think you quite understand," Leon said, lifting his hand as if to touch her cheek again. Crow felt the odd fluttering in her stomach and shook it off.

"Then explain it," she said simply, shrugging her powerful shoulders. Leon withdrew his hands, sensing her true innocence and shook his head.

"It doesn't matter," he said softly, almost sadly. Crow blinked then decided she had imagined it and led the way into the small tavern where people were gathered around many wooden tables, eating heartily and laughing loudly. Crow paid for the dinner and she and Leon ate and talked until many hours had passed. It seemed that she got on nearly as well with Leon as she did with Alexander, and the knight knew her secret. They talked over his time in Narul and his journey to Kyper and his reasons for being a knight. Crow described blacksmithing and what living with Jek was like. And when the meal was over, they kept talking until they could walk together without saying anything in perfect comfort.

The two walked back to the Palace in silence and Crow collapsed onto her bed, exhausted, as usual. She slept until just before the sun began to peek over the horizon. As Crow emerged into the cold morning air, she was jolted from her sleepy mood by Alexander who threw a quiver at her. Only instinct prevented Crow from being hit on the head and she grasped the quiver with arrows and a bow with confusion.

"Another hunting trip?" she grumbled, glaring at the beaming Prince. "It's a little too early for jokes."

"This isn't a joke and it isn't a hunting trip. My father thinks that I should go explore the kingdom. Get to know the lay of the land. So he's sending me to Westmont for a bit. You're coming with," the blonde man replied, a relaxed grin on his face. Crow grumbled again and shoved the quiver back at Alexander.

"Ask me again when I'm awake," she snapped and lurched towards the kitchens to get food for her and Jek's breakfast. She was feeling grumpy and hadn't slept well and her nearest target was Alexander, so he got the full brunt of her mood. The kitchens didn't fare much better from Crow's attack and she walked away with the kitchen maids shocked and somewhat frightened of Crow. That only made her all the more intriguing.

As Crow walked back to the forge with her hands full of some bread and fruit, one of the bolder maids followed. She was a fairly pretty girl with a slight, willowy frame and large doe eyes and she ran to catch up with the long legged Crow. "Good morning, Crow," she said cheerfully. The blacksmith shot a wary glance at her and mumbled a reply under her breath. Not to be deterred, the maid continued to follow.

Crow managed to reach the forge before the girl spoke again, "I was wondering if you could help me out?" Despite Crow's bad mood, she was, by nature, helpful. Sighing, she put down the food just inside and returned, running a hand through her hair and watching the maid with sleepy curiosity. The small girl blushed.

"What do you need, Deirdre?" Crow muttered and the maid straightened at Crow's knowledge of her name. But Crow knew everyone and everyone seemed to know Crow, so the compliment was mild. The maid took a step forwards and tilted her head back to look at the beautiful Crow.

"There are stories going around that you were raised by a band of gypsies in the Eastern Lands but that you were really stolen away from a royal family from the lands north of ours. Bytern. I tell people that they're being silly, that you were touched by faeries, but they don't believe me," Deirdre said, stepping yet closer to the wary Crow. Had she been fully awake and perhaps not still thinking over the events of the night before, she might have realised what Deirdre was trying to do, getting so close. After all, Alexander had warned her about such things just the day before.

As it were, Crow simply snorted in derision and shook her head. "This is what you wanted my help on? Sorting out rumours?"

Slightly stung, but nowhere near perturbed, Deirdre shrugged her delicate shoulders, "I just thought you might like to have your past straightened out. People are curious and they'll say anything to figure you out." The maid came closer, tentatively reaching out and touching Crow's arm. "I want to figure you out."

Crow stepped away from the girl and was suddenly awake, full force of her annoyance and anger resting on the maid. She glared out of her green eyes at the maid who stepped back as if slapped. "I will give you only one warning. Do not go digging into my past. I don't care if people think that I was raised by crows or mountain lions, if I was a slave in the Eastern Lands, if I was stollen away by elves. I will not sort out any rumours that are circling just to amuse you. Leave me out of your games," she growled and turned away. Deirdre stared at Crow with wide eyes and then fled back to the kitchens, full of fear and a story to tell.

Alexander appeared out of the forge after the maid had gone, a smirk on his lips. "I would say 'I told you so' but I don't think that quite covers all the angles here." Crow focused her glare on the Prince but he had been in its path enough times to simply shrug it off. Had she been really angry, that might have been different, but her anger was not directed towards him. "Would it have killed you to straighten out her stories? You would have gained quite a few friends in the kitchens. Not to mention the rest of the Palace."

"But now he's a challenge and a mystery," a new voice cut in. Crow sighed and realised her attempts at being done with the event had failed now that Leon was here. The knight wore a thick woollen shirt and his hair was covered with dew, indicating he had been up before dawn. "Far more appealing."

"The both of you can shut up," Crow snapped, walking into the house to prepare the morning meal. She fished out some cheese and meat from the day before and sliced them, putting it on the bread and onto a tray. She took the tray out to the dim fire in the forge and heated the bread, meat and cheese on top, until the smell was overpowering the usual smell of the forge. She took the tray inside where Leon was cutting into an apple she had retrieved and Alexander was already nibbling on the core of the other. Exasperated, Crow dropped the tray onto the table. She was about to tell the two men off when they each snatched up the bread and ate it. At the exact moment Jek decided to walk into the room.

"I smelled food," the big man mumbled, "but I see I was mistaken. Crow?"

Crow huffed, "These two lummoxes ate the apples and the bread before I could even sit down! It isn't my fault!"

Jek folded his arms and raised an eyebrow at Alexander and Leon. The Prince spoke first. "I'm trying to get Crow to come with me to Westmont. I figure that if I annoy him enough, he'll agree just to make me stop." Crow gave a strangled sound and muttered to herself under her breath. Jek sighed and shook his head at the Prince who only grinned in response.

"I'm just hungry," Leon explained. Jek looked at the knight and at Crow who slumped against a wall.

"Well, you can come to Westmont, too," Alexander said, having had taken a liking to Leon. Any man willing to annoy Crow in the morning was worth his weight in gold. The knight brightened and nodded.

"Sure, as long as Crow cooks," he agreed, licking the grease off his fingers from the breakfast that Crow had made. The black-haired smith gaped openly at Leon and then her stomach growled, ruining the effort she was making to stay aloof. Jek looked at her and she gave up.

"Fine, fine. I'll go if Jek lets me which," she added, holding a finger at her master, "I'm sure he will because he's 'managed fer years a'fore ye came, lad. Have some fun'." She managed to capture Jek's drawl immaculately and the great smith chuckled deeply. He waved his hand at Crow and she stalked off to her room, emerging a few minutes later with her pack over one shoulder. She gestured grandly to Alexander and Leon and the trio left the house and walked across the yard to the stables.

When the three were mounted and on their way through Kyper, Leon began the conversation anew, "So, Crow. What is your past? Stollen by gypsies is the story that I heard most often, but I have heard some pretty raunchy ones about you being captured as a young 'un by slavers and sold to some child-lovers. My favourite is the one where you lived with elves."

"No, no, that one's average," Alexander put in. "I like the one where you walked with nothing but your hammer across three lands, charming your way into royal homes where the princesses would fall madly in love with you. Then you would be chased out of town by their fathers for ensorcelling the women."

Crow opened her mouth to argue and Leon cut her off with a grin, "Oh, really? I thought that the princesses had you chased out of their lands for falling for simple kitchen maids rather than them."

"Will you two give it a rest?" Crow snapped. "Where do you hear these ridiculous stories anyways?"

Alexander shrugged, "If you walk down a hallway and then vanish, I'll hear ten stories about you within two minutes. Crow, no one knows much about you except that you claim to have come from Hotun and had a smith master that died."

"Well, it's the truth," she retorted, feeling indignant.

"That may be, but no one really knows about your past. You are the Palace mystery and many people are devoted to solving you. They want the truth of your past, and until they get it, wild stories are going to fly about where you came from," the Prince said, nodding his head to the guards at the gates of Kyper. "Especially if your past turns out to be nothing more than a boring childhood."

"Why do I have to be a mystery? All I want to do is go about my smithing, in peace! I don't need kitchen maids cornering me and asking me all sorts of ridiculous questions, regardless of their intentions," Crow said, pulling the wide green cloak tighter around her. She looked threateningly at the sky which was pregnant with grey clouds. She knew that the freezing rain which threatened to fall would soon turn into snow and the roads would become treacherous. She could only hope they made it back from Westmont before the weather turned.

"Because you don't talk about yourself," Leon replied. He shrugged at Crow's look, "I've only been here a day and I can tell you that."

"He's right," Alexander agreed. Crow huffed, feeling like she had been singled out for prodding. "You can remember any of a hundred facts about someone but they don't even know your favourite colour. You're good at listening and getting people to talk, but the fact that you don't talk about yourself in return allows for stories to fly."

"Well, that's silly," Crow said. "Plenty of people are secretive and if I don't want to talk about me, then they should let lie."

Alexander laughed and Leon looked at Crow, confused. She shrugged and watched the Prince with veiled interest, her insides warming at the sound, as they did every time he laughed. She wanted so badly to reach out and touch him, to have him pluck her from her horse and set her in front of him. She wanted to feel him harden and press into her back with his want. Crow, outwardly still grumpy, shook herself and reminded herself that she was wishing for the one thing that would never, could never, happen.

"That's not going to happen. I told you, Crow, you've got yourself a following of girls throughout the castle. At the banquet, I even heard many of the noblewomen talking about you. They find you attractive and you're too nice to them to throw them off. You'll help and listen and women can't seem to ignore that."

Crow frowned and looked at the saddle in front of her. The horse, the same sorrel she had taken on the previous hunting trip, moved steadily, having decided that Crow was a worthy rider. Her Scheren sat in its sheath against her hip and the quiver full of arrows was angled towards her to give her easy access. Crow was set in comfort and riding to Westmont was surely easier than walking. She should have been grateful, but all she felt was a longing. Alexander talked about how women were pining after her, a thought which she didn't like or agree with, but he didn't realise that she was pining after him. He would never realise. Crow resigned herself to her sadness and remained silent as the day wore on and conversation turned to other things.

The weather grew continuously colder as the day progressed into evening and by the time the sun set, all three were wearing their cloaks wrapped tightly around them. Crow had started the fire and Leon had hunted while Alexander cleared a spot for the camp. They dined on some scrawny ducks that had not yet migrated for the winter.

"Crow, you're from Hotun, right?" Leon asked. The blacksmith nodded and inched closer to the fire, pulling her cloak closer. "That's right near Shadow Lake, if I remember correctly."

"Yes," Crow said. "Why? That area's fairly pretty in

the spring, but there isn't much out there since the bandits came."

"Exactly!" Leon exclaimed, startling Crow. "I was traveling through Barem and I heard this story—"

"Haven't we had enough strange stories for one day?" Crow snorted, shaking her head. She was curious, though, to know what Leon was going to say, to see if he had heard what had happened, or if he was even close to the truth.

"This one's not just a story, though," the knight said, the flames flickering and casting strange shadows across his face. His brown eyes and dark skin in the firelight made him look like a monster out of a children's nightmare. "It's about the lost Duke of Shadow Lake."

"What?" Alexander asked. "I've never heard of any lost Duke."

"It was years ago, according to the people in Barem. Crow, you must have been fairly young when it happened, so I doubt you'd remember," Leon started. The knight had captured the interest of his audience, Alexander eager for a new story, Crow frightened to hear what Leon knew.

"I don't remember," she said resolutely. Alexander shot her a look and Crow glared into the fire, pulling her cloak closer to her lean frame.

"Well, according to these people, there was a Duke and his family out near Shadow Lake. He kept quiet because he had seceded from the Eastern Lands and didn't want to cause problems for the King by drawing attention from the Eastern Lands' shamans. I was told that he had a beautiful wife, with long black hair and the charms of a siren. He supposedly was skilled in the ancient arts of fighting, most lost to history. But this Duke kept quiet, sending in his taxes each month and essentially letting his people live in peace. One day, a visitor came to the Duke's palace and fell madly in love with the Duke's wife. She refused him and the man, who was a leader of bandits, returned to ransack the palace and steal her for his own.

"The Duke fought back and, even with all his arts, was overpowered. But he managed to deeply diminish the ranks of the bandits. His wife started a fire in the palace and killed herself. Enraged, the leader of the bandits attacked the people and then vanished, leaving the palace burned and empty of all signs of the Duke. Since the Duke was so quiet, almost a legend amongst even his own people, all history of him was lost. But it is said that there was a child, maybe seven or eight years old, that survived and he is waiting, biding his time until he can hunt down the leader of the bandits and then claim his inheritance."

The story was finished like a ghost story and a tense silence filled the clearing for a few heartbeats. Crow ended the silence in laughter, her clear, melodious tone flowing through the air. Startled, Alexander jumped backwards, his cloak coming undone. The Prince pulled it around him and Leon frowned at the ground.

"That's ridiculous," Crow said frankly, relieved that Leon's story was far enough from the truth to keep her history safe. "Sythfeld explained to me what happened.

There was no Duke, only a fat and angry Lord. He refused to keep his lands safe from bandits and the lands were attacked. The Lord's house was burned but he escaped. He had no heirs, no wife, and no one to inherit his land. Now it belongs to the people until an heir to his line can be found or the King decides to appoint a new Lord and that's that."

"I liked Leon's version better," Alexander said, fascinated by the story. "But it does sound a little farfetched. I would have known of a Duke and his family that just went missing."

"I liked it better, too," Crow conceded and Leon smiled. "It's not the truth, though."

Leon shrugged and the three started preparing for bed. Crow stoked the fire and made sure it was contained and then set out her bedroll, stuffing her cloak within. She pulled off her shirt and winced as the cold air hit her bare skin. Alexander and Leon stared blatantly at her wrapped torso.

"What's with the bandages?" Leon asked, piercing eyes guessing one of the reasons. Crow felt her breasts tightening under his accusatory gaze, but she knew that even with the bandages, she looked like a boy.

"Scars," Crow said as she wriggled into the bedroll. She remembered vividly the broad hand that drew the scars on her skin and the pain that had followed. "Just some scars."

CHAPTER 10

It took a week of travel to reach Westmont. By that time, all three travellers were cold and saddle sore. Even the unflappable Leon was feeling grumpy and it didn't help that the three had run out of things to talk about the day before. Crow would offer up nothing of her past, Alexander didn't want to get into the politics that he spent his days reviewing and Leon hadn't led a very interesting life. He came from Narul and had been trained by a retired knight that lived there. Upon turning twenty, he went to Kyper palace and found himself travelling with the fair Crow and the handsome Alexander.

The doors to the Westmont castle estate were barred against the cold and it took Crow's entire body weight to ring the hardly used bell. The three stood next to their horses desperately wishing that they had thought to bring fur-lined cloaks when the great wooden doors opened. A slender girl wearing a simple blue frock took in the three and gestured them inside.

"Welcome to Westmont. His Lordship is expecting you, Your Highness," the girl said, watching Alexander out of half-lidded eyes. The Prince, Crow noted, was watching the girl in return, taking in every feature that seemed to have been sculpted by a master. Her long brown hair curled delicately around her face and fell past her shoulders and she wore her slim figure well. "I am Eleanor, daughter of the Earl of Narul, at your service."

At the name of Leon's home town, Crow perked up, interested. She cast a questioning glance towards the knight and he shook his head; he didn't know her. Alexander straightened, shaking off the cold and inclined his head to the lesser noble. "I am Alexander Fenyr, as you know, and these are my travelling companions, Sir Leon and Crow," he introduced, indicating each in turn.

Crow bowed as low as was proper for someone of her status and Leon inclined at the waist, his bow slightly less deep than Crow's. Eleanor curtseyed to Leon and nodded politely to Crow. She turned and started walking away, "If you will come with me, I shall take you to His Lordship, Duke of Westmont."

The trio followed Eleanor, their horses and packs taken care of. For once, Crow was not in the mood to protest someone doing her work. She was tired and ached and was fairly certain she was catching a cold. She followed the pretty Eleanor in silence, dull and drained.

Westmont castle was old and beautiful but nothing like Kyper palace. There were fewer windows and more torches were needed to light the castle properly. The ancient and grand tapestries in Kyper were substituted with heavy drapery and the floor was covered with simple rugs. The trio was led to a large room with many books and a desk in a far corner. The Duke of Westmont sat, scribbling away at some papers while Thomas played quietly with a map.

"His Highness, Alexander Fenyr, Crown Prince of the Land and his travelling companions, Sir Leon, Knight of the realm, and Crow," Eleanor announced and the Duke turned. He had not changed at all since Crow had first seen him. He rose to greet his guests with a bow.

"Sire," the Duke said, his bow low and deep. Sir Leon received a smaller bow and Crow was greeted by the Duke coming over and clapping her on the shoulder. "So," he said, "you survived. I was worried for a bit that Jek wouldn't take a liking to you and send you out to one of the lesser foundries."

"I survived, your Grace," Crow said with a weary grin. "Jek treats me well and introduced me to silversmithing."

"Crow," said a young voice and she turned to face the young Thomas who was staring up at her with arms folded over his finery.

"Lord Thomas," she replied with a bow.

"Did you bring me anything to play with?" the boy asked eagerly, forgetting that he hadn't liked the smith upon their first meeting. Crow blinked, astonished at the audacity and was even more surprised when his father did not reprimand him. She had been around Alexander and Jek for so many months and before that Sythfeld, who was no noble, that such obtuse mannerisms had been forgotten. Leon, though, stiffened beside

Crow and said nothing. There was propriety to follow, after all.

"I'm afraid not, my lord," Crow said, feigning a sad tone. "But tomorrow, I shall find your local forge and see if I can convince the master to let me make you something." The only possible solution for such an unforeseen slight.

"A sword!" Thomas exclaimed and Crow was once again taken aback. She looked at the Duke briefly but saw no admonishment there. So, instead, she inclined her head and left the matter at that.

Once the introductions were over, the weary trio was led to their quarters. Alexander received the largest, with plush rugs and a large, four poster bed and enormous fireplace to warm the room. Leon was given a spare room by where the soldiers were quartered, also fairly nice with a comfortable bed and a fireplace. Crow, being not of their class, was led through winding corridors and darkened hallways to a room besides the other servant's quarters. It was small, barely big enough to hold a bed, and the only light came from two candles set into the wall. The stone floor was cold and the blankets barely adequate. Crow snorted and shook her head.

No matter how the Duke seemed to like Crow, she was a peasant and therefore not worth anything but the cursory effort. The fact that she was travelling with the Prince allowed her a room to herself, but there was no place to bathe and she would be lucky if she didn't freeze during the night. It was barely afternoon, so Crow set down her pack and put on another layer before grabbing her cloak and money and heading out of the castle. Perhaps she could find better luck in town.

Finding the stables was easy, but finding a hostler willing to saddle a horse for a peasant was impossible. Crow did the work herself and mounted the sorrel before heading out of the Westmont estate. She followed the road to the nearest town and set about buying a fur-lined cloak and seeking out food, hot mead, and the local forge. The cloak she found in a small shop where a plump old woman with silver hair was knitting what looked like a blanket inside the store's warmth.

"What'll it be, young man?" she crooned, putting down her knitting to admire Crow. The smith wandered through the store and returned to the woman.

"I need a fur cloak and a thick blanket," Crow said. The woman eyed her warily until the black-haired girl pulled out an appropriate amount of coins. Only then did the woman shuffle off to a corner and pull down some fabric lined with rabbit fur. Clucking, the woman held it up to Crow's height and shook her head. This happened twice more before a proper fit was found. The blanket was simply picked out of a pile.

Crow paid and put on the cloak, her thinner one going into a saddle bag with the new blanket. She led her horse, rather than riding, further into the village, stomach growling. She was certain that Alexander and Leon would be fed while they bathed, but there would be no such luck for her. Once she remembered the way of nobles, it was easy to figure out what Crow could expect from her host. And that was not much.

She found the forge before she found food. The glowing heat drew Crow and she saw a dark skinned man with long hair tied into a horse-tail bending over an anvil. Crow tied the horse to a post and entered the forge, looking around. She was caught up in admiring a twisting piece of metal hung to the wall when she felt a looming presence behind her.

"I don't take kindly to intruders," the smith said, voice breathy and deep, frightening. Crow turned and faced the man who was holding a still glowing blade in one hand and hammer in the other. "Especially scrawny boys who don't know their way around a forge."

Indignant, Crow huffed, "I know my way around a forge. That's why I'm here." The smith scoffed and shook his head, pointing to the exit. Crow held her ground.

"Boy, I suggest you get out or I'll beat your head in with a hammer," the man snarled and Crow knew, immediately, that he would do so. He probably had done so in the past. Still, she stood her ground.

"I'm Crow, apprentice to Jek at the Kyper palace," she retorted, narrowing her eyes and feeling her anger start to boil. She could accept being disregarded and underestimated by nobles; that was what they did and it would take quite a bit of time to change that. But smithing was her life. It was what she knew and she would not be denied.

"Jek doesn't take apprentices," the man snapped, stepping closer with the weapons. The blade was beginning to stop glowing but Crow knew it was still plenty warm. The hammer was more dangerous, though, because it could easily break bone.

"He took me, at the urging of the Duke of Westmont," Crow said in reply, her anger fuelling her courage.

"I'd have to have the Duke himself walk down here and tell me so before I believed you," the smith replied, wariness creeping into his tone. Who was this whelp that dared stand against him? Crow met the smith's gaze easily, her green eyes blazing.

"Or I could just show you," she said simply, holding her hand out for a hammer. "Lord Thomas told me to make him a sword and this is as good a time as any."

Laughing in derision, the smith sneered and handed her his hefty hammer. Crow held it deftly and grabbed a piece of metal for a sword the right size for a boy. As she had done so many months ago for Jek, Crow proved herself, heating and shaping the sword until it was complete, gleaming in the flickering light. The smith watched in silence as she worked, her strokes skilled and precise, time irrelevant in the face of her work. After working as swiftly as she could manage, Crow doused the blade and cleaned it on a cloth. She held up the blade for inspection and the smith gave a grudging humph.

"So you know your way around a forge," the smith grumbled, taking back his hammer possessively. Crow held onto the blade, handing the smith a few small coins for his materials. "That doesn't mean much of anything. Why are you up at Westmont if you have a smith master?"

"The Prince asked me along," Crow shrugged,

hungry and ready to move away from the forge. She was tired of the ill treatment by the townspeople and the nobles. She wanted nothing more than a good meal and a hot drink and that was what she was determined to do. She slipped the blade into a saddle bag and walked out into the chill.

"Heh. That's funny," the smith smirked. "What would the Prince want with a scrawny lad like you?"

"Don't ask me," Crow snapped, untying the sorrel and mounting deftly. She glared down at the smith in anger. "I have no idea why he spends time with me. Could be that we're friends, but..." she trailed off, leaving the end of her sentence unsaid. "I wouldn't expect to see me again, if I were you."

Angrily, Crow rode back through the town, ready to search out a place for food. Most of the taverns seemed a little too busy for her usual tastes, but then, she was in a sour mood and busy meant she wouldn't be bothered much. The smith found a fairly nice looking one and dismounted, tying her horse to a post by the water. A young lad eyed her horse eagerly and Crow dug around in her pocket for a coin. "See that he gets fed," she said, handing him the money. "Take care of him and there's more where that came from."

Satisfied that the sorrel wouldn't be stolen, Crow marched into the tavern, relaxing slightly at the loud chatter and heat that filled the room. She pushed her way through soldiers, villagers, farmers, travellers and made it to the bar where a stocky man with a lazy eye watched the crowd calmly. "What'll it be?" he asked, gesturing for a woman with wrinkles of stress on her face to come over. Crow assumed it was the man's wife.

"A hot meal and some warm mead," Crow said, raising her voice to be heard above the din. The man nodded and his wife led Crow to a small table in the corner. It was away from the fire, but with the many people, Crow didn't mind. She sat and the woman returned with a large stein of mead, a plate of shepherd's pie in the other hand.

"Just holler if you need anything else. I've got some girls who would be glad to give you company, if you want. They like handsome men, even if you are more feminine than rugged," she offered, leaning close to Crow.

"No," she said flatly, turning away from the woman and picking up the stein.

"Suit yourself," the woman said, walking away and touching a few men on their arms, probably to make the same offer she had made to Crow. In her desire to avoid going back to the Duke's estate and be subject to blatant disapproval, Crow ate slowly and drank more than she was used to. She talked with some of the people near by and slowly began to relax, feeling warm and well-fed at last. Thoughts of her friends and the respect they were getting vanished from her mind and all that was before her was all she wanted. Time seemed to pass swiftly and not at all and it was near midnight when someone tapped her on the shoulder.

Crow, having moved to sit at a table with five other men to play a game of wits, looked about, startled. Leon stood there, brows furrowed in confusion as he took in the flushed features of Crow and the small pile of coins she had amassed in front of her. She waved a hand to him and turned back to her game. If she was surprised to see him, she didn't show it. "Next riddle," she called out to the man across the table, a merchant wearing dark leather and a smirk on his face.

"Very well," the man replied, putting two small bronze coins on the table. Crow matched him and the two locked eyes. "Give me food and I will live. Give me water and I will die. What am I?"

Crow snorted and said, "Fire. Really, your earlier ones were much better. Besides, you shouldn't ask a smith anything involving fire." She swiped the merchant's coins towards her pile and the man on her left looked at her and grunted.

"Riddle from you, Master Crow," he said slowly, voice thick from his spiced wine. Leon moved to put his hand on Crow's shoulder and the smith shrugged him off. She turned to the man, considering. Carefully, she lifted a bronze coin from her pile and placed it on the table.

"Crow," Leon hissed under his breath. She ignored him. The man with whom she was going to match wits put a larger, silver coin down and Crow raised her brows at him. She exchanged her own coin out and thought. There was a tense silence around the table as she thought, though the room was still rowdy and loud.

"What can run," she began, almost chanting, "but never walks. What has a mouth but never talks, has a head but never weeps, has a bed but never sleeps?" Her opponent paled and licked his cracked lips, reaching for his wine. Crow waited, eyes locked with his. The man said nothing as he kept his gaze even with Crow and a single bead of sweat rolled down his nose. Finally, he broke his gaze and Crow grinned triumphantly. She pulled the two silver coins towards her and stretched.

Leon gripped her shoulder, hard, and Crow turned to face him. "What?" she snapped. "I'm busy."

"Crow, you've got to come back to the estates. Alexander was wondering where you were and it's late," the knight murmured softly to her. Crow frowned and folded her powerful arms.

"Why would I want to go back there?" she said, the drinks that she had quaffed making her tongue loose, but not so loose as to lose her head. "I'm sleeping in a tiny room with barely passable blankets, no fire, and there is no way that I will be allowed to spend time with you two. You'll be busy going on adventures with Eleanor and the Duke and I'll be sent to the kitchen to help out. I'm having fun, here, and I can just get a room until we leave."

"That's enough," Leon snarled, face flushing with annoyance. "I was sent to fetch you back and I will do so. Your horse is ready outside and you are inebriated."

"I won't go," Crow replied easily.

"You will," Leon hissed, voice dangerous. Crow blinked at his tone and shook her head. "If I have to carry you there myself, you will come with me."

A slight hint of fear bit into Crow and she realised that Leon was serious. She could fight him, but it wasn't worth it. She sighed and gave in, turning to put her earned money into her money bag. With a wave to the other men, she stood and pulled on the fur-lined cloak she had placed at her feet. In stony silence, Crow followed Leon out, feeling for the first time the dullness to her senses her mead had given. She mounted the sorrel horse with little trouble and demurely walked back beside Leon.

"What were you thinking?" the knight finally asked, watching Crow's slumped posture with a sad look on his face.

"I didn't lose any money," Crow murmured in response. "And I was having a good time."

"I could see that," Leon sighed, moving his horse closer to hers. He peered into her face and saw that her pale skin had returned to its normal colour. Crow was sobering up but would still feel the weight in the morning. "But why did you run off in the first place? Alexander wanted to hold up dinner until you got there. Our host managed to convince him otherwise, placating him with the promise of a servant to go find you. He may not know your secret, Crow, but he still cares about you. You are his best, and perhaps his only, friend. He likes me, but without you, we would never have crossed paths."

Crow lowered her head, staring at the saddle in front of her. She glanced sideways at Leon, pain rich in her eyes. Had she been in her right mind, not free with drink, she would have veiled her hurt. Leon reached out and touched her arm through her cloak, a comforting gesture which Crow appreciated.

"I didn't mean to cause problems," she said at last.

"I've been in noble houses and I knew I would find no dinner for me. I needed a new cloak and blanket for my bed, seeing as there's no fire, so I went to town. And then I met the smith, a real bastard, if you ask me, and got dinner. One drink turned to more and," Crow shrugged. "I just didn't want to hang around the judgement that was being doled out to me."

Leon shook his head, "Crow, you've dealt with this more than I have, but you didn't have to go and get drunk enough to play riddles with some strange men."

Crow snorted, "It's not like they were going to do anything to me. I'm a boy to them, remember? And even drunk, I can hold my own in a fight. I had my Scheren with me the whole time. I also had enough money to cover any debts I might have incurred."

"That's not my point, Crow. You're acting out of character and I don't like it," Leon snapped, moving his horse away. Crow didn't say anything and simply let the knight lead the way back to the Duke's estates.

She knew the reason she was acting so uncharacteristic, even if she didn't understand the cause. She couldn't sort out her feelings for Alexander any more and she didn't know why she had lost control. She was afraid of him finding out about her secret, about her past, about her emotions. She had never needed to deal with anything like this before and that alone frightened her. So Crow remained silent, letting the cold night air blow her short hair and redden the tip of her nose.

Leon and Crow made it back to the estates with no trouble and Crow stabled her horse, carrying her new blanket and sword to the small quarters she had been assigned. Leon followed her, ready to help her if she wobbled, but Crow held her drink well. He stood in the small doorway and squinted through the gloom of the two candles as Crow spread her blanket.

"Will you be okay?" he asked quietly. Crow nodded, pulling off her layered shirts to sleep in her bandages. She removed her boots and kept her breeches on, only a couple inches of her navel showing. "Then I'll see you tomorrow, okay?"

"Night," Crow said and shut the door, crawling into her bed and wrapping her new blanket around her. She stared at the blackness for a few minutes before the exhaustion she had been staving off with food and games and mead took hold. She was asleep within instants after that.

Morning found Crow with a headache and a forced smile on her face. She wore a green shirt and a thick pair of breeches, her skin clean after having begged the use of a private tub. As morning wore on, Crow's headache lessened and she felt her stomach rumble. But there could be no breakfast until Alexander emerged, according to their host. He looked at Crow with a half-fondness, the sort of look you give a stray cat.

Angry and indignant, Crow wandered through the castle until she came upon Alexander's room. With a couple of rapid knocks to announce her presence, the beautiful smith burst into the Prince's room, ready to demand that he come down to breakfast so she could eat.

Instead, she was silent as she took in the scene before her.

Asleep on the bed, completely unaware of her presence or the knocks she had given, lay Alexander, a blanket wrapped around the lower half of his legs but otherwise bare. Even in sleep, Crow could see the Crown Prince reaching for his companion. Asleep as well was Eleanor, her long brown hair tangled from a night of passion. She was bare but for the other half of Alexander's blanket covering a small portion of her back.

Crow took in the scene and when she had done so, a sudden stab of pain so violent it caused her to stumble into the wall took hold. She felt tears springing to her eyes and blinked them away rapidly. Quietly, she turned and fled the Prince's bedchamber, closing the door gently behind her. She kept her eyes dry as she began to run, a sprint meant for escaping terrors. She was not bothered or spotted by anyone who would question her presence as she raced from the castle and onto the grounds.

The pain worsened as she ran into the forest and her heart felt like it would burst. Finally, Crow collapsed against a tree, succumbing to the sobs that had threatened her during flight. She leaned against the oak, letting tears run down her face as she tried to make sense of the muddled emotions that coursed through her. With Jek back in Kyper, Crow turned to the only person she could. As Leon approached, having followed her, she lunged and buried her head into his broad shoulder, crying deeply. The knight said nothing and simply wrapped his arms around her.

"I d-don't under-s-stand what's h-happening to me, Leon," Crow said through gut wrenching sobs. "I d-don't understand these e-emotions or what I'm sup-o-ssed to do. Why d-does it hurt, Leon? I'm so lost."

"Hush," Leon murmured, pressing his lips to Crow's hair and then resting his chin on her head while she clung to him in desperation. "Did no one ever explain to you about love or what it means to be a woman?" Crow shook her head and the sobs subsided, tears falling heavier in their absence.

"I've been a boy for so long," Crow said pitifully, breathing in the earthy scent of the knight. The scene with Alexander played over and over in her head and the pain she could not explain returned.

"Oh, Crow," Leon said softly, rubbing his hands over her lean back. "You just need someone to teach you, to make things make sense."

"What?" Crow asked, lifting her head to meet Leon's gaze. His brown eyes hardened with an emotion Crow could not name, but it was not dangerous. Just the opposite. As the salt water left her eyes, Leon leaned in and pressed his lips to hers. Crow was startled, but the knight would not let her pull away. Crow found herself responding instinctively and realised she didn't mind it at all. She had never been kissed before.

"That, dear Crow," Leon said as he pulled gently away, "was a kiss. Have you ever been kissed before?" Crow shook her head and Leon gave a small smile, eyes narrowed in pleasure. "Then let me do it again." And she did.

CHAPTER 11

Crow did not return to the castle to eat breakfast. She was not ready to face Alexander and she didn't want the quiet ministrations Leon paid her to end. He stroked her face, pressing gentle kisses along her cheeks, her forehead, her neck. He ran his hands through her short hair, trying to get a grip but failing. His actions made it easier for the images of Alexander and Eleanor to quiet inside her mind. Crow let him dull the ache she was feeling inside, but it did not go away completely. She doubted that it ever would.

"Leon," she murmured as the knight stopped his kisses to wrap his arms around her, staving off the cold that threatened. "You have to go back. The Duke will not let breakfast begin until you are there."

"And I won't go back until you do," the knight replied. Crow sighed, letting him share his body heat with her, but she gave and effort of will and pulled away. Staring at him, Crow shook her head.

"I'll be fine. I think I'll just go find something to do to work off this headache. You can tell Alexander that I came back drunk and need to get rid of the lingering effects," she said and started back to the castle. Leon trailed closely behind, saying nothing, though his expression was admonishing. Crow felt his presence and allowed herself to be comforted by it until they reached the open space just around the castle. Then, she built up her walls again and shut the pleasant feelings regarding Leon away. She didn't understand them anymore than she understood her feelings regarding Alexander, but at least these were more enjoyable.

"Then I'll find you later, alright? I'm not done teaching you," the dusty skinned man said, walking away from Crow and heading towards the main doors. She watched him walk away with a graceful stride, his posture proud and shook her head. She admitted to herself that she didn't mind being taught such gentle, pleasant things. She had never been involved in such a way and longed to learn more, to understand why her emotions were doing what they were. Maybe then she could sort everything out and things could go back to the way they always had been.

Distracted, Crow walked around the back of the palace until she found the practise yards. They were much smaller than those of Kyper and were composed of hard dirt instead of grass, but already there were a few soldiers about, training with wooden weapons or dulled metal ones. Crow shook her muscles loose and grinned.

This was what she needed, she thought as she waltzed onto the dirt.

At her entrance, all of the people there turned to look at her. Most were rough looking soldiers with unshaven faces and hard gazes, but there were a few more elegant men who were obviously knights stationed at Westmont. One, a brawny man wearing no shirt despite the coldness of the morning, moved away from the group he was with and approached the pale smith.

"What are you doing, boy?" he said, spitting on the ground next to Crow's feet. She didn't blink but met the man's gaze in a challenge. "This place is for warriors. Not scrawny younglings like yourself."

"I'm looking to spar," Crow said, ignoring the insult. It was nothing she hadn't heard before. And this time, she could prove herself worthy. "And I can hold my own."

The man laughed, his chest heaving as he roared. "You would get flattened by any of my men. Go run along to the stables, boy. You'd be of better use there."

Crow narrowed her eyes, green fire beginning to burn. She was using her pain at finding Alexander and her anger at being judged to fuel the rage that begged to be let loose. She walked over to the side of the practise yards and picked up some spare bandages that were lying about next to a bowl of white chalk-like powder. She wrapped the bandages around her hands and halfway up her forearms before turning back to the man who had watched with feigned disinterest. He was bored and beating some sense into Crow would lighten his day.

"Two bronze bits says I can win," Crow barked out, voice rising to fill the yards. The bare chested man scoffed but nodded and he looked around.

"Who do you wish to fight?" he asked, amusement plain in his voice. Crow set her gaze on the man and shrugged almost lazily.

"Pick someone. I'm not choosey," she said, adding her own dark humour into her voice, letting the rage heighten her senses. The man looked about and settled his gaze on a scraggly man with powerful arms and a crooked nose. The chosen warrior nodded and began prepping for a fight, pulling off his shirt to reveal scarred skin and a strong core, wrapping bandages around his own hands.

"Sven will be your opponent," the leader said, stepping out of the sparring ring and gathering his men in a circle around Crow and Sven. Crow pulled her own woollen shirt off, revealing the tightly wrapped bandages. Some men scoffed and others murmured in admiration. What other reason would a man have for wrapping his chest than to cover some grievous past wound?

As both fighters took their positions, the men began chanting, unintelligible grunts timed with the stomping of their feet. Crow let the pulsating rhythm set her motions and she bowed to Sven as he bowed to her. When they straightened, the fight began. The scraggly man lunged right off the bat, hoping to gain a blow by the element of surprise. Crow dodged left and swung her arms forward as if to beat her fist into the man's stomach.

Sven pulled back as Crow's fist would have hit him, but Crow was no longer where she had been. She used the momentum from her punch to spin around and pushed off the ground with her long legs, lifting into the air enough to land a kick on Sven's back. The big man flinched and roared in agony as one of his ribs cracked, but did not fall. Crow rolled as she fell back to the ground and was on her feet again, hands raised to protect her face.

All of her attention was focused on the fight and Crow watched with narrowed eyes as Sven started to weave back and forth, taking a step forwards every time he shifted his weight. He feinted right and punched left, but barely managed to graze Crow's arm as she twisted and bent around him. She pulled Sven's weight onto an outstretched leg and rolled him over her hip, putting him to the ground. Before the big warrior could move, Crow was standing over him, one foot poised above his abdomen, a calm look on her face.

"Concede," Sven said and Crow let him up, helping to pull the man to his feet. He looked at her and saw the truth of lean, wiry muscle that he had missed upon first appraising the pale skinned youth.

"Sorry about the rib, by the way," Crow said as she clasped arms with Sven. "I didn't mean to put so much force into the blow. I haven't done this for a while."

"You haven't done this for a while? Then I must be hopeless," Sven chuckled and the two turned towards their audience. Excited murmurs filled the air as the soldiers and few knights talked about what had happened. Crow met the gaze of the leader and gave a smile, walking over to him.

"Two bronze bits," the man said, "as promised."

"Thanks," Crow replied, taking the money. "But I wasn't really looking to make money. Just needed to blow off some steam." She stretched out her arms and turned slightly, planning on walking away.

"Then maybe you'll give me a chance to make my two bits back," the man said, folding his arms across his broad chest. Crow looked at him curiously and he grinned, "I haven't seen that kind of fighting since I was near the border of the Eastern Lands. I'd like to pitch some of my men against you, see if they can hone their fighting techniques. And if I make a few bets, well then."

Crow chuckled, the agony of her morning nearly forgotten. "I can't promise anything. I haven't done hand to hand sparring for a while. And the last sword fight I got into was with Sir Gavin."

"You're the one who beat that poor man into humiliation?" a one-eyed man said, one of the knights stationed at Westmont. Crow shrugged and the knight shook his head, a smile playing on his harsh features. "He got beat worse than he said, if that's true. He made it sound like it was some monster of a man. You're just a boy!"

"He was overconfident and slow," Crow replied. She flexed her fingers and looked at the leader of the men. "I think I can manage a few more fights this morning."

"I was hoping you'd say that. What's your name, boy?" the man said, holding his hand out for Crow to shake. She took it and met his gaze.

"Folks call me Crow," she replied and that earned her quiet laughter from the men in the circle. She was paired with another warrior and the fighting began. For the remainder of the morning and into the afternoon, Crow either sparred with the soldiers, taking them on and winning, one by one, or she sat on the side-lines to regain her breath as she watched the others fight. At some point, warm cider had been passed around and bread, meat and cheese was brought out by a young servant to feed the soldiers.

Crow had, at first, watched the betting with mild interest, feeling flattered when men bet on her. But after a while of prodding, she began to take place, looking over the men with a critical eye. She made a fair bit of coin but lost occasionally and always lost with grace. She was laughing loudly at some raunchy joke the one-eyed knight had made, head tossed back and face flushed from the fighting and the cold, when two new figures stepped into the practise yards. All activity stopped and the two warriors that had been preparing to spar straightened, turning to look at the newcomers.

"Alexander, Leon," Crow called, her forgotten pain pricking her as she spotted her friends. She ignored it, deciding that it could not have been avoided as Alexander would never know. The sight of Leon admiring her lean frame and bandaged wrapped chest helped as well. "Come meet Vaughn, captain of the Westmont soldiers."

The Prince eyed Crow warily, but stepped forwards, walking through the sparring ring to stand near Crow.

The leader, Vaughn, held out his hand and appraised Alexander's fighting form. "Crow?" the Prince asked, looking curiously at his friend. "What are you doing?"

"I'm fighting, off and on. Making some money on bets, having some hot cider," she shrugged.

"Your friend is quite skilled," Vaughn said, nodding his head at Crow who simply chuckled and shook her head. Alexander nodded, posture tense. He looked at Crow and moved away from the other men. Crow sighed and walked over to where the Prince stood, fidgeting nervously with his shirt.

"What's going on?" she asked, handing him her cup of hot cider. Alexander took it as if grateful to have something to do with his hands, but he did not drink. Instead, he looked at Crow as if he didn't recognise her.

"I could ask you the same thing," he muttered and Crow tilted her head slightly, confused. "I brought you along because you're my friend and I wanted you to be around so I wouldn't have to deal with Westmont and could have someone to talk to. But we got here and then you ran off to town to, according to Leon, end up playing riddles well into the night. And this morning, I don't even see you at all but have to actively seek you out and find you fighting and betting with soldiers. What's gotten into you, Crow?"

Crow bit back a sharp retort, offended at Alexander's tone. She hid the pain in her eyes and slid her hands into her pockets, bare arms brushing against her bandaged torso. "I've had enough of being judged just because I'm not of noble class. The Duke may have introduced me to

Jek, but it was the only alternative to paying me and he sees me as an interesting project. I'm stuck in the servant's hall in a room no bigger than I can swing a cat and while you and Leon are fed, I'm left to fend for myself."

"You could have found me," Alexander said, exasperated. He hastily took a sip of the cider to keep from saying something that would hurt Crow and cause an argument. Crow fixed him with a hard look in her eye, mouth set in a straight line.

"That wouldn't have done much. The Duke would have easily found a way to keep you from consorting with peasants. I didn't like how I was treated, so I removed myself from the situation and decided to do things my way. If that means acting uncharacteristically and going to a tavern for a few drinks and playing riddles with fairly pleasant people or spending my morning with soldiers, practising my hand to hand combat, then so be it," Crow said simply. She was still feeling the pain of her earlier sight of Alexander but she was able to hide it, ignore it, instead focusing on her friend.

"I would have made sure you were with Leon and me, no matter where we went," Alexander muttered, suddenly feeling badly for not noticing the treatment of Crow. He recognised now, as Crow detailed the situation for him, that what she said was true and was feeling self-conscious for not noticing.

Crow shook her head slightly, a forgiving expression alighting onto her features, "No, Alexander. You wouldn't have been able to stop this. But that's alright. In a week, we'll be heading back to Kyper and I won't have to deal with petty nobles. Come on, these soldiers have been an embarrassment to the name of fighting and you need to teach them a lesson." Alexander sighed and considered Crow. She certainly had been miserable during their journey to Westmont. And the placations of his host as well as the various insinuations against her person only made everything more clear. But here, she was smiling and happy. So he obliged, determined to do at least one good thing for his friend this trip.

The Prince followed Crow back to the sparring ring and the black-haired smith grinned at Vaughn. "You up for another fight, Crow?" he asked and Crow was certain she saw money exchange hands as she considered. Shrugging and swinging her arms slightly, bouncing on the balls of her feet, she nodded and grinned.

"I'll do another one, but I think you need to see Alexander with a sword, first," she said, stepping out of the ring to leave a stunned looking Alexander in her place.

"What? Crow, I'm really not in the mood for thi—" he tried to protest, but Crow shoved a longsword into his hands, a mischievous grin on her face. The Prince stuttered and tried to hand the blade back but Crow simply stepped around him and pushed him into the ring. He sighed and Crow took up a spot next to Leon.

"Crow?" Leon said, stepping closer so their shoulders were brushing. Crow could feel a charge through Leon's shirt and her bare skin developed goose pimples, making her fold her arms against the cold. She looked at Leon, a slight smile on her face and the knight chuckled. "You have a mean streak."

"I don't know what you mean," she sniffed, watching Alexander speak to Vaughn. The brawny man said something and then gestured for one of the men to enter the ring. He was one of the knights, an elegant looking man with his dark hair slicked back on his head. He had a rapier rather than the normal longsword or broadsword most knights preferred. Alexander shot an angry look at Crow and then turned to his opponent, bowing.

"Putting Alexander in the sparring ring to exact your revenge isn't what I'd call nice," Leon said, turning to look Crow in the eye. She grinned and chuckled softly.

"I'm not exacting revenge. I'm making some money," she replied and raised her voice. "Hey, Sven, three bronze bits says that Alexander will have your knight down in less than three minutes, by the hourglass you have sitting next to you."

Sven, his rib wrapped tightly, laughed and then winced, "I think you're kidding yourself, but I'm happy to take your money." Crow grinned and as the Prince and his opponent straightened, she turned her attention to the fighting.

With almost lightning speed, the knight lunged at Alexander who, having learned something from Leon's style, moved out of the way almost as quickly. He was larger and stronger than the other knight but his speed suffered for it, though not by much. So, pressing the advantage of size, Alexander bore down on the knight with a quick swing. The two blades latched at the hilts and it became plain to see that the rapier was no match for the longsword. In a move of desperation, the smaller knight broke away, darting past Alexander's side.

The Prince, by instinct, turned and brought his blade down on the back of the knight, hitting him with the flat and causing the man to stumble. The moment of unbalance let Alexander move in, slipping his sword over the man's shoulders to stop at his neck. The smaller knight froze and nodded his head slightly in acquiescence of Alexander's victory. Crow grinned in triumph and marched across the ring to where Sven sat, the hourglass at his side.

"Well?" she asked, flexing her fingers. The scraggly man sighed and handed over the money, dropping the bits into Crow's hands. As the last piece fell, a sharp voice called out over the practise yards.

"What is going on here?" The question caused Crow to spin and she saw the tense form of the Duke, standing with his hands at his sides, fingers clenched so the knuckles were almost white. He was glaring at his men with insolence and disgust in his eye. "I expect you to take my offer of service more kindly. Perhaps you would better spend your time training than gambling?"

Crow felt herself bristle and she pushed the money back into Sven's hands, stepping forwards to confront the Duke. The noble narrowed his eyes at Crow in obvious dislike and then he spotted Alexander. "Your Highness," the Duke said with a touch of civility in his tone. Alexander straightened his posture and raised his eyebrows at the Duke. "Perhaps your time would be better spent away from people of such a low class. These soldiers are little more than peasants skilled in the art of fighting and they are not worth your time. That they engage in such lewd activities such as gambling is despicable and they will be punished."

Crow stepped into the centre of the ring and visibly crossed her hands in front of her, a stance for fighting. The Duke didn't recognise the stance and simply looked down his nose at the lean smith with her chest wrapped in bandages. "I thought that I did a service in introducing you to Jek, but I see I was wrong. Highness," he continued, turning his attention to Alexander. "I apologise for bringing this, this commoner into your presence. He is not worthy of such an honour."

Crow drew back her lips in a feral snarl and felt her muscles relaxing as she prepared to attack. She could feel Leon's presence approach behind her but ignored it. Alexander, however, did not simply remain quiet. He frowned and raised his longsword enough to be a threat to the Duke. Crow blinked, startled by his reaction.

"I was sent here to remind you of my father's power over you, Westmont. You have become insolent and rude in your regards with the throne and I was sent to make sure you were paying what taxes ahave not been payed and to remind you of your station. I was treated graciously and with luxury, but I see that I was wrong. My friend, Crow, whom I brought with me by special invitation, was subject to a stone closet for quarters, no heat, no food, and disregarded by you and your notions of polite behaviour. He was made to ride into town and buy his own blanket and fur cloak, eating dinner in one of the local taverns because you did not see fit to treat him as a host should. I realise that nobles and peasants are not of the same class, but they are all humans and deserve some respect. Especially when I, Alexander Fenyr, Crown Prince deem it so. You disgust me, Westmont, and your treatment of your own people is despicable. My party and I, Crow included, shall impose on your hospitality for one evening more, feasting in my chambers. We will depart on the morrow to deliver the news of your treatment of the crown to my father. You will be severely punished," Alexander hissed, voice low and deadly. He looked every bit the part of regal and powerful Prince and his golden hair shimmered in the weak sunlight of near-winter. Crow felt her heart flutter and, despite Leon's presence beside her, wished that he had been the one to kiss her that morning.

The Duke of Westmont did not have a response to Alexander's speech and instead spluttered and muttered hurried apologies to Crow and the soldiers, his eyes wide and begging. While the King would not directly bring down force upon the Duke unless a revolution was mounting, he could easily see to it that Westmont was made to pay more of the taxes he collected from the people, would be burdened with companies of soldiers returning from the borders, have few men to defend his lands and be snubbed in noble society. Such things could lead to Westmont's ruin and his land would be turned over to the people if he were not fit to hold it. That or another Duke would be appointed to take his place.

Crow straightened, her need to fight over, but she felt strangely unsatisfied. Alexander walked over to her, his anger simmering in his blue eyes. He thrust the sword into the ground and growled angrily. Crow looked at him with curiosity and confusion. "You didn't have to do that," she said quietly as Alexander came up to her. She went and picked up her shirt from where she had first disposed of it and pulled it on, unwrapping the bandages around her hands and forearms. "I could have defended myself."

"Crow," Alexander said softly, stepping in between Leon and the smith. The knight sidestepped smoothly and Crow saw a hint of frustration in his eyes. "You would have challenged Westmont and been executed for such daring. You know the laws, in these circumstances, perhaps better than I."

"I would have figured something out," she muttered, staring stonily into Alexander's sculpted face. He sighed and his features softened, taking in his friend who was so righteous, determined to find justice.

"Crow," he murmured, clapping his hand gently on her shoulder. She longed for him to pull closer, to press against her and kiss her, brushing his lips against hers with a serene gentleness and patience that would lead to a passionate embrace. Startled by her train of thought, Crow mentally shook herself, wondering where her feelings were coming from that they were so strong. "You don't have to be strong all the time. It's okay to let others help you."

"I know," Crow muttered and Alexander smiled sadly,

all her emotions closed off to him. He stepped away and the trio walked back to the castle, the Prince leading the way and Crow trailing behind with Leon, desperate for him to explain what was going on in her head, to touch her and make all her other thoughts go away. She felt slightly guilty that she was using her friend in such a way, taking advantage of his experience and his kindness to let her experience a few moments of peace and enjoyment at being treated like a desirable object. But that was what Leon wanted, wasn't it? To teach her, to treat her like a woman?

Such thoughts continued to roll through Crow's head as the three ate in Alexander's chambers, served the most expensive dishes the Prince could think of out of spite. Crow tried to pay rapt attention to the conversation, smiling at funny stories, shaking her head at Alexander's fury towards the Duke. But she could not keep her mind from wondering and she remained silent, not trusting herself to speak.

As she prepared for bed, later that evening, Crow turned, startled, as the door opened to her small stone room. Leon stood before her, wearing little more than a pair of breeches and he closed the door behind him, watching Crow's face with apparent interest.

"Leon," she murmured, standing there in her bandages and breeches, taking in and admiring his well-cut chest, tempted to reach out and touch him. "I don't understand these feelings, these thoughts going through my head."

"That's what I'm here for," he said, voice deeper than

usual and containing a husky element. Crow shook her head, pressing her hands against her temple. "Ask me anything, tell me what you're thinking. I'll make it better."

She tentatively took a step towards him, lowering her head to stare at the floor before her feet, her hands before her, fingers touching nervously. "Is it alright for me to... to use you and what you're offering to clear my head, to make me feel...wanted?"

Leon bridged the gap between them, grabbing Crow's hands and pressing them against his chest. Crow opened her mouth slightly as she felt the shock between their skin. She wanted to stand there all night, tracing the lines of his muscles, his veins. Crow looked up into Leon's eyes, pulling back slightly, afraid. The knight looked back at her, lust vibrant in his eyes, illuminated by only the two candles in the niches in the wall.

"Crow," he said, pulling her closer, keeping her hands on his warm skin. He leaned in and put his mouth to her ear, nipping the lobe slightly. "That's what I'm here for." He pulled away from her and then closed on her open mouth, seeking hungrily for something Crow could not yet understand. She relaxed into his hold and deepened the kiss, thoughts of Alexander momentarily silenced.

CHAPTER 12

Morning found Crow wrapped tightly in her blanket, wishing desperately that Leon had stayed and kept her warm. But he claimed that he wanted to take things slow, make sure his lessons sank in, before anything more. Crow grumbled and untangled herself from her bed, standing and stretching out her sore muscles. She hadn't fought so much for a long while and her body was protesting the abuse. Crow dressed and packed her belongings, shouldering the pack and holding the fur-lined cloak on one arm before vacating the small stone room, happy never to have to see it again, even through the bleary eyes of morning.

She found Alexander and Leon already outside near the stables, preparing the horses for the return journey. Neither seemed pleased about being up early, but there was an extra bag of provisions taken from the Duke's store room to placate them for a while. The three said little to each other in the first hours of the morning, instead riding along in silence and hoping that the sun would warm their cold bones.

"So, Crow," Alexander said at last, handing over a meat pie to the well-bundled smith. "How much money did you make in all your activities?"

"Enough. It all comes to about ten gold coins, if I ever exchange it out," she replied, drawing her horse into a faster walk, eager to put Westmont behind her. Leon kept apace with her and she could often feel his eyes watching her with an eager admiration that made her almost flush. Crow contained her emotions and sighed, watching her breath condense in the cold air.

"Well, at least one of us had fun on this trip," the Prince muttered and Crow couldn't help but chuckle, shaking her head. "What?" he asked, turning to look incredulously at Crow.

"So Eleanor wasn't fun?" she teased, feeling only a slight sting in her heart when she mentioned the topic. Alexander, to her amusement and pleasure, flushed deeply, whipping his head around and fixing his gaze on the road.

"I won't ask how you know about that," he spluttered. "But it meant nothing. She was lonely and I was...hungry. She knows that it meant nothing and there are no expectations. I..please don't tell my father. He'll kill me for sleeping with a noble with no intention of marriage. I'm supposed to find a queen from among nobles, not a good time."

"Relax," Crow admonished, inwardly elated that Alexander was only whetting his sexual appetite with Eleanor. She reminded herself that she shouldn't be so pleased, that she would never mean anything to Alexander and that there was no hope of him ever thinking of her like she did him. "I won't say a word. I'm just messing with you."

The relief which Alexander expressed was obvious and Crow felt a sudden stab of pity for the Prince. That he was so afraid of enjoying himself for fear of what his father would do, of what people would think, was sad. Crow ate her meat pie and they rode on in relative silence.

"Have you ever played riddles?" Crow asked as they were beginning to slow for the day, the sky turning grey from cloud cover and the wind beginning to pick up and bite through their clothes to chill the bones. Each was ready for any distraction and a game of riddles seemed best. They modified the rules to play on horseback and Alexander was about to start when a slight thud caught the attention of the riders.

"Oh," Alexander said, voice slurring a bit. He turned and pulled out a brightly coloured dart from where it stuck in his shoulder and blinked groggily a few times, licking his lips as he took in the projectile. He looked at Crow in confusion and then tumbled from his horse, unconscious.

Crow pulled up her sorrel and with little regard for her own safety, dismounted, hurrying over to the unconscious form of Alexander. Her concern was great enough that she focused on little else but her Prince and then barely noticed when a dart pierced her cloak and hit her shoulder. Crow turned, her mind already coming under a fog and looked at Leon. The knight also had a dart sprouting from him and was beginning to tumble to the ground. Crow managed to stave off the effect of whatever drug was in her system long enough to watch as a group of people walked up to them and then slumped to the ground, slipping into unconsciousness.

Crow awoke on her knees, her hands tied behind her back with thick, scratchy rope. Her head was beginning to clear but she still felt odd and her mouth was dry. Blinking away the disorientation, Crow swung her head slowly around to see the situation. She saw Alexander to her left and Leon to her right and it was plain that the three were in some sort of temporary camp, as there were makeshift shelters and fires burning around the fairly large clearing. The people inhabiting the area were thin and looked as if they had seen better days. Even the few children Crow saw had a hard look in their eyes, the look of ones who had seen too much and had to fight for every advantage.

She turned her head enough to see that their horses were unsaddled and tied to a tree, the saddles on the ground, bags spread around a bulky and oddly shaped man with a thick neck and small, beady eyes. He had Crow's Scheren on his lap and was holding the blade, much to Crow's dismay, with the knowledge of one who knew how to use it.

"Oh, good, you're awake," a voice said, causing Crow to tilt her head upwards. She was met with the sight of a fairly buxom woman with unkempt brown hair, a few bird feathers sticking out at odd angles. Her eyes were painted darkly and she had three gold hoops through one ear. Her clothing consisted of tight breeches which left very little to the imagination and, despite the cold, a sleeveless tunic which allowed her fairly muscular arms to be shown. Crow furrowed her brows and looked about the clearing some more.

To her disgust, she saw a large cage on cart wheels with people covered in dirt, haunted looks on their faces, chained to it. They were huddled together near the wheels and by the way they were standing, Crow could tell they hadn't been out of the cage for a while. Slaves. She felt Leon stir next to her and Alexander soon followed suit. The woman, their captor and what looked like the leader of the group, grinned, revealing teeth that were slightly yellow, one on the bottom missing.

"You managed to hold up to the tranquilliser very well," she said, crouching down to examine each of her prisoners with obvious interest. "I'm pleased."

"Where are we?" Alexander croaked, his voice raspy from a dry mouth. Crow licked her lips, attempting to get some moisture to them as the woman beamed at the Prince.

"Not far from where you were riding," she cooed, reaching out to stroke the Prince's face. Crow felt anger bubbling beneath the surface as the woman caressed the Prince's handsome face. Alexander looked disgusted but he was too weak to do much of anything about it. Even as she felt the anger, Crow realised her strength was coming back. She twisted her wrists around in the rope and found they were well tied.

"They're slavers," Crow said, her voice slightly raspy but clear. Alexander balked and tried to recoil from the woman. She simply laughed and ran her hands through his golden hair, taking obvious pleasure in her prisoner being unable to fight back.

"Slavers?" Leon rumbled, causing the woman to look at him, her eyes bright and excited. Crow could see where her nipples were hardening in lust under her tunic and curled her lips in disgust. "I thought there were no more slavers. The King had them killed and keeps patrols..."

"Patrols? From old King Byron? What a joke," the woman scoffed, rising slowly to her feet. Alexander ground his teeth but said nothing. If the woman knew what sort of a treasure she had in her hands, she would take the Prince to any of the warring nations a couple of countries beyond and they would pay handsomely for him. Crow glared at the ground, slowly twisting her wrists around to try and loosen the rope. She knew that she could break her bonds, as she had years ago under a different hand, but the situation was not yet so dire. She would not relive those moments for nothing.

"It is so nice to have such fine specimens. Good stock is hard to find. And with such handsome men as yourselves, I may not even sell you for a while, just see what you taste like first. Perhaps I'll make some extra money off of you in the fighting rings," the woman purred, resting a hand on Leon's rugged hair. He glared up at her but, like Alexander, was too busy fighting off the effects of the drug to do anything.

"Hey, Alkai," the big man who had been rummaging through the packs called. He stood and held up Leon's cloak, the one distinguishing him as a knight of the realm. Crow breathed a sigh of relief that he had not found anything incriminating in Alexander's bags. She needed to have the Prince's identity kept secret. The big man walked over, Crow's Scheren in his hands, and handed the cloak to the woman.

Alkai grinned, running the fine cloth through her fingers. She looked with cold, cruel calculation at her prisoners and inhaled the scent of the fabric. "Which of you is the knight?" she said, crouching low again to stare each in the face. None of them spoke. Her grin wider, the woman inhaled again and pressed her nose against Alexander's neck, breathing in his scent. She pressed her lips to his throat and let her mouth linger, eyes burning with desire. But then she moved on to Crow, breathing deeply. It took much of Crow's willpower to keep from resisting her, even when Alkai trailed kissed up Crow's neck and bit her ear. She slid over to Leon and did the same, her hand grabbing a fistful of his hair as she pulled his head back and kissed him on the mouth. "You," she said as she pulled away.

Crow watched the scene with disgust but trained her attention on the big man who was still holding her blade. She saw the hilt of a thin sword at his side and frowned when she realised he was carrying his own Scheren. "Alkai, one of them's been carrying this," he said, catching the attention of the woman as he held out the blade.

She took the blade and pulled it from its specially made sheath, eyes widening as she took in the gleaming, razor sharp metal. "What do you make of it, Mac?" she asked, handing the Scheren back to the man.

Mac took the hilt and pulled the blade free of its sheath, examining the entire length carefully. Crow felt her rage burning as the man fingered her sword and narrowed her eyes. "This is extremely well made. Best I've seen since the Shaman's tent, and he paid three hundred crown for it," Mac said, referring to one of the leaders of the Eastern Lands. "I'd say whoever's carrying this knows how to use it."

Alkai looked interested and she turned back to the three kneeling before her. Crow blinked in surprise as she saw a tattoo on the woman's shoulder, the picture an image of a lynx with a snarl on its face, feathers in its fur. Crow stiffened and in her surprise, she lost control of her brimming anger. The rage took over, making her still and forcing her muscles to relax. Memories, memories that Crow kept locked away deep inside of her, began to emerge and Crow met Alkai's gaze as the woman crouched down. "I doubt the knight knows how to use a Scheren, so which of you two owns the blade?" she purred, reaching out to touch Alexander's shoulder. The Prince had regained enough of his facilities to flinch away and Alkai laughed, shaking her head. She turned to Crow and recoiled in shock as she met the burning green eyes before her, murder plain in their intent.

"I know you," Crow hissed, voice no longer raspy, complete control over her body returning as her rage burned the remainder of the drug away.

"What?" Alkai asked, standing and backing away a couple of steps. Mac stood next to her, hands grasping Crow's Scheren as insurance against attack, just in case. He, too, saw the murder in the pale, lean prisoner's eyes, her beautiful features turned into a deadly sight but still alluring, demanding.

"I know you. As sure as I breathe, I know you. I name you Alkai "Bloody Feathers" Maruk," Crow said, twisting her wrists in such a way that the left one popped, leaving enough of a gap in the rope for her to pull her hands free. She kept them behind her back, ignoring the throbbing pain as she stared down Bloody Feathers.

"How do you know that?" Alkai whispered, backing away even more, hands rising in defence. She looked frightened and ready to fight, to kill Crow.

"Because," Crow growled, rising to her feet as she kept her hands behind her back, straightening to her full imposing height and looking down at Alkai. The slaver got a full glimpse of the power within Crow's shoulders, her arms, the strength in such lean muscle which was corded over Crow's back, her stomach, her legs. "I am the spawn of the Jackal and he demands revenge."

"No," the woman said, shaking her head so that the feathers that stuck there shivered with the movement.

"That's not possible. The only member of the Jackal's family that survived was taken by the Mazemaker. You are lying." Alkai, believing her victory, allowed a smile to come to her face. Her smile soon disappeared as Crow continued to stare her down, face blank of all emotion but for her eyes. Her eyes were full of some hidden desire, rage, murder.

"The Mazemaker," Crow snarled. "He would have succeeded in killing me, just like all of his other victims, terrorised, beaten, held onto the stone ground with chains pulling their limbs in four directions so he could carve his designs into their skin without their movement. He would have succeeded in killing me," she said, her voice dripping with venom, "had he not underestimated my will to live."

"No," Alkai "Bloody Feathers" Maruk breathed, her breath shaking with terror. She stepped back again, letting Mac stand before her, letting him bear the brunt of Crow's wrath. But the big man stood stone still, disbelief and fear on his face. Crow continued to stand where she was, legs spread slightly to give her balance as she kept her hands behind her back. Seeing Alkai begin to retreat, she let her lips curl ferally, exposing her white teeth, the canines gleaming dangerously. Crow took a step forward and then another, hypnotising her captor with the fire in her green eyes. Nothing else mattered but the prey before her, the hunt that was certain to ensue.

"The Mazemaker did what he wished to me, spending much more time and care in the pictures he carved into my skin than any other of his victims. While he played with them, boy and girl alike, he kept me clean, chaining me to the wall while he simply watched me, terrorised me. But he underestimated my anger. The Mazemaker," Crow snarled, bringing her hands forwards to clench at her sides, "is dead these past six years, because he chose to ignore my potential."

In an instant, Crow, actions and mind under the powerful control of her rage, leaped and snatched the Scheren out of Mac's hands, swiping the triangle blade across the big man's chest and opening deep gashes there. Stunned, the bulky man watched as Crow cut him down, and then fell to his knees, unable to do more than groan in pain. Mac immobilised, Crow turned her attention towards Alkai.

"You," she snarled at the slaver, "were the one who led them to my father. The Jackal, who trusted you in a position where trust was dangerous to give, would have lived had he not let Alkai "Bloody Feathers" Maruk deal with getting rid of those fool bandits. You were the one who betrayed him for the promise of his land. And he died trying to get you to repent. It is your fault that the Jackal is dead."

"No," Alkai begged, continuing to walk backwards as Crow advanced, her hands held up in surrender, in fear. "I did not kill him," she said in desperation, backing into a tree. Crow narrowed her eyes and then tilted her head back and laughed a cruel, cynical laugh.

"You may not have been the one who put the blade through his heart, who eviscerated him and left him for the scavengers to eat," Crow growled, her chest rumbling like a wild-dog. "But had it not been for you, you and your schemes of power, he would have lived. You would have been rewarded and I would not have spent three years of my childhood being shaped inadvertently by the Mazemaker. Where is your power, now?" Crow threw out her hands, indicating the clearing around her. "Where is your promised land? Your title? Your loyal subjects?"

Alkai trembled as she watched Crow come closer, closer, closer. Crow bent down so that her lips nearly touched the slaver's ear, her voice little more than a whisper, "Gone." With that last word, Crow pulled back her arm and thrust her Scheren forwards into the heart of Bloody Feathers, a quick death. As she removed the blade, the pale, beautiful, dangerous girl wiped its tip on her shirt and wrestled her rage under control. She turned back to where Mac knelt on the ground, bleeding slowly.

"Bandage him," she called to one of the other slavers, all of whom had watched the event in complete silence. Many had run off after Crow had cut into Mac, but those that remained trembled visibly. "He will live. And you will leave this land, spreading word to all your kind that Crow, spawn of the Jackal, lives and will tolerate nothing." Her voice was sharp and the slavers immediately did as she ordered, hurrying to avoid her wrath.

A moment later and Crow recalled herself and her friends and turned away from the desperate slavers. Slumping from the weight of her memories and her actions, her nightmares having come to life as they had so many years ago, Crow returned to Alexander and Leon, cutting them free with a few quick slices and then sheathing her Scheren, carefully packing up her belongings and re-saddling the sorrel. She said nothing and did not meet either of their gazes, worried that they would see the anger and fire still burning there.

The Prince and knight were stunned but did the same, the three of them riding away only after the slaves had been freed. Crow made sure to keep a certain distance between her and her friends, afraid of what their looks would say. Neither Alexander nor Leon bothered her, too shocked to do much more than take in what had happened.

Crow remained silent for the next few days and the only conversation between the group happened between Alexander and Leon. To her disappointment and sorrow, Leon did not attempt to come to her, to kiss her, to even speak with her. But on the third morning, Alexander spoke to Crow, breaking her out of her sorrow.

"I'm sorry," he said. "I wish there were something I could do." Crow looked at him with unshed tears in her eyes and nodded. "But no matter what, you'll always be my greatest friend, Crow. Know that."

Crow smiled, her heart throbbing in her throat as her feeling swelled to the Prince. Leon looked at her with sadness and quiet peace and, rather than saying anything, rode close to Crow, their knees almost touching. She was forgiven for keeping her secrets, for losing control, for her past.

When they reached Kyper, Crow immediately went off to go soak herself in water and try and wash away all that had happened. Leon went off to do the same, though his mind swirled with thoughts of how beautiful and dangerous Crow had looked as she confronted her nightmares. Alexander, though, walked up to Jek and asked, very quietly, "What do you know of the Jackal and the Mazemaker?"

CHAPTER 13

Jek stared at Alexander. The Prince grew frightened when the smith grew pale. With a slowness that betrayed Jek's trepidation, the big man put down his current project and gestured for Alexander to follow him. The Prince followed, expecting to go into the house and was surprised when Jek led him to a quiet alcove in the palace walls. There were trees sheltering the area and it had obviously not been traveled in quite some time. Jek sat on the ground at the base of one of the trees and Alexander followed suit, sitting across from the smith.

"Where did ye hear those names?" Jek said, voice quiet and trembling. Alexander wondered if he should protect Crow, but he trusted Jek and the smith was the closest thing Crow had to family. So, as quickly as possible and trying not to highlight the shock and fear he felt while watching his closest friend drive a blade through the slaver, Alexander relayed the entire incident, looking at his hands the entire time.

When he had finished, the Prince looked up and saw that Jek's eyes were closed and sweat had broken out on his brow, a worrying look on his face. Silence prevailed and Alexander wondered if he should ask his question again, but Jek opened his eyes and met the gaze of the Prince, a sharpness within. He spoke, the uncultured tones that Jek worked so hard to keep, gone.

"The Jackal is a nightmare come to life. It is said that he was born of a slave in the Eastern Lands, a woman who escaped the hold of her master for one evening to give birth to her son..."

Pasha ran through the darkened corridors of the Shaman's palace, careful to place her steps as quietly as possible. She had her dark, raven hair bound with a cloth of deep blue and her pale skin glimmered in the half-light as she ran. She was beautiful and yet her face looked older than her age, the skin wrinkled around her eyes, deep frown lines around her mouth. She ran, breath heavy, a hand on her stomach, fighting off the pains of childbirth until she could reach the outside.

It seemed ages until Pasha managed to get out into the expanse of the wilderness, the land flat and with few trees. In the distance, more vegetation grew and gradually, the land changed from desert to oasis. That was where Pasha ran. She had held off the contractions for as long as she could, though, and she was but a quarter mile from the Shaman's palace when she collapsed on the ground with a gasp of pain. She landed, luckily, on her side, and managed to turn herself over, giving in to the pain with a wild howl. The birthing was long and painful and Pasha barely lived, her breath ragged, eyes wet with tears of joy as she gazed at her newborn son.

He had her features; the raven hair, the milk-white skin, and it was obvious that he would be handsome. His face was scrunched up in the beginnings of a cry, but he made little noise. As Pasha soothed him, brought him to her breast to feed, she stroked him and whispered his name.

"Kamal," she said, her voice little more than a whisper. The baby, the beautiful child that his mother named perfection, blinked open his eyes to reveal a deep, piercing blue. His mother smiled and her body convulsed, causing her to lose her grip on Kamal. She dropped him a few inches to the ground and tried to grab the dirt as she convulsed. Her cries caused her son to cry loudly and she attempted to soothe him, only to convulse in pain again.

The cries of a dying animal drew the wild dogs that lived in the desert and they eagerly awaited Pasha's demise, circling with excited yips, growling and barking at one another, females driving off the males only to be driven off in return. Pasha tried to ward the animals away, but she was weak and dying. Her son cried out in dismay as his mother reached for him only to fail and slump to the ground, dead.

As soon as Pasha's breath left her body, the dogs attacked, beginning to tear into her flesh with yellowed fangs. Kamal cried all the louder as he watched, too young to remember, the dogs eat his mother to the bones. He was ignored for the larger feast, but once the corpse of Pasha was disembowelled and most of the meat gone, some of the dogs began to turn on the wailing thing that scented of new life. Shrieking his anger, Kamal waved his hands and feet, trying to drive the creatures away.

A sudden, sharp rapping sound caused the dogs' attention to turn to a man wearing long, desert wandering clothes. He brought down a large staff on the head of the boss dog and the bone cracked, leaving the dog dead. The others growled and started to advance, but the man waved his stick again and they ran off, yipping, into the night.

"So, you are Kamal by your mother's last breath," the man said, leaning over the newborn boy and picking him off the ground gently. Kamal's cries ceased as soon as he was held and he stopped waving his hands to open his eyes and stare the stranger in the face. The man was older, weather worn and had a scar running across his face. His eyes were hard and cruel and yet he chose to look on the boy with affection, not malice. The man would become Kamal's father, mentor and bane.

Kamal grew, raised by the leader of a band of desert brigands, sometimes slavers and above all, thieves. The boy, with his pale skin and raven hair had few friends and the man who had once looked at him with affection only sought to make the boy become great. Kamal did as he was instructed, spending the time while the older men were on raids, practising with a full sized Scheren, working until his hands were raw and bloody, his legs collapsing underneath him. When he could fight with a Scheren no longer, he ate and returned to the place where he practised, honing his hand-to-hand combat skills.

By the time that Kamal was seventeen, he was undefeated in a fight and had led more than his fair share of raids. All had been successful and it was obvious to the desert brigands that Kamal would be their next leader. However, the man who had raised him saw only mistakes, a disappointment where others would praise. No matter how well Kamal did, it was not good enough. He, in the hopes of making him better, was sent off into the desert, alone. At the end of three months, he would be allowed back into the group granted he brought back a suitable amount of money and new weapons.

Kamal did as he was asked, getting the money and weapons within days of his departure. But no matter that he had done what was required, he would not be allowed back until the three months was over. So, Kamal followed the brigands, eating snakes and small mice along side the wild dogs that he claimed as pack mates. When three months had elapsed, Kamal went back to the brigands, stronger and carrying a hefty sum in his hands. Still, though, his adopted father was not pleased.

Furious that he had not been accepted, Kamal drew his Scheren and cut down his father with a slice to the back. For three days, the man languished, his wound getting infected due to lack of treatment. Kamal, though the others of the group begged, would let none treat the leader, instead staring down at the man day in and day out until he saw the lights die in his eyes. Too afraid to do otherwise, the desert brigands allowed Kamal to take his place as their leader.

Not to say that he wasn't effective; he was extremely adept at what he did. And many of his people admired him for that, calling him the Jackal for being cunning enough to take what they wanted out from under the Shamans' noses. Those who did not agree with his methods or questioned his judgement, though, vanished under strange circumstances. Corpses would occasionally be come upon half buried in an ant-hill, the features carved away with precision so as to be unrecognisable. A pack of wild dogs took to following the brigands around, their bellies filled frequently.

Kamal was cruel and he enjoyed seeing those who opposed him suffer. He would occasionally exercise mercy and let his victims live, often with a missing ear or limb. Parents in desert villages began to forbid their children from going out at night should Kamal take them and train them as his father did he. Those too weak to keep up with the brigands were abandoned, a single knife left in their possession. None survived.

The nightmare that was Kamal became local legend, stories told about him to frighten children into behaving or to tighten the hold of the Shamans on the villages. However, most of the stories told were true and it was said Kamal dined each evening with a goblet full of blood, willingly given by his followers. The tale was only half-true as the blood was from snakes and mice rather than humans. But the pale-skinned, raven haired monster thrived, despite attempts otherwise. He was far too skilled in combat and he was paranoid.

The Jackal's wild reign of the deserts ended when he captured a group of women for slavery. Most were old or ungainly, but there was one that caused Kamal to pause. She was beautiful, her features like a deity, her green eyes glowing and proud, her figure pleasing. But what struck Kamal most about this woman was that her hair was as black as his, though her skin was darker. He took her to his tent and watched her for an evening, saying nothing, making no move to harm her, just watching.

Eventually, the two began to talk and slowly, Kamal's heart was given to her. She was his more reasonable side, persuading him to give up his more obvious shows of cruelty. The promise of cruelty, she claimed, was more effective than the act. Kamal, the Jackal, the nightmare, became more reasoned. He no longer drank blood in the evenings, no longer captured children to train, no longer abandoned those too weak to follow. Instead, he became fiercely protective of his people and was said never to raise a hand in anger except to his enemies. To them, he was quietly ruthless.

It was his quiet cunning, his almost silent way of manipulating people to do as he wished that truly made Kamal a nightmare, but to him it did not matter. His wife, for the slave had become his bride, was carrying a child and he held more power in his hands than any Shaman. Because of such, he claimed a land in the oasis, a valley in the shadow of mountains. He became more powerful and dangerous, more intelligent and sly as time passed and he raised his child with a mix of compassion and hardness which granted the child a tempered personality and a deadly skill with fighting.

One evening, though, the small group of bandits which Kamal kept close beside him turned, desirous of his power. They led another group of brigands into the heart of his domain, burning his home and taking his wife to rape and kill. Kamal, in a quiet rage, slew many of the bandits and declared that none would ever scent his power. He was shot down in a coward's blow, an arrow to the heart while his opponent taunted him. The corpses of Kamal and his wife were thrown onto the burning pyre of his home and the bandits were faced with the child, seven years of age.

What they saw in the burning green eyes was a fury so refined, so potent, that it would easily be far greater than that of Kamal's. The child was not only skilled in combat, but was far more dangerous and deadly than the father. The Jackal was dead, but the child would have revenge and the thought frightened the bandits so much they fled Kamal's domain, never to be seen again. The child, a slight thing which was their only opposition to Kamal's power, lay untouched...

Jek looked into Alexander's eyes as he finished the tale and the Prince found his throat tightening, his fear acute. "The child of Kamal... is Crow?" he breathed and Jek's brow raised into a pain-filled expression.

"I wish it weren't so, but from what ye said, I think it's likely," the smith replied, voice catching in his throat.

Alexander saw that the big man was holding back tears and would have moved to comfort him had he not been immersed in his own disbelief.

"But Crow.. doesn't act like that," he said, holding out hope. Jek swallowed and nodded his head.

"Crow is a good 'un. I haven't seen a lick of cruelty in 'im since I've known 'im," the smith said, choosing his words carefully. Alexander brightened and nodded. Jek continued, "Crow may have been born under the flag of Kamal, but there's no reason why 'e can't be a good person."

"I'm glad you think so," said Crow as she entered the alcove. She had caught most of Jek's tale and though Alexander searched her eyes for a refutation, it was plain that it was true. Crow leaned against the trunk of a tree and slid to the ground. "I have done my very best to lock away those memories, to live my life like Sythfeld taught me rather than what the Jackal imparted. I cannot pretend that I was not taught by my father. You've seen evidence in my fighting. But I don't want to be like him. I'm doing everything I can to be nothing like him. You must believe me."

Alexander turned his head to meet the gaze of his friend, the one who kept secrets of bloody histories, and saw that Crow was crying, body shaking with suppressed sobs. He wanted to hug Crow, to protect his friend and make everything okay, but the knowledge of what Crow came from caused Alexander to hesitate. He saw vividly the way that Crow had lost control over the rage and easily killed Alkai. No matter that the slaver had been guilty, her death quick, the thought of his friend having murdered someone was terrifying.

Crow saw his reluctance and choked out a cry of pain. She pulled her knees to her chest and buried her head between them, her cries muffled by the cloth and her body. "I had hoped that you would judge me based on what you knew of me, of my character. I did not lie to you in what I am like," she said between sobs.

"Crow," Alexander said, reaching out to touch her back and pulling away at the same time. He was hurt by the fact that Crow had not told him but he also pitied the blacksmith apprentice for carrying the weight of such a burden, knowing that if it were ever revealed, she would be judged for the crimes of her father.

"No," she said, wiping away the tears on her sleeves and standing on shaky legs. "It's okay. I always knew what would happen if this got out and I'll manage. It hurts that you would think so poorly of me as to judge me based on things that happened that were out of my control, but I'll manage."

Alexander furrowed his brows, confused at Crow's words. But when she ran from the copse, the meaning became clear. Crow fled from her smith master who had looked at her like a daughter and now looked at her with pain and the Prince to whom she had become attached, become friends, who turned away from her. She ran to Jek's small house and nearly collided with Leon who had been coming to see her.

"Crow?" he asked, clamping his hands on her arms and holding her steady. She tried to pull away, but the big knight wouldn't let her. He pressed a gentle kiss to her forehead and she desperately wanted to do nothing more than put her head on his chest and cry, but she heard footsteps approaching and wrenched away. Leon released her as Alexander approached and Crow darted into the house, to her room where she grabbed her pack and hastily shoved her belongings into it.

She had it nearly done when the Prince entered, standing in the doorway so as to block her exit. He had his hands loosely at his side and his eyes were wide with hurt. Crow looked away, continuing to pack as quickly as she could. "Crow," the Prince said, voice sharp, making the pale-skinned girl who took so much after her father flinch. "Don't."

"Don't what?" she snarled, wishing she could just vanish. Her humiliation was visible in her face and she felt badly for hurting her friend. It was anything but what she wanted and as soon as Alexander looked into her eyes, he saw that. "Don't be the child of Kamal the Jackal? Don't act like I'm not a monster ruled by skills forced into me by my father? Don't regret what happened to me to make me barely be able to keep control over my emotions? Don't pretend that I didn't murder someone?"

Alexander recoiled at the pain in Crow's voice and was afraid of seeing the rage in her. But there was no anger, no fury that was not directed inwards. Crow looked upon Alexander only with guilt and regret and sorrow. She stood there, chest heaving beneath tight bandages, the pain of what she was etched on her heart forever more. The Prince saw all this and also saw Crow as she was. The cheerful, just and good friend, willing to do anything for those she loved. Crow, who was stubborn and determined and cared about smithing more than money. Crow, who would never harm someone who did not deserve it, who was modest and a good listener and a mystery to those who lived at Kyper. Crow, who trusted Jek and Leon and the Prince himself but was careful with her affections though she was kind to those around her. Crow, not a monster created by the mythical Jackal, but a good person in spite of her difficulties. Alexander stared at Crow and saw this and then blinked, taking in the pack held in her hands.

"Don't leave," he whispered. Crow staggered from the weight that his words took from her and she wished she could run and hug him, pressing her mouth to his, seeking forgiveness. Instead, she smiled, sniffing slightly as she forced back unshed tears.

"Alexander," she said and the Prince simply stared at her. "Thanks for being my friend. For seeing me and not what people would suppose."

"You're welcome," Alexander replied, lifting his hands to run through his hair as he took in all that happened. "I wish that I could say that everything will continue on as normal, but it won't."

"What? But I thought—" Crow said, taking a step backwards. Could Alexander be so cruel, offering her hope of continuing the friendship with the man she valued so highly and then snatching it away because he couldn't reconcile her past? Alexander lowered his blue eyes and shook his head, groaning quietly.

"I know you're a good person, Crow, and I know that we'll still be friends, but it's going to take me time to figure everything out. I have to be able to understand how your past fits in with you now. I just... need time," Alexander said, frustration at himself showing in his quiet words. Crow blinked but nodded.

"I understand. But if you're going to take everything into consideration," she whispered, memories of a nightmare worse than her father filling her head, "then you should know more."

"What? What else could there possibly be?" Alexander asked, stepping forwards to peer into his closest friend's face.

"The Mazemaker," Crow breathed, her body trembling at the name. Alexander swallowed; he had forgotten the other part of the exchange with Alkai upon finding out about the Jackal but curiosity swelled within his chest. "If the Jackal is a nightmare come to life, than the Mazemaker is the Jackal's nightmare."

CHAPTER 14

Crow gestured for Alexander to sit on her bed and stood before him, anxiety making her nervous. She had pushed the memories of the Mazemaker far away and wished ardently never to live through them again. But it was necessary. She closed her eyes and opened her mind, allowing the terror of so many years before to live again.

"After my parents were killed and my home destroyed, I had nowhere to go. The people in the village near my father's domain would not welcome me and I was living in the forests on what skills the Jackal had taught me to survive. About a month after my parents' death, I returned to the site of my home, hoping to reclaim what was mine by birth. That was when the Mazemaker found me..."

Crow returned to her memories, no longer the strong girl who was friends with a Prince but a weak, shivering, angry thing of seven. The rage that her father shaped in her still burned brightly and her black hair was ragged, cut short in a moment of frustration with its tangles. She had numerous scrapes on her skin and she was hungry. As she climbed among the ruins of her home, she searched for weapons and money, anything that would help her. Instead, she found a man, larger than any man she had ever seen before. His body was layered in corded muscle and his shoulders were enormous. He wore dark breeches and an ill-fitting tunic that stretched over his broad back and chest. His face looked as if it had been sculpted by a poor artist and his jaw jutted forwards. His hands, though, were delicate and precise.

Her breath hitching in sudden, sharp fear, the young Crow tried to back away without the man's notice, but it was too late. He turned to look at her and a grin split his features into the visage of a gargoyle. His bottom lip was split and his teeth were stained. His eyes were cruel and full of mirth upon seeing Crow and he lunged, crossing the distance between them with a quickness of foot that surprised the young Crow. "So," he growled, his whole body vibrating with the force of his voice, "you're the spawn of the dreaded Kamal the Jackal."

Crow writhed and tried to claw the man's face, "My father taught me enough to kill you, monster."

The man roared with laughter, shaking Crow where he held her in the air. "Your father is dead, little one. And now you are in my clutches. One so pretty as you should not be wasted..."

"He took me to his hideaway, a large system of caves in the mountains near my home. There, I saw his horror and knew him to be more than a monster. He was a demon. The Mazemaker prided himself as an artist and his favourite medium was the skin on human bodies. He would strip them down and tie them, spread eagle, to the floor of his cave, preventing them from moving. He would take his knives, sharpened to the point of being almost paper thin and begin to draw on their skin, watching as the blood flowed off of their bodies and into the shallow depression beneath them. He would ensure the formation of scars by rubbing ash into the open wounds. Often times, people would die before he could do more than draw the beginnings of a maze on their bellies.

"His mazes were intricate and almost impossible to unravel and they were the work of a sadistic genius. For those victims that were still children, captured as they strayed from their parents or bought at illegal slave markets, he would not carve up their skin until he had satisfied his cruel tastes, feeding them and spoiling them before beating them, leaving them unable to move.

"I," Crow said, her eyes still shut as the memories filled her head, "was special, though. He would not touch me until I had been fed. He never beat me but made me watch as he did things to others. And, when I was strong enough, he tied me to the floor and began drawing on me. My designs were more intricate, more complicated than any he had ever done before and he took great pains to keep me alive. Each day, my hatred grew, my pain threshold increased until he managed to carve the entirety of my back in one day without me giving a single cry. Then, he let me heal until the maze was little more than scars whiter still than my skin.

"The Mazemaker's intention," she continued, feeling the rage she so carefully pushed away rise to the surface, pushing at her boundaries, demanding freedom. Crow took a shuddering breath and kept talking, unaware of how Alexander was looking at her in horror. "His intention, I think, was to have me succeed him. Who better to continue his work than the already broken and cruel child of Kamal the Jackal, the most dangerous man to have lived? He let me loose, keeping me in the caves with a chain around my ankle and as he carved up his victims, he talked to me. Talked about what knives were best for certain types of mazes, what the different designs signified, how best to keep a victim alive. What he didn't know was that my hatred and skill forced into me by my father was building. He underestimated me and until the day when I broke my ankle to get out of the chain, he didn't realise how strong I was.

"I was free and standing on both my feet, the pain from my ankle negligible, holding his favourite knife in my hand and he had the gall to simply laugh at me. He said that it was about time I took my place as heir to his name and I broke. I flew at him and before he could fight back, I had slit his throat and stabbed him in the chest. He died with an expression of shock on his face.

"After that," Crow said, pushing the memories away as she had so many times before, the pain of his carvings lingering after the others had gone, "I went to Hotun and got apprenticed to Sythfeld. He pitied me because I constantly hung around the forge and paid an excessive amount of attention to him, trying to mimic his movements in the dead of night. He took me on and that's that."

Crow's tale done – excepting the details she left out about waking in the middle of the night with a cruel laugh on her lips or anger making her beat her work into a shapeless mass, about how many years it took for Sythfeld to teach her about what it meant to be kind and good rather than furious and cruel – she opened her eyes, looking at Alexander with a numbness that encompassed her entire body. The Prince was sitting stone still, his blue eyes wide, mouth open slightly in disbelief. He said nothing but simply stared at Crow, completely shocked. Crow desperately wanted for him to say something, anything, but she did not press the matter. Alexander collected himself, returning to the reality of the moment and stood.

He walked to the door of Crow's room and turned to look at his friend, "You are quite the man, Crow. I'll see you later." He left and Crow collapsed onto her bed, pressing her lips together to hold back the tears. She tried to swallow the pain that Alexander's words had caused and failed. He knew the entirety of her past, her darkest secret, the truth of what she was except for one thing. To him, Crow was still a boy, nothing more than a friend. That was the most painful thing of all.

Crow, to keep her mind off of what Alexander must be thinking of her, unpacked and then fell onto her bed, praying that exhaustion would grant her the ability to sleep instead of thinking. She was not so fortunate. The hours passed and Crow knew that the Prince was still awake, piecing together all of the things he had learned and deciding what to do about Crow. He had made it clear that he would never see her in the same way, but what did that mean? Would they still be friends? Would Crow be forced to watch as the Prince turned away from her? She didn't realise she was shaking until Leon entered her room and placed a hand on her back.

"Crow," he breathed, kneeling on the ground by her head. She looked into his brown eyes and saw the confusion that swirled there. She reached out and wrapped her arms around Leon's neck, breathing in his scent. He pressed his lips to her forehead and held her and that was fine with Crow.

She knew that she should tell Leon what had been discussed about her and her past but after watching Alexander walk away, she didn't want to lose another person who was close to her. She wanted to feel Leon's presence as he kissed her or talked to her about what a person was supposed to treat a lady like. She knew that it was wrong to keep her past a secret from him, but she wanted him close.

"Don't go," she whispered, squeezing her arms around his shoulders. Leon shifted, releasing her for a moment and Crow thought he was going to leave, despite her plea. But he simply stood and crawled onto her bed, an awkward feat since it was really far too small for two people. But Crow lay half on Leon and he held her close, so they managed somehow.

"Crow, I'm worried about you," the knight said, staring up at the roof. Crow said nothing. "You're always so strong, but now I'm seeing you break. I want to ask you what's going on, but I know that I would lose what I have with you if I did. I'm afraid that you're moving away from me, right under my nose and that one day, I'm going to come and see someone I never knew."

Crow blinked and squeezed Leon in the dark, as much a comforting gesture as she could manage. "I'm no different, Leon. I'm still me, still Crow. Don't worry about me changing, I'm just figuring things out."

"If you're sure," Leon said, moving again so that Crow was pinned underneath his weight. Even in the dark, she imagined she could see the burning in his eyes. "Then I have no reason to doubt." He leaned closer and closed on her mouth. She hesitated for a moment, the pain of what had happened to her fresh in her mind. Her heart still ached over Alexander's words, but the thoughts were soon driven away by Leon's insistence. Crow soon gave in to his demands, allowing him access with his tongue as his hands ran over her body, scrabbling at the fabric in the way.

Crow felt a sudden, burning desire and arched her hips to rock against his. Leon, moving away for only an instant, pulled Crow's shirt away and then was back, his lips running along her jaw, her neck, her collarbones, until he reached her bandages. Growling in impatience, Leon sat up, hands working at the fabric.

Crow recollected herself and pushed Leon's hands away, lowering her hips to the bed as she leaned up on her elbows. "Leon," she said softly and the knight leaped away immediately, running into the wall in the dark.

"I'm sorry," he said quickly. "I'm so sorry. I didn't mean to—it just-"

"Leon," Crow said again, more sharply. Leon fell into silence and she could hear him pacing across the floor. "It's not that I don't want to... um.. but Jek is in the other room and I thought that...perhaps..."

"Oh," he replied, voice mollified. Crow chuckled and rose, feeling her way about the familiar room and stopping when her hands met Leon's chest. She stepped closer and reached for one of his hands, bringing it up and kissing the knuckles lightly.

"Another time," she whispered, tasting the tip of his index finger. Leon trembled beneath her touch and Crow pleasured in the fact that she held so much power.

"Another time," he agreed, moving to leave. Before he could do so, Crow closed the last remaining inches between them and pulled his head to her, kissing him with all the force of the emotion in her. He gasped and Crow smiled though he could not see. She kissed his hand again then pulled reluctantly away, her pain and memories returning with each step that Leon took further away from her. "Goodnight, Crow," he murmured and then was gone, leaving her standing in her room.

Crow went back to her bed, mind no more able to sleep than it had been before Leon's visit. Only, now, she had the feelings of guilt regarding her use of the honourable Leon to plague her. Crow knew that she did not love Leon as he described in their discussions. She knew that she was using him for the relief he brought from her thoughts. She did feel attraction to him, but her thoughts and feelings did not revolve around him as they did Alexander.

The man she could not have was the one she was destined to love, Crow mused scornfully. And the one who could love her and was within easy reach was one she could not love. She felt not a small amount of resentment at the twist of fate that had made things as such. But thinking of Alexander reminded her of the fact that he was likely never to be as close as they had been before. He would forever be thinking of her differently, forever be guarding his words and actions should she snap and turn her terrible skills against him.

These thoughts filled Crow's mind as she finally managed to drift off into sleep. She woke feeling much the same and went about her normal duties as quietly as possible. It was impossible not to notice the look that Jek gave her as he followed her movements around the forge, but, much to Crow's joy, the looks faded into an expression Jek used with her normally. That simple act made her practically float around the forge, grinning as she worked on projects.

The ability that Jek had to look upon Crow no differently than before did not occur quite so naturally in Alexander. He spent much of the next week considering and coming to a conclusion only to change it again and reconsider. But time passed and he finally went out to the forge, watching in silence for a few minutes as Crow worked away, putting delicate pieces of metal on a belt buckle.

"Hey," he said at last, startling her into dropping the metal. She winced at the ruined piece and then glanced up at Alexander. Obvious shock filled her eyes and Crow immediately became guarded, afraid of what she would see.

"Hey," she responded, unsure of what else to say to the Prince, her closest friend. Or not, she amended.

"I've been thinking," Alexander said, tilting his hair so that the weak winter light caught it and made it gleam. Crow felt her insides softening as she gazed on him, guilt gnawing away at her for putting the serious, pensive look on his face.

"Is that good or bad?" she asked, waving her hammer about as she raised her shoulders in question. To her delight, Alexander chuckled and shook his head at her in amusement.

"I've decided that you're alright, Crow," he said. "You're alright." Crow beamed.

The friendship between Crow and Alexander was changed by what had happened but not necessarily in a bad way. It allowed both to be more open, realising that the other knew about the darkest secrets they could hold. Crow never spoke about her past regarding the Jackal or the Mazemaker again, but would spend time telling the Prince about how Sythfeld had raised her. Leon was often included in the conversations between smith and Prince and the bond between the three was strengthened as a result. However, the knight could not match the friendship between Crow and Alexander and he never tried.

Between Crow and Leon, things changed very little. They talked, they kissed, occasionally they would scramble to de-clothe the other before pulling back. Leon, it seemed to Crow, became more attached, more caring and attentive and though Crow wished she could reciprocate, it was beyond her power. Her heart had been claimed by Alexander, though she was reluctant to admit it and loathe to accept the fact that her deepest dream could never be.

Time passed, as it usually does, and any rifts between the three were healed. Winter was at its highest peak when Alexander came running through the courtyard, slogging through the snow as quickly as he could. Crow was trying to coax the fire into growing warmer, but the gusts of cold air that seemed to continuously blow through the forge did not help her cause.

"Crow," Alexander called, halfway across the courtyard. She looked up and gave up on her task, instead ploughing her own way through the snow to meet the Prince outside the forge. He stared at her with wide eyes, fear and excitement warring for control over his features.

"What?" she asked, folding her arms against the cold. It was worse away from the forge and the thigh-high snow drifts certainly didn't help. Shivering, Crow didn't wait for a response, instead turning and following her tracks back to the slight protection the forge offered. Alexander followed, breath coming out in hot puffs.

"My father," he said, "has decided that I need to have

a party for my coming of age. A banquet like none that we have held before. He is calling for bringing gypsies here to have a festival, a tournament that would bring people from all corners of the realm."

"Sounds great," Crow grinned, thinking longingly of the warm, sweet cakes that were often found at tournaments and festivals. Then she frowned, "Of course, that means I'll be on double duty, fixing armour, making knives, arrow-heads and such. What's the bad news?"

Alexander blinked as he saw Crow raise her eyebrows in knowing and frowned, the fear winning over. "If I don't win the tournament, I'm going to be a disgrace to my father and my kingdom and the people will never truly accept me. Besides, Lady Yvonne will be there and we all know how annoying she is."

"Oh, goody," Crow said, voice flat as she recalled the simpering, annoying beauty that was Lady Yvonne. She had no desire to meet the blonde woman again and shuddered at the frustration she knew would come with her. Crow looked at Alexander and knew immediately that it was not Lady Yvonne that was worrying him, but the tournament. She reached out and patted his shoulder in comfort. "Relax, alright? You're the best swordsman I know," she soothed.

"Discounting yourself," the Prince teased and Crow considered.

"Discounting myself," she admitted and shook her head. "You have nothing to worry about. And you should know that."

"I know that I've been well taught and that I'm pretty good—" Alexander started and Crow snorted.

"Pretty good?" she asked, folding her arms as she looked at him incredulously.

"Alright, fine, I'm quite good. But there will be warriors from lands all around and I don't know if I can beat them. I need you to teach me."

"Teach you?" Crow said, completely shocked. "Teach you what, exactly? You already know how to fight in hand to hand combat and your skill with the sword shouldn't be in question."

"I want to learn how to defend myself against Scheren fighting. I want to learn how to fight with a Scheren, fight like you do," Alexander pleaded, seeking approval in Crow's face. Instead, her features hardened.

"Do you know what you're asking?" she demanded. "You want me to teach you what the Jackal taught me?"

"I'm sorry," Alexander said, placing his hands on Crow's shoulders and looking into her eyes. "I know it's hard for you." Crow's insides melted, her unrequited feelings making her soften to his request.

"It's okay," she said softly. "Fine. I'll do it. I'll teach you what my father taught me."

"Thank you," Alexander said gravely, fighting to keep a grateful smile from his face. Crow looked at him and sighed.

"I'm going to teach you Mak'tal," she said, shaking her head. "Well, huh."

CHAPTER 15

"Twist your wrist," Crow snapped, circling around Alexander as he stood in the practise yards, holding her Scheren. Teaching Alexander the art of Mak'tal, despite his being a good fighter, was extremely difficult. Crow had to make Alexander unlearn things that he had ingrained in him and now, he was struggling to master a basic wrist flick. "Again. More speed, more snap."

"Crow," Alexander growled, sweat gleaming on his bare back as he tried to comply while holding the crouching stance Crow had taught. "Can we take a break?" Crow whirled on Alexander, green eyes hard, unfeeling. She, too, wore no shirt, only her bandages, and despite the cold, she did not shiver. The snow had been plowed aside by the two at the beginning of their training session and the muddy ground beneath their feet provided an unstable footing for the Prince.

Crow lunged, attacking Alexander unexpectedly. He

tried to defend himself with what he had learned, but Crow easily ducked around his efforts, moving almost slowly to simply evade him. She wrapped an arm around Alexander's sword arm and pulled, bringing him flying over her hip to fall to the ground, winded. The Scheren flew from his grasp and Crow caught it by the blade, ignoring the stab of pain that came when the razor-sharp edges cut her palm. "We keep practising until you get this right," she ordered, not really seeing the Prince but her father as he had taught her so many years ago. "We keep practising until your hands are raw and bloody, your legs are literally collapsing underneath you and all your muscles can do is go through the motions. And then, we practise some more."

"Crow," Alexander said, voice quiet but demanding. She blinked, snapping green eyes to his face, startled and slightly confused. "You want that?"

"No," she said, pressing her free hand to her temple. "No, I'm sorry. It's so hard separating then and now with what we're doing."

"I know," the handsome man replied, standing and gently reaching out for the blade. Carefully, Crow gave it to him, gasping when she realised her hand was bleeding. "Come on, we'll go get that wrapped and get something to eat, okay?" Crow nodded and Alexander put a hand to her back, pushing her gently away from the practise yards and to the forge where Jek was polishing some armour. He glanced up as the two approached and frowned when he saw Crow's hand.

"What happened?" he asked flatly, standing and

lumbering over to his apprentice. Crow looked at him sheepishly and shook her head.

"Crow grabbed the Scheren by the blade," Alexander explained and Jek made a surprised choking sound in his throat. His apprentice was never so careless. He went into the house and returned with a bandage and some water. Cleaning the cut, which was shallow, luckily, he wrapped it and folded his arms.

"I don' like what yer doing if it means injurin' yerself, a'right?" Jek growled, glaring down at the lean muscled Crow. She blinked and stared at her hand, seemingly confused.

"Sorry, Jek," she muttered, looking up and meeting the blacksmith's eye. Her own were growing less hard, less confused, more clear. "I forget myself sometimes," she replied and moved off to the kitchens. "I'll get some food."

As soon as she was out of earshot, Jek turned to Alexander and brought his face within inches of the Prince's. "I hope ye know what yer doin' to 'im," he snarled, narrowing his eyes. "Yer openin' that lad up fer a whole slew of nightmares, all to do with 'is past. No 'un should have to live through that more 'n once."

"Crow agreed to this with his eyes open," Alexander said softly, backing away from the smith master carefully. "He knew the risks."

"I don' think 'e did," Jek said, glaring at Alexander but making no move forwards. "I don' think 'e realised that 'e'd be confused with 'is father. Did ye?"

"No," Alexander said, leaning his weight against the

wooden post at the entrance to the forge. "I don't think Crow did realise that this would happen. And I'm sorry for it."

"Then stop," Jek said, voice almost a plea. "Don' do this to i'm."

"Don't do what to whom?" Crow asked, returning with one hand full of a pitcher of warm cider, the other balancing some bread and warm meat against her, three rare winter apples nestled in the crook of her arm. She stepped inside and deposited the food then set about getting cups and stoneware plates. Alexander and Jek joined her, a tense silence between the two. Crow picked up on it immediately and crossed her arms over her bandaged chest. "Don't do what to whom?" she repeated, narrowing her eyes at the two men.

"I don' think ye should be teachin' Alexander like this. Ye forget yerself," Jek said softly, reaching for his lunch to cover his worry. Crow sighed and sat across from him on the wooden bench that served as a chair.

"Jek," she said, pouring some cider for herself. "Relax. I can handle this, okay? It's just taking some time."

"You don't have to keep going with this," Alexander said, looking at Crow. She shook her head and frowned.

"I do. Not because you've asked me and I want to help, but because I need to figure this out. I have to be able to differentiate between the Jackal and myself. I'm getting there," Crow said, shrugging. "And besides, you really are not very good. So if we want you in shape for the tournament, you're going to have to work a lot harder." This was said with a smile, enough to make certain

Jek and Alexander saw that she was fully in the present, not stuck in the past with her father.

Alexander grumbled good naturedly and the three ate their lunch with the conversation going no darker than whether or not to play pranks on Lady Yvonne when she came. Jek and Crow were of a mind she needed it, Alexander was inclined to agree, but he remembered his station and duty.

For the remainder of the day, Crow drilled Alexander in the practise yards, well away from any of the soldiers and knights. Occasionally, she would push Alexander too hard, her eyes becoming hard and almost cruel, but the Prince always brought her back with care, his eyes pleasant and kind to his friend. Crow wished that he would look at her like that more frequently, with more love in the blue depths, but she knew she was kidding herself. The fantasy almost made delving into her nightmares more bearable.

At night, just before the evening meal, Alexander excused himself and Crow returned to cook for Jek then go to the forge, working until near dawn on projects she could not get to during the day. She was tired, physically and mentally, but she slowly got through it. Each day came with Crow stronger and more grounded in reality rather than haunted by the past she was exploring. And each day, Alexander became better at fighting Mak'tal. This routine continued for many weeks, with Crow and Alexander working during the day and the blacksmith pounding away at her work during the night. Leon, when he wasn't drilling with the knights or on patrol, would join Crow and Alexander. He never took part in the training but watched as the two worked, sparred or were jolted back to reality. During the night, though, Crow belonged to him.

He would come each evening after Jek had gone to bed, often with a light snack to keep her energy up and the two would talk while Crow worked. When she paused, to wipe the sweat from her brow or while waiting for the metal to heat, Leon would lean over and grab Crow's shirt front, pulling her into him for a prolonged kiss or to rub his hands slowly up her arms. It pleased him to feel her responding to his touch and Crow was glad for the attention and company of Leon.

"Why are you making so many silver pieces?" Leon asked one evening, munching slowly on a sweet cake. Crow had been working on her finer projects with gusto and she had quite the collection, more than any orders that had come in.

"When the fair and tournament happens, I want to have things to sell or trade," Crow said. "I'm able to charge a lot more than I spent on materials or the like. This one's my last one for a bit. I have to make swords and blades as well and I have to make something for Alexander's birthday."

"I would think that knives and swords would sell far better than jewellery or belt buckles or buttons," Leon said, taking in the impressive wall of swords that Crow had already made, her Scheren among them.

"Actually, no," Crow said, tightening the coil she had made as the finishing touch on her final piece, a decorative sheath for a long dagger. "Despite the fact that men are far more interested in my weapons and armour and such than fancy tidbits, they have daughters and wives and sisters and the money goes to that far more than is probably healthy."

Leon chuckled, "I'll keep that in mind when I shop around. I can probably get a good price on weapons and equipment, then." He watched as Crow rolled her eyes and took the still warm sheath to cool over on a sideboard. She then grabbed a large, ungainly lump of metal and thrust it into the fire, preparing different baths and pulling out a larger hammer. Crow grabbed her tongs and pulled the heated lump from the fire, drawing it out into a long blank with expert skill. She dipped it into one of the baths and then reheated the metal.

The process went on for a long time, the metal, over the course of many nights, beginning to take the shape of a grand, elegant and powerful sword. Its length gleamed and the edges were sharp enough to cut a hair Crow plucked from Leon's head. She began then to work on the hilt, an elaborate piece that would fit one hand and one hand only. It was meant for Alexander and Crow put all of her skill into making it, the detail on the hilt exquisite, designs of fantastic creatures etched into the metal. She didn’t need to measure his hand or fighting style, as she might have if making a custom blade for others. Crow knew his measurements perfectly and there was no doubt in her mind that it would fit him. The designs were in a style that suited him and would stand up to heavy wear. The blade, when finished, was fantastic and would stand up to a lifetime of use, perhaps more.

The day following Crow's completion of the blade, the gypsies arrived, their wagons and laughing children, loud dogs, goats and the like filling the courtyard of Kyper Palace with enough space remaining for people to move about comfortably. They were greeted by Alexander and some servants in charge of organising the set-up of the fair. The tents and tables the gypsies set up spilled out into Kyper town and the whole village was converted to fairgrounds, people clearing space for dancers, theatre productions, even contests for the peasants who could not take part in the tournament. The main area was in the courtyard. Crow revelled in watching the set-up, staying contentedly out of the way until she was called to help carry things around and pull up tents.

The practise yards were cleared of all the straw dummies, sparring areas and the like to prepare an area for the tournament. There was enough space for a jousting ring, archery range, and a place for general combat. There were stands set for nobles to watch and an area cordoned off for peasants. The fair would begin in two days time and nobles were already beginning to arrive.

Crow was leaning on a post outside the forge, watching the gypsies mingle with the townspeople, setting up wares and talking loudly. They were dark haired and dark-skinned people and they laughed and talked almost constantly, it seemed. Since the coming of the fair, the training sessions with Alexander had stopped and the Prince moved through the people, greeting them with a smile and polite questions. Leon was equally busy, training with other knights and soldiers for the tournament, patrolling the grounds and keeping an eye on everything. He was too busy to talk with Crow and wouldn't be free until the third day of festivities. So Crow was alone, watching with a content smile on her face as the people moved about, horses carrying finely clad nobles arrived or people from neighbouring lands came to try and win a name of honour for themselves and their lands.

The fair featured smith was caught unawares, however, when a beautiful woman wearing the latest fashion stepped through the people and came to look at the forge, a necklace with topaz and butterflies sitting at her throat. "Crow," Lady Yvonne crooned, stepping forwards and putting her hand on Crow's arm.

"Lady," Crow acknowledged, bowing stiffly as she was meant to do. She tried to pull away and go help someone with anything, but Yvonne dug her claws into Crow's arm and kept her there.

"Crow, aren't you going to show me around? I got in very late yesterday and I haven't had a chance to see anything!" Yvonne simpered, pulling Crow along. Since Alexander hadn't asked Crow to be nice to Yvonne for his sake, the smith did not move.

"I have work to do," she said coldly and strode away, using her long legs to escape from the noblewoman and get to a man trying to coax a donkey through the maze of tents and tables and areas where people milled about. Crow set her hands on the beast's rump and helped to move it to a small corral of animals for auction. She saw Yvonne approaching out of the corner of her eye and moved off, disappearing into the crowd to go busy herself.

The desperate dance between Crow and Yvonne continued for the remainder of the day until Yvonne pranced off to go enjoy a sumptuous dinner and Crow ducked into the kitchens, running straight into Deirdre. The kitchen maid blushed but held her ground as Crow tried to awkwardly sidestep into the kitchens.

"Who was that following you around all day?" she asked of Crow, narrowing her eyes in what she hoped was a seductive look. She let her lower lip pout a bit and shifted so that she was closer to Crow. Frustrated at Yvonne and Deirdre for ruining what could have been a perfectly pleasant day, not to mention feeling hungry, Crow put her hands on the maid's shoulders and moved her aside.

"Lady Yvonne," Crow said as she snatched some bread from a table and a small pot of stew she had prepared earlier in the day. She tried to brush casually past Deirdre but the maid was nothing if not stubborn.

"Lady Yvonne? What does she want with you?" she asked, reaching out to pluck some imagined lint from Crow's shirt, letting her hand rest on her shoulder. Crow shrugged it off, aggravation growing with each minute and forced her way back into the open.

"I don't know," Crow snapped. "Why don't you ask

her?" She started weaving her way through the people to go back to the forge and small house but Deirdre stopped her, words sharp.

"Do you like her because she's pretty?" she asked, voice betraying her hurt. "And because I'm not?"

Crow sighed and turned, shifting her hold on the pot. "Listen, Deirdre. You're very pretty. But I'm not interested. I have my smithing to keep me busy and you would do better to find someone else. Trust me." To her surprise, the maid began to sniffle, barely holding back tears.

"It's because I'm just a maid and Yvonne's a noble, isn't it?" she accused and Crow frowned, her annoyance acute.

"Alright," Crow said slowly, deliberately, "I'm going to explain this once and once only. Yvonne is nothing but an annoyance. You are quickly becoming an annoyance as well. I'm not interested, Deirdre. Go back to your work." Blinking, Deirdre recoiled and hesitated before running back to the kitchens, tears falling freely. Crow huffed and turned around, walking resolutely to the house. Leon appeared at her side.

"You know, now you've just opened yourself up to a whole set of new problems. Since you don't want Deirdre, everyone's going to assume it's because you want someone else and they're all going to assume it's them until you give them reason to believe otherwise," Leon said, holding the door as Crow slipped inside, setting the pot on the table and taking out a couple of bowls.

"Well, that's just great," Crow grumbled. "Just what I need. Are you staying for dinner?"

"No, I can't," Leon replied, rubbing Crow's shoulder in comfort. "I have to go eat with the others and the Captain so that our plan of action, should anything go awry, can be discussed, again. I'll be free later tonight, if you want, though."

"And that would be when I can't," Crow said, feeling indignant at the hand she was dealt. "I have a few more specialty items to make and one noble who got here yesterday is determined to have a whole new cutlery set by the time she leaves. I have to get started on it or I'll never be able to keep up with the orders that will come in over the next few days. You should see what Jek has to deal with."

Leon winced and looked at her in sympathy. Crow straightened and stepped closer to the knight, trailing a hand over his dusty coloured neck, cupping his jaw. She pressed her mouth to his and was startled by the hunger with which Leon responded. He wrapped his arms around her and held her close, preventing her from leaving as he feasted on her, breaking away from her mouth only to press his lips against her jaw, her neck, then going back to her mouth.

Crow melted in Leon's arms and was glad for the support he gave to her. She wrapped her fingers into his hair and pressed her chest against his, feeling his pulsating desire. After a few more moments, Leon slowly pulled away and Crow regained her ability to stand without help. She grinned at the knight who was smiling back with a sly look in his eye.

"I love it when you do that," she said, turning back to the stew and ladling some out into the two bowls she had set on the table. Leon put his hand on Crow's shoulder and leaned close to her ear.

"I love you," he whispered and before Crow could react, he was gone. She stood holding a spoon with a blank look on her face as she tried to process the information. Leon loved her? She was still standing with shock written in her eyes when Jek came in, sweaty from having helped to set up the stands around the jousting ring.

"What's got inter ye?" he asked, waving his hand in front of Crow's face. She blinked and took stock of where she was. In a moment of need, she reached out to Jek and hoped that he would help her shoulder the burden.

"Leon said he loved me," she said quietly as she sat down at the table and set the spoon into her bowl, playing with the stew. She had been ready to eat after a hard day, but her appetite had vanished as soon as shock set in and her heart was a tumult of emotions. Jek stared at Crow, almost as shocked as she then slowly shook his head.

"How hard it is," he said, a hint of sadness in his voice as he watched Crow, "to have a daughter who is so close to ye and then poof, she's gone."

"Jek," Crow said, a well of gratitude sweeping over her as she considered the man who had become her true father after Sythfeld died, after her problems with her past. She loved the bulky, barrel-chested man, there was no doubt. Jek waved away her sentiment with his spoon.

"The real question is if'n ye love Leon," he said gently and Crow met his gaze, eyes full of unreadable emotion and confusion. She shifted her eyes to the table and played with her stew for a moment.

"I..I don't know," she said honestly. "I'm so confused. I thought that I didn't, but now there's so much inside and I just don't know."

"Then ye'd better let 'im know," Jek replied, shovelling his own dinner into his mouth. Crow shook her head desperately.

"No," she whispered, fear plain in her voice. "Because the only thing that might be worse than me not knowing whether I love him is that I might know. And I'm not sure how he'd react."

CHAPTER 16

The morning that the fair began, Crow was busy setting up a small display table directly outside the forge. She wasn't able to move far away from the forge in case orders came in for weapons or armour or anything that might be necessary for the tournament. She had Alexander's sword wrapped and hidden and had finished setting out her belongings when the first few people began to wander through the fair.

The gypsies had musicians scattered around to add to the liveliness. Crow caught the strains of a high-spirited violin as she inspected her work. Her necklace, the one she would wear when she no longer needed to hide, was hidden away, as yet uncompleted and Crow thought of it with longing and fear as she took in the other necklaces she had made. None had anything more expensive than cut glass or pretty rocks, but they twinkled in the early morning sunlight.

"You have an eye for fancy things," a crooked old

woman said, reaching out to finger the fine work as Crow watched. She wore the garb of the gypsies and her eyes glinted cunningly. Crow murmured her thanks and moved into the forge, stoking the fire and bringing it to a dull roar. She kept an eye on the woman as she did so, but the woman only gave Crow a wink and a cunning smile before moving on. The gypsies were like that, Crow mused, saying something casual and meaning far more than you ever knew. She thought of Alexander and the woman's words and sighed. Sometimes these people were too discerning.

For most of the morning, Crow divided her time between a few smaller tasks around the forge and talking with people who came to the table. A few had come from far away to speak with Jek; these were the other smiths and they seemed surprised at Crow's presence and her skill. She sold three pieces of jewellery within the first few hours and two knives as well. Some people came by to place orders or to ask about prices. For some of the peasants, they had saved up all their money to be able to buy something made at the royal forge and Crow invariably lowered her prices for them, allowing many a family to walk away pleased.

The day passed quickly with all the extra work that Crow was doing and she was feeling exhausted by the time the evening meal came around. Jek stopped her as she was about to heat some more metal and pushed her away from the forge.

"Go find Leon and drag 'im away from whatever 'e's doin' so ye can get somethin' to eat, a'right?" Jek said and

Crow looked at him in surprise. The big smith had worked just as hard as she had during the day, filling orders and pounding out dents in armour as it was brought to him. He must have been hungry and was letting Crow free for the evening? She caught a loving glint in his eye and grinned, grabbing a small bag of money to spend while looking around.

She ran from the forge, not stopping to look at any stalls or entertainment until she came upon one of the knights who was on guard. He was a newer recruit and looked bored. Crow walked up and folded her arms. "Wow, Terric, you get to stand around and look at the fair and just keep a watchful eye out and you look bored? Something's wrong, here," she teased, shaking her head in mock disappointment.

Terric grumbled and shifted his weight, "I've been standing here, in this same spot, for the last hour. What do you want, Crow?"

She frowned, "Fine, snippy. I'm looking for Leon."

"Over by the tournament, watching Prince Alexander fight like a man possessed. A really scary man possessed. I never knew he could do all those things," Terric said, picking up a thread of conversation that he enjoyed. Crow simply tilted her head and smiled slightly. Terric paled. "You taught him?"

"See you around, Terric," she said, waving as she walked away. She chuckled at the fearful look on the young knight's face and started running off again, snaking her way through the maze of tents and people to the transformed practise yards. She ducked through the crowds of peasants who were watching the current fight and found Leon at the far end of the fence, an impressed look on his face. Crow slid in next to him and grinned.

"Hey, Crow," Leon said, flicking his gaze to her and then back to the fight.

"What's got that awed look on your face?" she asked, poking fun at him. Leon, in all seriousness, simply nodded towards the combat field. Crow turned to look and saw Alexander deep in combat with an ebony skinned man from a land far to the west. He was using an odd, curved blade that was shorter than a normal one and his fighting style was similar to that of most people who fought with a longsword or broadsword. His face was sweating profusely despite the chill in the air and it was plain to see why. Alexander, wielding his longsword, was attacking with the precision of a wolf. He was using mostly his normal fighting style but it was modified with things that Crow had taught him.

In a flash of movement, the ebony skinned man lost his blade and was brought to his knees. Alexander touched the man's throat and the battle was won. A great shout rang out and the Prince turned, acknowledging his people with a modest nod. He caught sight of Crow and she grinned widely. Alexander beamed and Crow's innards melted at the prowess of her Prince, the look of deserved pride and gratitude in his eye directed at her.

"That's really quite scary," Leon said, diverting Crow's attention. She met his gaze and was overcome with a desire to kiss him. Only by a great effort of will did she stop herself from doing so and moved away from the crowd.

"I'm glad you think so," she said primly, stuffing her hands into her pockets. Leon laughed and slung an arm around her shoulder; it was all the contact they were allowed with so many people around. Crow looked up at him and smiled. "Jek gave me the evening free and said that I was to drag you off to get some food."

"Well, I think we can manage that. I don't have to go back to my duties until sunset, so we have at least an hour," Leon replied. Crow nodded and smiled as they wove their way back through the fair, stopping to admire things and entertainment, buying food at a stall which sold all manner of sweat breads and meats. The pair ate and left their fingers sticky and all was right with the world. Crow and Leon laughed at each other and it was nearing sunset when they were interrupted.

Leon was looking at a flower stand, teasing Crow about some lilies that she liked when Alexander walked up, hair mussed from fighting, a frustrated look on his face. "Oh, thank goodness," he said upon finding Crow and Leon. "You have to hide me."

"Hide you?" Crow asked, raising her eyebrows. "Is one of your opponents mad that you beat them? Or are we talking Yvonne problems." The look on Alexander's face told her that it was the latter and Crow sighed in sympathy. She grabbed his arm and started to drag him away, Leon following with a slight frown marring his features.

"I have to get back to the Captain," he said and

waved goodbye to Crow and Alexander before walking away. Crow let her gaze linger after him for a few seconds then returned her attention to the Prince who was looking around desperately. She led him back to the forge and stuffed him in an out of the way corner where he was not likely to be seen, much to the surprise of Jek.

"Yvonne," Crow explained before starting up her work again. She looked happily at the table of products she had made and noted that some of her finer pieces were gone. "Did you sell anything?" she asked, looking at Jek.

"There were a couple of people from other lands that were interested. They said they'd stop by later to see if they could catch you," the smith replied and Crow grinned. She rearranged the table and took out some other pieces, letting her fingers linger on the sheath she had made.

"You make weapons?" a voice said and Crow turned her head to meet the gaze of a fairly average looking man. At least, he was average in terms of features and height, his hair a shiny black, his skin the colour of clay. He wore loose clothing in multiple colours and had an exorbitant amount of jewellery on his person: rings on his fingers, in his ears, on his toes, a many tiered necklace weighing down his neck and gold paint gilded on his eyelids. A Shaman of the Eastern Lands. Crow had never seen such a person, but she had heard many stories from the Jackal and his gang and she grew immediately wary.

"I do. I've made many blades, knives, swords and the like. There are a few hanging up inside the forge, if you're interested," Crow said, gesturing to the entrance to the forge. The Shaman hummed for a moment, picking over the selection Crow had on the table then slowly, deliberately, moved into the forge, ignoring the sudden increase in temperature as he moved to the wall of swords. Alexander joined Crow, as curious but perhaps not as wary as she at the Shaman. He examined each sword, taking them off their hooks to run his hands over the blades and hilts, testing the quality. Crow stood up to his inspection until the Shaman took in the next blade in his inspection; the Scheren.

Immediately, the man paled then flushed, anger obvious in his mien. Crow blinked, surprised and nearly recoiled when the Shaman spun to face her. "How dare you," he hissed, the Scheren in his hand. He hadn't even bothered to inspect it before turning it on its master.

"Um," Crow said, not inclined to be polite at the moment, "What?"

"How dare you own a Scheren. Only people of the Eastern Lands, of the blood of my people should dare to own this, let alone presume anything about handling it. And here you stand, claiming to have made it," the Shaman spat, waving the three-pointed sword at Crow. She dodged easily and glared, her arms at her side in a relaxed, casual pose. Alexander saw this and moved to the outside of the forge to give Crow space. Jek followed his example.

"I do not claim, nor presume," Crow said flatly. "I did make it and I do know how to use it."

"Such insolence from a western inbred," the Shaman

snarled, straightening and trying to look imposing and regal. "If you were under my rule, you would be flogged and thrown to the wild dogs for such disrespect."

"Well," Crow said, throwing off his attempts at superiority with a look of her own. "I guess you'll just have to make do."

"You will be punished for this," the Shaman said, narrowing his eyes. Crow met the man's gaze evenly, managing to look slightly bored though her inner anger was thrumming and threatening to break free. She tightened her control and said nothing. The finely dressed Shaman took her silence as insolence and raised his hand, moving forwards until he was fairly close to Crow. He slapped her openly and showed his crooked teeth. "I challenge you," he said.

"I accept your challenge," Crow replied without hesitation, piercing his gaze with her green eyes.

"You must defeat a warrior of my choosing in the arena, at sunrise tomorrow, with only your precious Scheren to defend you. My warrior will be similarly outfitted," the Shaman said and then flung the Scheren away, stalking out of the forge. Crow caught the blade in her already bandaged hand and it cut through the fabric, luckily stopping before it could cut her hand again.

She emerged from the forge into the dying light and was greeted with glares from Alexander and Jek. "Are you insane?" the Prince asked, gesturing to the retreating Shaman.

"Generally," Crow replied smoothly. "He challenged me. I could not refuse unless I wished to forfeit my honour and all rights to my Scheren. Besides, he smelled funny."

"Crow," Alexander said. "I know you are incredibly skilled, but you've lived here for your entire life. His warrior has been in the Eastern Lands, the birthplace of Mak'tal, for his entire life. You may have been trained by the Jackal, but you'll be facing someone equally skilled. You could very well lose, tomorrow."

"Ye could die," Jek interrupted, voice sharp. Crow looked at her master and then at the Prince, touched by his concern. It meant he cared about her, at least somewhat, right? She pushed that thought away and shook her head.

"Then I die well," she replied. "I'm touched, really, that you think so highly of me as to fear for my safety, but I'll be fine. And if I'm not fine, then at least I go defending my honour." She marched past the two and started packing up her table of wares for the evening, making sure to store the items carefully. Alexander and Jek watched with fear then the Prince muttered a goodbye to Jek and walked off to the Palace. Jek watched his apprentice then shook his head and moved to get some food from the fair. As the sun set, most people left the fair, but there were a few that stayed later into the night. Crow wandered around for a while, hoping to find something to keep her mind away from the morning's match. She had begun to fear that what Alexander had said would be true and she mentally prepared herself.

"Crow?" Leon said, startling her from where she had been examining a table of drawings. She looked up and saw concern written on the handsome knight's face, concern for her. He knew and Crow figured he was coming to talk her out of it. He wasn't wearing his regalia, so she assumed that he was done for the evening.

In a moment of inspiration, of desperation and need, Crow reached out for Leon's hand and pulled him into the shadows. "Come, sit in the shadows with me, for tomorrow I may die," she whispered and Leon stiffened slightly, shocked at her request. But he wrapped Crow in his arms and she felt him soften, his body mould to hers.

"Of course, my love," Leon whispered and started walking, leading Crow through the dark streets of Kyper town. The fair there had not been quite as loud or as late in the courtyard, but there were still people milling about, their tongues softened by the darkness. Crow wanted Leon to stop walking, to tell her where he was taking her, to kiss her, possess her, but the knight resolutely kept walking.

They walked until they reached the gates of Kyper and were met with the two guards stationed there. They were complaining about having to keep the gates open at night because of all the people who had camped around the walls of Kyper so as to attend the fair. Leon and Crow slipped out, barely noticed. Crow could feel her sudden trepidation, for what the morning might bring and what she would let Leon do, her heart pounding in her throat, her chest a mixture of emotions. Leon, walking slightly in front of her, his hand grasping hers, seemed cool and collected as he looked back at her every few moments.

They walked until they were far enough away from Kyper to not hear the nighttime revels of the people and were well into the trees of the forest on either side of the road. Leon kept moving until he found a small clearing, the grass soft with the beginnings of spring, remnants of frost on the tips. He slowed and stopped then turned to face Crow. She was afraid, now, of what would happen, of what she was doing. Leon saw the fear and his expression softened. He stepped forwards once, twice, then put his hands on Crow's cheeks, tilting her head so she looked him in the eye.

"Trust me," he breathed and then kissed her. It was gentle, soft, teasing, demanding and Crow was left breathless, her heart pounding, her mind swirling with emotions that left her confused and scared and passionate. Leon kissed her possessively, drinking her in slowly, gently. He let his hands wander down her face, caressing her neck, her shoulders, her sides, until he grasped the hem of her shirt. Without moving away, he pulled the shirt over Crow's head, breaking the kiss only for a moment. Crow, the beautiful, lean, powerful, strong girl melted under his gentle touch and even as he stroked the bandages around her, she deepened the kiss, reaching for his shirt.

Leon reacted first, pulling his shirt off and tossing it carelessly to the ground, his hands grabbing Crow's shoulders and pulling her to him so he could press against her lips with his tongue, probing, pleading, demanding until she opened in a gasp. Crow felt the thrumming passion through Leon's skin and she began to wonder where she was. It was as if she had been drugged; all that mattered was the touch, the need. She reached out and touched Leon's face, feeling the sheen of sweat on his jaw. The knight growled and pulled Crow closer, pressing his lips against Crow's jaw, nipping her shoulder, the base of her neck.

Crow gasped and arched her hips as Leon tugged at her hair, bringing them altogether closer, though it seemed impossible. She did not protest as Leon pushed her to the ground, fingers running rivulets along her arms and the bandages, the cold wind making her tense, the lust and desire making her receptive. She kissed Leon, alternately gasping as he leaned over her, teasing and tempting but never quite fulfilling her pleas. He lowered his hands and scrabbled at her bandages then pulled roughly away.

Crow sat up slowly as he did so, untucking the end of her bandages, slowly unwrapping it. She felt her need pressing between her ribs and her muscles felt like water. He growled, moving closer and helping her to unwrap the fabric, skimming his palm over her exposed navel, feeling the thousands of scars that had been drawn there. As more skin was revealed, he took more, pressing his lips to her skin, feeling her hard muscles between his teeth as he nipped her. She unwrapped the last bit of her bandages and he lunged, pushing her back against the ground as he fondled her breasts, teasing them and making them tighten under his touch.

She was in the throes of passion as he kept his lips on hers, one hand cupped possessively over a breast, teasing the nipple into form, the other snaking down to rest on her hips. He explored and she begged, not knowing where she was and just wanting him to let her go, to let her move that last little step towards release. As his fingers danced on her skin, she felt a stab of panic and cried out, arching her back as she became torn with fear and desire.

He pushed further, trapping her legs beneath his, the weight making it seem as though his pulse were hers. "Say my name," he panted, moving to nip at her jaw. She groaned and arched against him, begging him to let her go. "Say my name," he demanded, poised and ready, resisting for a few more seconds as she pressed against him.

She groaned and breathed, "Alexander."

In a snap, Leon pulled away, his heart breaking as he took in the waiting Crow, every beautiful feature from her eyes to the terrible scars which laced her body. She gasped and pressed a hand to her head, reality crashing to her. Slowly, she sat up and met his brown eyes, so full of hurt and pain and understanding with her own green ones, tears falling freely.

"I'm sorry," Crow breathed, voice soft and yet cutting through the night air. Pain lanced her heart as it did Leon's, but she knew that it was nowhere near as deep. She cared for him, maybe even loved him, but not like that. And, as Leon looked at her, he knew it, too.

"I know," he replied, sitting back and staring with sadness at Crow.

"It's just... I love him," she said, voice deteriorating

quickly into sobs. Her body shook and she pressed one hand against her belly, the other against her mouth.

"I know. Oh, Crow, I wish with all my heart that you were able to feel about me like I feel about you," Leon said, reaching for his shirt and pulling it over his shoulders. He stood and stared for a few moments at the copse of dark trees around him, his breath coming out in bursts of steam. He knelt down and wrapped his arms around the scarred, beautiful Crow.

"I wish I could, too," she replied, no longer bothering to check her tears.

"That man is going to hurt you. He's going to hurt you badly, Crow," Leon said, sighing and trying to ignore the pain in his chest.

"I know," Crow choked out. "And I can't help but let him."

CHAPTER 17

Crow stood in her small room, absently looking out to the garden as she dressed with care. She wrapped her bandages tightly around her chest, pulled on a comfortable, well-fitted pair of breeches and a shirt that hugged her lean frame and wouldn't get in the way during her fight. Her eyes, as she wrapped more bandages around her hands and up to her forearms, were glazed. Her chest throbbed with passionate emotion; guilt, for hurting Leon, anger at herself, for being unable to change it, anger at Alexander, for being all she wanted and for being unattainable, anger at the Shaman, for presuming where he should not, anger at her father, for imparting his curse upon her, anger at the Mazemaker, for teaching her to work through pain when all she wanted was to curl up and let the world pass around her, fear, in case she was just not good enough, love, for those who cared for her, who dared to love her despite her faults, who were there.

The sky was just beginning to lighten when Crow stepped out from the house by the forge, her Scheren, the finest blade she had ever crafted, at her side. She walked through the silent tents, posture straight and proud as she ignored the people who watched her. They were the gypsies, the servants, the townspeople, the soldiers, the common folk and they watched her with a quiet hope. One of their own was standing up against a noble, and a foreign Shaman at that. She walked resolutely to the practise yards and stepped into the arena, suppressing a mild shock as she took in all the people that stood quietly to watch her. The stands for the nobles were filled with people, peasants and the upper-class mingling together. The ground was covered with warm bodies, unmoving and staring at Crow as she took her place.

She saw Alexander sitting in the royal box beside his father, a pensive look on his face. When Crow met his gaze, her heart leaped involuntarily and she wanted to smile as Alexander gave her an encouraging look. She did not smile, but shifted her gaze to where Leon stood next to the Prince, his gaze hurt but forgiving. He understood. Crow felt her barely suppressed rage rear towards herself and swallowed it down for another moment, waiting for the warrior of the Shaman to come and face her.

The sun rose over the horizon and the chosen warrior walked into the ring. He wore the thin metal armour favoured by the people of the Eastern Lands and had power in his every step. His body rippled with finely honed muscle and, despite Crow's height, he stood taller. His face was marred with the scars of many fights; that he was still alive proved he had won. His head was bald and Crow noticed that he had no facial hair either, giving him an eerie, skeletal look. This was a man to be feared.

The Shaman diverted her attention from the warrior as he climbed into the royal box, taking a seat on the other side of Alexander. The man's finery was even more extravagant than before and his eyes gleamed with arrogance and rage. He raised his hands, "You fight today to claim right to the Scheren of my people. You will die a terrible death at the hands of my warrior. Have you anything to say for yourself?"

Crow knew that the Shaman expected her to surrender, but she simply gripped her Scheren tightly and looked the Shaman in the eye. Even at a distance, the regal man of the Eastern Lands could see the immense, burning rage within Crow's eyes. She spoke, voice carrying easily over the silent crowds. "I am the child of the Jackal," she called, pleased at the surprised gasps from some of the nobles, the look of complete shock and horror on the King's face and the sudden terror on the Shaman's. "I have as much a right to fight with this blade as you. I will not yield."

The Shaman, voice shaking, managed to call out, "So be it." He lowered his hands and Crow turned to face her opponent. They bowed low to each other and straightened and the fight began. The man's Scheren darted towards Crow with blinding speed and Crow managed to dodge by the skin of her teeth, narrowly avoiding a cut to her arm. She retaliated and crouched, pushing off the ground to leap at her opponent, swinging her Scheren at his shoulders. The man countered easily, his blade meeting Crow's and she twisted mid-air to avoid being stabbed through the belly.

Her rage grew and took control over her motions. Crow and the Shaman's warrior lunged at each other, blades meeting in a clanging of metal, leaped backwards, circled, attacked, defended and each tried to gain the upper hand. Crow, for being leaner and smaller, was faster, but her opponent had more strength. He could wear her down then push his advantage when she lost an inch of speed.

Crow gained a cut on her shoulder, for which she delivered a stab at the man's leg, cutting where the armour did not protect. The two exchanged blows like that for what seemed like ages and it was soon apparent that they were evenly matched. Crow's anger was ruling her every movement and she fought like a demon, using every trick she knew, funnelling her father's teachings towards her enemy, teeth gritted and fire burning in her green eyes. She was strong from working in the forge, but the man was stronger.

I just need a little more strength, she thought desperately as she swiped her Scheren at the man's chest only to barely cut through the armour, delivering little more than a scratch. For her efforts, she was cut across the belly, a long, shallow cut that stung deeply. Crow growled, searching for any last instance of strength, of power, she could find.

Suddenly, it seemed she was no longer fighting the Shaman's warrior but dragging a Scheren nearly as long as her, a five year old girl. Her hair was longer and slick with sweat, even as she walked through the rain back to the castle of her family. Her father had finally released her for the evening and she barely managed to find the strength to walk up to her room, collapsing on her bed. She screamed into the pillow on her bed, anger filling her marrow.

"Hush, dear one," her mother's voice soothed, a gentle hand on Crow's back. The child turned and with rage-filled green eyes, she looked up at her mother. The beautiful woman looked back with only kindness and sympathy.

"Why should I? Father says to use my anger as a weapon, to hone it and sharpen it until I can use it to stab through the gut of my enemy," Crow responded, her features beautiful even as a child. Her mother sighed and wrapped her arms around her daughter, pressing a gentle kiss to the black hair as she did so. Crow relaxed, the only time she ever did back then, into her mother's arms.

"My darling," the beautiful woman, once a slave, murmured, eyes fixed not on her daughter but on the wall opposite, "your father is partially right. Anger can be a very potent weapon, granting strength in times of need and giving you a drive to keep going when all seems lost."

"Then why should I stop screaming? I'm screaming because I'm angry," Crow replied, half-haughty and half-confused. Her mother stroked her hair and closed her eyes for a moment.

"I said your father was only partially right. Anger is powerful, able to grant you a strength beyond what you might normally be able to achieve. But if you let it grow, let it take control over you, it will become bitterness. You will be strong, yes, dangerous, yes, but your full potential will be suppressed," the woman said, holding an exhausted child in her arms.

"I don't understand," Crow replied, leaning her head on her mother's breast, rubbing her small hands in circles on the beautiful dress.

"Anger is powerful and can grant you strength. It can keep you going when all seems lost. But there is something even more potent, something that cannot exist while you let anger rule your life," she replied, voice soothing.

"What's that, Mama?" Crow asked. "I want to be the most powerful person there is."

"Oh, my child," her mother responded. "You are letting anger blacken your soul, letting your desires be shaped by rage. Do not let your soul be governed by anger or you will never be as strong and good as you could be. You will never be as powerful, if you wish, or as kind, as you would like."

"Why would I want to be kind?" Crow asked, screwing up her childish face in a look of disgust. Her mother sighed and lifted Crow onto her lap.

"Because kindness gets you loyalty, gets you a place in people's hearts that is far more prestigious than that of fear of your anger. That is not to say you should be always kind. Temper your nature with the wisdom to know when a person deserves to be forgiven, or taught. Kindness allows you to become loved. Love is what is so much more powerful than anger, my dear. It can grant you more strength and wisdom and goodness, righteousness, than anger ever could. It lets you forgive others of their mistakes because you know they are only human. It lets you forgive yourself because you cannot expect to be perfect. Love lets you be patient, unassuming, strong and beautiful, inside and out. It will grant you loyalty and friendship and so much more. Anger, my child, is potent, but it will only let you get so far. So let go of your anger for love and you will be free and strong and beautiful and you will live well."

"I will, Mama," Crow replied, not sure how to do what her mother asked, but determined to try.

"I know you will. Because I can see that you will be greater than your father. And that was the one lesson he never learned."

Crow blinked, pushing away the tears that gathered in her eyes as she defended herself against another attack. That was the only lesson her mother had taught her, repeating it over and over, as much as possible to ingratiate it into Crow's blood, her being. And Crow had forgotten it, instead embracing the anger because it was so much easier to be angry at herself, at her past, than it was to forgive.

She felt the anger ebbing in favour of a more passionate, beautiful emotion and she thought of her father, of the Mazemaker, of Sythfeld, of the Duke of Westmont, of Jek, of Leon, of Alexander. She let her anger directed at each dissipate, allowing herself after all this time to forgive them for things that were beyond their control or well within their grasp. The past could not be changed and it was time she stopped trying. She forgave them and then, as she pushed her Scheren against the other, sheer strength keeping both blades still, she forgave herself.

Crow heaved and threw the other man away, watching as he stumbled backwards, surprised at her sudden strength. He looked into her eyes, expecting to see a more fearsome anger burning there than what he had been fighting. He would expect no less from the child of the Jackal. But what he saw scared him more, because there was no anger in Crow's eyes. There was a serenity there that proved she had accepted her life, forgiven and accepted what she could not change. She had stopped staring at the past. Now, she looked forwards.

Crow watched the man in return, at peace with herself and the world. There was a hush over the arena as the two warriors faced each other, pausing their fight for a few precious seconds. Alexander leaned forwards, watching Crow desperately, searching for any sign of a serious injury. Crow stood, relaxed, as her opponent crouched and clutched his Scheren, wary against attack. Crow slowly, surely, deftly, raised her gleaming blade. And she began to dance.

Her movements seemed graceful, elegant, as she attacked. She appeared to be more skilled at the art of

Mak'tal than before she had begun and her opponent stood no chance. Crow moved swiftly and with a serenity that bespoke the fact that she knew she would prevail. With a simple flick of her wrist, Crow circled her Scheren around the other and her opponent's blade went flying. He stared in shock as Crow pointed the tip of the Scheren at his chest then fell to his knees, bowing his head.

"You have won," he said and Crow lowered her blade. "Kill me to save me from dishonour."

Crow thrust her Scheren into the ground and grabbed the man's arm, hauling him to his feet. "There is no shame in losing. I will not kill you," she said and turned to face the Shaman. A few cheers and claps broke out in the watching crowd then it seemed that everyone took up the call, praising Crow for her victory. She smiled, pleased with the fight, then looked the Shaman square in the eye.

Where he had seen anger before, the Shaman saw none and for a moment, he relaxed. Until, that is, Crow began to speak, "I was brought here today to defend my right to carry a weapon because I was not worthy. I have proven my worth, by my heritage, but mostly by my skill. Shaman, I demand recompense from you."

Startled, the Shaman gave a coarse bark of laughter, "A commoner such as you demand recompense from me?" He shook his head and stood to go, only to find Alexander and Leon barring the way, the King directly behind them, fury burning in his eyes.

"You came into my lands invited and insulted my

people. Crow has defended himself well and he is well within his rights to demand recompense from you. For your insolence, you will pay him a sum that you would pay my son, the Crown Prince Alexander. You will do so within the day, or I will want to know why," the King said, his hand resting on the hilt of his sword. His voice carried over the voices of the people and all stared at him.

"Yes, your Majesty," the Shaman muttered and scurried off before anyone could stop him.

"Sir Leon," the King said, "follow him and make sure he is collecting his money and not his men to leave."

"Of course, your Majesty," Leon bowed and rushed off after the Shaman, easily catching up to the man. Alexander stood by his father's side and Crow was struck with the similarity of their features. She felt her heart pounding in her chest, the force of her feelings for Alexander no longer subdued by her anger.

Crow turned to leave, to go set out her wares and continue her day's work when she was stopped, the regal and demanding voice of the King preventing her from leaving. "Master Crow," he called. She turned and bowed deeply, feeling gratitude and respect for the man, despite the fact that he had never spoken to her let alone noticed her. "I would have a word with you."

"Yes, your Majesty," she said, pulling her Scheren up from the ground and moving over to the royal box. She saw Alexander look between her and his father with fear in his eyes and the King looked at his son.

"Alexander," he said calmly. "Go enjoy the festival. Find a show to watch or get something to eat."

"But, Father—" Alexander protested. He was silenced with a wave of the King's hand and obediently did as he was told. Crow felt a sudden stab of fear and pushed it aside, standing and regarding the King.

"You fought well today. I expected no less from a child of the Jackal," he began. Crow bowed her head politely.

"Thank you, your Majesty," she murmured, tempted to shift her weight uneasily. Or, perhaps, to run.

"I expected no less, even for a woman," the King replied, watching Crow's face to gauge her reaction. She blinked, startled and stumbled backwards, preparing to run. "I was the only one besides your immediate family who knew of your gender. Your father sent a courier to me on the day of your birth, to thank me for the land and title I granted him as well as to renew his pledge of allegiance. I cannot say that I particularly liked the man, but he was quiet, granted me no trouble and always payed his taxes. I was saddened by the news of his demise, if only because I would lose such a loyal subject."

Crow swallowed and lowered her head, staving off the impulse to run, if only for a few moments. "My father was a cruel man," she said carefully.

"I know. That much was apparent, even blatantly obvious when he rode to my Court, to petition a joining of his land with mine, breaking away from the Eastern Lands. No Shaman would oppose him, and so I agreed. I did not know of the fact that you survived until today.

And, now that I do, I must question your motives for coming here," the King said, deep voice quiet and yet demanding Crow's attention. A voice that Alexander would possess, and already had much control over.

"I have renounced the Jackal's way of living many years ago," Crow said. "I wanted nothing more than to be a blacksmith and so I had to act the boy. Women are not blacksmiths. It was never my intention to come to Kyper—"

"Indeed," the King said, voice holding none of the disbelief that Crow expected. She blinked in shock and continued her explanation.

"I was on my way to Barem and surpassed it. The Duke of Westmont introduced me to Jek," she continued. The King shot her a look at that and Crow shrugged. "I have been here ever since."

"I have heard many things about you, Crow, from both Alexander and Jek. Granted, my son has been far more eloquent and frequent in your praise, but on the few occasions when I have spoken with Master Jek, he has said only good things about you. You are friends with my son," the King said and Crow nodded. The royal frowned and sighed. "Since you came, Alexander has been happier and more easy. He never had an easy time making friends and to find one that is so close and good in you was...not my ideal. You were nothing more than a peasant boy, never mind being exceptionally good at smithing, but Alexander was happy. I could not begrudge him his friendship, especially when it was doing him so much good. But now..."

"Now you question my integrity because I am female and because the Jackal is my father," Crow said, her voice soft rather than sharp. She sighed and slumped against the wall of the royal box, much to the surprise of the King. To act so familiar in his presence! Crow met the King's eye and he all but jumped from shock. For her to meet his eyes was surprising, given their respective stations, but that the green depths held none of the anger he expected from her was nothing short of astonishing.

"I ought to have you punished for your deceptions," the King said, breaking away from her gaze. "But I cannot. You have done no wrong but to keep your gender hidden for the sake of your craft. I trust that you did not mean to become friends with Alexander, but now that you have, I cannot punish you for his sake. I must ask one thing, though. What are your designs concerning my son?"

"I had none when I first met him. I simply enjoyed his company and his conversation. But that has changed. I will admit freely that I am in love with Alexander. I have tried to fight it, tried to seek elsewhere, but I cannot change it," Crow said, voice dull. The question had not astonished her, though that the King was so direct was surprising.

"My son will come of age in three days, the final day of the fair. Afterwards, he must begin in earnest to find a queen. She must be of noble blood," the King said carefully, eyeing Crow. She laughed, the sound derisive but understanding.

"You want to make sure that I will not stake my claim now that you know my heritage," she said softly, folding her arms and looking at the floor.

"You have enough money, what with the recompense from the Shaman, to rebuild your home. You can claim your birthright without the money and there is no denying what you are. I allowed the Shadow Lake region to become part of my own when your father offered, in exchange for making him a Duke. You are the heiress to your father's land and wealth, to his title as well. I am only looking out for Alexander," the King replied, feeling an odd sensation for the poor girl. He might have called it sympathy. He watched Crow and noted with no sense of pleasure the sadness on her face.

"If only it were that simple," Crow said. "Alexander does not know that I am anything but a boy and I fear that if I were ever to reveal myself to him, he would hate me. Just because I am a Duchess does not mean that Alexander will up and marry me, no matter how ardently I may love him. I doubt that you shall have to fear your son loving the spawn of the Jackal." She did not wait for a response but walked away, her heart heavy in her chest as she accepted the truth of her feelings for Alexander. They would never be shared by him, never be seen by him. He would fall in love with a beautiful noblewoman, perhaps even Yvonne, and she would be his queen. Crow would lose him.

"Leon was right," she muttered. "He is going to hurt me and I cannot seem to prevent it."

The King watched Crow walk away, posture straight

despite the burden he could see on her shoulders. He felt for her, saw with no shadow of a doubt that she was nothing like her father. The Jackal would not give up something he loved simply because of the feelings of the other. But Crow had. And, the King knew, that if Alexander knew her secret, could be made to see her feelings and her sacrifice, that he would be very much in danger of loving Crow as she loved him.

CHAPTER 18

Due to her sudden fame from winning the fight, Crow's products sold faster than she could make more and people were stopping by the forge just to look at her. At first, making money outweighed the annoyance of people, but Crow soon grew aggravated.

"Can't they just leave me alone?" she snarled as yet another group of people walked towards the forge, eager looks in their eyes. They were parents of a boy who was tall and wiry for his young age, and as they approached, Crow knew exactly what they were going to ask.

"Master Crow," the father began, tugging at his coarse shirt. "We commend you on a great fight and congratulate you on your win."

"Thank you," Crow said stiffly, cleaning a workbench for the next project. The man seemed to take her reply as leave to continue and he did so eagerly, if nervously.

"We know you are busy with your duties, but... our

son, Nolan, is in need of a teacher... would you take him on as an apprentice?" the man said, his wife stepping up to grab his arm. Crow felt sorry for the disappointment she was about to impart but she did not want to mislead them.

"I will not teach the art of Mak'tal," she said, trying to make her words gentle. The father blinked and shook his head.

"You misunderstand me," he said. "We want to know if you would take on Nolan as a smithing apprentice."

"I'm a quick learner," Nolan added, eyes shining. Crow blinked, startled. She had been approached many times to be asked if she would teach young boys the art of Mak'tal, of fighting with a Scheren. To be asked to be a master smith to an apprentice was startling.

"I cannot," Crow said, much more sincere. "I am only an apprentice myself and am not allowed to take on an apprentice until I am made a master. I might be able to recommend a few good smiths in town, though, if you wish."

"Oh," the man said, obviously disappointed. "We had hoped that you would make an exception for Nolan. He is a talented lad and you are the best. Price is no object, if that is what you need."

"No," Crow repeated firmly. "I can't make an exception for Nolan, no matter what I want. As to money, I do not need it. Speak with Master Faraday, in town. He's a very good master and man and Nolan should do well with him."

She was thanked profusely, though with obvious

disappointment and when the family was gone, Crow's shoulders sagged in relief. She gave an exasperated sigh and looked at Jek. He stood with shoulders shaking from silent laughter. "What?" Crow grumbled, looking indignantly at the smith.

"Next thing ye know, ye'll be playin' matchmaker for people," Jek said, voice tight with laughter. Crow frowned and grumbled and went back to work, doing her best to ignore the numerous people that came by. One person, though, did catch her attention.

"Jek," a quiet, raspy voice said. Crow looked up from her arrowheads and blinked when she saw a well built man wearing dark clothing and a fine cloak, gold rope at the neck, black fur trimming the ends. Jek looked up and grinned at the sight of the man, standing and going to clasp arms with him.

"Ye haven' changed a bit, Charles," Jek said. The stranger chuckled and Jek retreated into the house, leaving Crow alone in the forge. She worked in silence for a while; the fair seemed to have claimed those who would come find her. Crow was left in relative peace as her mentor held conference with the stranger.

After what seemed like hours, the stranger emerged with Jek not far behind. They exchanged farewells then Jek looked to Crow. "I know that technically, you're not supposed to get this until you're at least eighteen, but..." he handed her a bill of paper, tied and sealed with black wax. The seal was elaborate and Crow looked at it with interest.

"The guild?" she asked, looking at Jek. He shrugged

and she opened the paper carefully. Shock had her reaching for something to balance on and joy had her feeling as if she could fly. The paper was an official certificate, releasing Crow from her apprenticeship and making her a master smith. She blinked and looked at Jek with a wide grin.

"Congratulations, Master Smith," Jek said, reaching over to ruffle Crow's hair. Crow stared at the paper, smiling and feeling nothing but happiness.

"Master Smith?" a sweet voice asked. Crow turned and spotted Lady Yvonne standing at the entrance to the forge, a seductive smile on her face. Feeling slightly put-out but still happy, Crow waved her papers slightly and nodded. Yvonne purred, "Congratulations, Crow." She walked forwards and in a sudden movement which caught Crow unawares, her hands were on either side of the smith's face, her mouth crashing on Crow's.

Without a second thought, Crow pushed away and hurriedly wiped her mouth. Yvonne stumbled backwards and into the wooden post at the entrance, face gleaming with anger. "You'll regret that," she said simply, her voice trembling with anger and hurt at being rejected. Crow narrowed her eyes.

"Regret what?" Alexander asked, folding his arms as he emerged from the people and approached the forge. "I saw you kiss him. Obviously, Crow doesn't want you Yvonne. Why don't you go seduce some soldier or something, okay? You're not wanted here."

"You are just some worthless peasant," Yvonne hissed

at Crow as she started to move away. "Whereas I am a Lady of the Court. You will regret this."

"Suit yourself," Crow said, shrugging. She picked up a blade she had finished recently and ran her finger along the edge. "But I can do as much with this as I can a Scheren."

With a growl of indignation, Yvonne stalked away, her back straight, nose raised. Crow laughed at her retreating back and shook her head. Alexander grinned as well, "I have been waiting a very long time to do that. She'll be miffed for a while and I'll probably get a lecture from my father, but it was worth it. So, Master Smith, eh? Well done."

"I wasn't expecting to get it so soon," Crow murmured, admiring the decorative lettering on the certificate. She stroked the page reverently and shook her head.

"Well, since you did, and since we happen to have a fair here with entertainment at every possible moment, I say that this calls for a celebration," Alexander said. Crow nodded then remembered herself and looked at Jek. The big man shook his head.

"Crow, ye ain't my 'pprentice any more. Ye can do what ye like," he said and Crow nearly balked from the realisation. She grinned and bounded into the house, stowing her certificate and grabbing a small bag of money before returning to Alexander.

"Let's go find something strong to drink. I feel like celebrating until I can't feel my head, no matter that I'll regret it in the morning," Crow announced and strode off, the Prince at her side.

They wandered the fair and ended up in Kyper town at a local tavern, the place brimming with people of all walks of life. During a fair, people seemed to lose their inhibitions about mingling with others of different ranks. Crow and Alexander found a low bench and called for drinks and food, eating and celebrating with smiles and raucous laughter.

"So," Alexander said, carelessly waving his second stein of ale, the other hand holding some sweetmeat. "What exactly did my father want with you after the fight?"

Crow scoffed and shook her head, "He wanted to figure out whether or not I was like my father. Apparently, they didn't get along despite the King's claims otherwise."

"And? What did he decide?" Alexander asked, eyes riveted on his fair friend. Crow shrugged and took a sip of her drink, pleased with the feeling of it going down.

"That I'm acceptable," she said, fixing her voice so that it was full of arrogance, "good enough to remain as your friend. That I can fight and that I'm still fairly dangerous."

"Ha," Alexander scoffed. "As if my father could determine my friends. He may be the King, but I am the future King and I have some sway."

Crow's eyes grew serious for a moment and she fixed Alexander in her gaze, "Don't underestimate your father. He can be very cunning."

"I suppose," the Prince said. "Alright, now, you fought with more.. something. I've never seen you that good or that quick before and at first, I was sure that you two were just going to keep going until one of you didn't have the strength to stand. But then you, I don't know, changed or something and all of a sudden, you're unstoppable."

Crow snorted into her drink, trying and failing to hide a chuckle, "I highly doubt I'm unstoppable. A good poison in my drink and I'll be as dead as a rose bush in winter. And twice as pretty." Her casual humour brought the mirth back into the conversation and the two continued on for most of the day.

By evening, Crow and Alexander were staggering back to their respective beds, completely worn out. They had drunk far too much and eaten little. They had wandered around the fair, admiring the products, laughing at the entertainment or watching the gypsy dancers. Crow had even had her palm read and was told she would find a beautiful young girl which wanted her help and would be the one she would marry. Alexander didn't understand why she was laughing so much at the prediction and Crow was too secretive, even inebriated, to explain.

She slept heavily and woke with a pounding headache just before dawn. Groaning, Crow rolled out of bed and went through her normal routine of dressing and preparing the morning meal and stoking up the forge before she remembered her good fortune from the day before. Her pleasure dissipated some of the pain, and the arrival of Leon pushed away the rest.

"Leon," Crow smiled, searching his face for any sign of resentment or hurt or anger. She saw only a distinct sadness and felt guilty for being the one to put it there. The knight met her gaze with a small smile and held out a box. Crow furrowed her brows but took it and set it on a workbench.

"Your recompense," Leon said. "I practically had to shake it from the Shaman, but he gave in eventually." Crow opened the box and could not hold back a gasp when she saw the amount of money contained within. The coins were all gold and shimmered in the morning light.

"Oh, wow," Crow said quietly, thinking of the possibilities for such an amount of money. She could rebuild her estate, claim her birthright. She could go home. The thought of returning to Shadow Lake, the place of which Leon had spoken in a story so long ago, was overwhelming and bitter sweet. Crow desperately wanted to return, despite – or perhaps because of – the horrors she had experienced there. She knew that as long as she was in love with Alexander, as long as he was her friend, she could not go.

"You deserve it, Crow," Leon said softly, putting his hand on her shoulder in a comforting gesture which made Crow want to cry for the hurt she had caused him. She did not and simply looked up at the dusty skinned knight in gratitude.

"Thank you," she replied, then, "I'm sorry." Leon

smiled at her and Crow was hit with the force of his despondent emotions.

"I know. It's just..." Leon started and trailed off, his gaze travelling to the gates of Kyper palace. Crow saw a glint of longing in his eye and lowered her gaze.

"Where will you go?" she asked, leaning her weight against the workbench as she watched Leon. He looked at her, startled and tilted his head, mouth open to ask a question. Crow beat him to it, "I recognise the signs of a wanderer. You need to search until you are healed, to find a place where you belong. You can be a knight errant."

Leon chuckled, the smile not quite reaching his eyes, "And do what? Save a damsel from danger?"

"If that's what it takes," Crow replied. She plucked twenty gold coins from the chest and handed them to Leon. "Take this. A gift between friends, if nothing more."

"I can't take your money," Leon murmured, looking at the coins in his hand.

"Then, when your travels are over, come find me and pay me back," Crow said firmly. She pulled Leon into an embrace and kissed both cheeks in a brotherly—or sisterly—manner and the knight watched her with sorrow.

"Goodbye, Crow," he said and put the money into his pocket, walking away just as Alexander appeared, his face set in a slight grimace. Crow remembered her own headache and felt for the Prince.

"Where is Leon going?" he asked, looking at the knight who had failed to return his greeting.

"Searching," Crow said with a shrug. "I don't know any more than that. But I doubt I'll see him again."

"Why do you say that?" Alexander said, massaging his temple with one hand. Crow wanted desperately to run her fingers through his hair, smoothing the slight curls and gently making his headache go away. Instead, she shrugged and closed the chest, carrying it inside the house and returning to the Prince.

"Just a feeling," she replied and Alexander shrugged. He looked in distaste at the fair that stretched out before him, regretting his revels of the day before. Crow was of a mind to agree with him.

"Let's go riding," Alexander said. "Maybe the fresh air will get rid of this fog in my brain."

"Don't you have a tournament to win?" Crow asked, folding her arms and looking at the Prince incredulously.

"No. Today is my day off. Mostly they're doing jousting and there's a general competition for peasants and such. I don't really have anywhere to be. Besides, this whole celebration is in my honour," he said, sweeping his hands to indicate the fair. "I think if I do what I want for one day, I'll be okay."

Crow shrugged and led the way to the stables, pausing for a moment to say goodbye to Jek. He waved her off and she ran into the dark, hay scented stables, finding Kayn and telling him their needs. The hostler saddled Alexander's horse and Crow's preferred sorrel with deft hands and soon, the pair found themselves far away from Kyper and well into the woods.

"Too bad we forgot our bows and arrows or we could

hunt some early spring fowl," Crow said, leading the sorrel in a prancing step through a newly melted stream.

"With all the festivities going on and feasts nearly every night, I'm sure the kitchens wouldn't have minded," Alexander replied, watching as two geese fled from a bush by the stream. Crow followed them with her eye.

"And that would have gotten me high favour with them. Darn," she muttered. "I guess I'll just have be nice to them."

"Very funny," Alexander said dryly. "So, what are you going to do with the money that you stole from the Shaman?"

"I did not steal it," Crow replied immediately, a hard edge in her voice. "My father stole. I earned."

"Sorry. I was just saying that the Shaman is going to claim you stole it. But what are you going to do? With the amount you have, you could easily have a similar financial situation as an Earl or something. Not that you'd have the title, but still. You could get a nice estate and build it up," Alexander said. Crow frowned and shrugged.

"I could," she replied. "But I doubt that I'll do anything. If I were going to do something like that, I'd rebuild my father's estate, claim my heritage. More than likely, I'll just stay here until I figure out where I'm going. After all, I'm a master smith, now. And we smiths need a forge."

"I'm sure you could stay here," Alexander said, pulling his horse up so that the two walked side by side. "Jek seems to like you and you could take over the forge after he's too old. It would be like a new heritage or something."

"I don't know," Crow murmured, looking at the trees on either side and wishing that she could stay for a different reason, wishing she could stay because Alexander loved her and wanted her. "Would you want me to stay?"

"Of course! You're my best friend, Crow," Alexander said immediately, his words only making Crow's heart sink further. She appreciated that he cherished her as a friend and was glad to have his love in any way that she could, but she wanted more. "I wouldn't want you to leave. Then, I'd have to travel a lot more than I do to visit you and it's really not much fun when you're alone."

"Alright," Crow said, putting a resolute tone into her words. "I'll stay until you decide that I'm too much trouble."

"I doubt that'd happ—" Alexander started. He broke off as Crow staggered in her saddle. The world seemed to slow down and all the Prince could hear was his heartbeat in his ears. Crow looked at him with complete shock and pain written on her face. She looked down at the arrow that was protruding from her stomach and looked up at Alexander, obviously confused.

"Oh," she said softly, as if it were the most natural thing in the world. Already, Alexander could see a slight blooming of blood around the arrow and he reached out to Crow, trying to catch her. He was too late, though, and Crow fell from her saddle, body completely limp as she went into shock.

Alexander looked around wildly and saw no one, no attacker. No other arrows came through the trees. He flung himself from the saddle and tried shaking Crow's shoulders. Crow simply stared at him with wide green eyes, movements slow and shaky. Yelling an unintelligible cry, Alexander picked Crow up as gently as he could, surprised at how light the smith was. With a great heave of effort, he mounted his horse and turned, kicking his heels into the horse's side, moving it into a gallop as he rode back towards Kyper. The sorrel was ignored in Alexander's desperation. He clutched Crow tightly, keeping her stable as she blinked in shock, the pain from the arrow spreading.

"Don't you dare die on me, Crow," Alexander snarled, angry tears falling from his eyes. "You're my best friend, dammit, don't you dare die."

Crow flexed her fingers and licked her lips, finding it odd that they felt so funny. "I won't," she said carefully, slowly.

As the pair rode furiously back to the palace, a big, oddly shaped former slaver with three cuts on his chest from a razor sharp triangular blade lumbered away through the trees, a bow in his hand. He had avenged his mistress, his beloved Alkai, and the spawn of the Jackal who had spared his life in a moment of mercy would very soon be dead.

CHAPTER 19

By the time Alexander thundered into the courtyard and carried Crow to Jek's house, she was shaking, mouth set in a determined line and skin even more pale than it already was, which seemed impossible to Alexander. Jek was working in the forge, deftly twisting a piece of metal into the shape of a sword hilt when he saw Crow, the arrow protruding from her belly. He dropped the metal and cleared the way through the throng of people gathered around, allowing Alexander passage.

"Go fetch the healer," Jek snarled at a young gypsy boy who took one glance at the smith's face, contorted with fear and rage, and darted off to fetch Matharus. Alexander took Crow into Jek's house and lay her on her bed, where the shaking promptly grew worse.

Crow floundered, her muscles clenching from the pain and she arched on the bed, voice strangled in her throat as she tried to call out. Her green eyes were wide and desperate and she fixed her gaze on Alexander, gritting her teeth as she began to shake again. Jek stared at the arrow and the growing circle of blood around the wound and lunged from the room, returning with a thin knife and some bandages. He turned to Alexander who was standing, hair mussed and face shocked, afraid, as if he were dead.

"Alexander," Jek said, voice pulling the Prince back to reality. "Hold Crow down. I'm going to cut the shirt and bandages away."

"Jek," Crow groaned, panting with effort, her eyes telling her pain. Jek caught the gaze and turned again to the Prince who was moving as though not under his own command, preparing to hold Crow down.

"Perhaps you should leave," the smith said, all the practised uncultured tones vanishing in the face of the emergency. Crow shook her head wildly and gasped, growling deep in her throat as she fought from the pain and loss of blood. She managed to sit partly up and looked Jek dead in the eye, her will clearly stated. In the next moment, she was back to groaning, muscles tensing again. "Never mind, just keep a tight grip," Jek ordered and Alexander pressed down on Crow's shoulders and upper body, keeping her still.

Jek carefully began to cut away Crow's shirt and when that was safely discarded on the floor, stained with Crow's blood, he stared at the bandages, hesitating. Alexander looked at the smith, "Hurry! He's going to die if we don't do something. Now." His voice held all of the regal tones that his father commanded and the obvious power of persuasion was present. Jek took a deep breath and gave Alexander a look of pure sorrow.

"Just know," the smith said quietly, "that it was never about you. It was always about the smithing. It wasn't about you."

"Cut the bandages away, dammit!" Alexander barked, confused and frightened. Crow looked up and watched Alexander's countenance as Jek lowered the knife and began cutting away the bandages, from her navel upwards. Alexander's grip lessened slightly as he took in the thousands of paper-thin scars that were drawn onto Crow's skin. The lines connected and turned and wound their way around her stomach, onto her back, forming the most intricate maze Alexander had ever seen. And, at the centre of the maze where a small square normally would have been, the arrow protruded. Jek kept slicing away at the bandages, muttering under his breath the entire time, saying over and over again what he had told Alexander.

"It was never about you. Always about the smithing. Never about you," he whispered, voice shaking. Alexander moved his hands, Crow managing to keep herself still while Jek worked with the knife. As he moved farther and farther up her chest, she captured Alexander's blue eyes with her own and opened her mouth to speak.

"I'm sorry," she breathed. Alexander shook his head, reaching out to touch Crow's shoulder in comfort. He froze, watching in horror as Jek cut away the last of the bandages, revealing the two small, perfectly formed breasts that trembled with Crow's every shaking breath. Crow's last sight was Alexander staring at her, face contorted with horror and disgust and fear and pain. She heaved a breath and slipped into blackness.

When she awoke again, her mouth felt like desert sand and there was a throbbing pain throughout her midsection. She saw, by the light in her room, that it was early morning. Carefully, Crow looked around for water and gasped when she saw Alexander standing in her doorway, face an unreadable mask. The act of gasping had Crow wincing in pain and she noted that, while her wound was bandaged, the rest of her was not and she was wearing only a light shirt. The Prince looked at her, eyes cold, and sat on a stool in the corner.

"Why?" he asked simply, voice betraying the hurt and derision there. Crow closed her eyes for a moment and turned away, licking her lips to draw as much moisture to her mouth as she could. She opened her mouth to speak and began coughing, the sound a dry rasping. The next thing she knew, a ladle of water was being pressed against her lips. She drank eagerly, swallowing the cool water in great quaffs. In gratitude, she looked up at Alexander and smiled. He turned his head away, features stoic.

"They don't let girls learn how to be blacksmiths," Crow replied to his question, laying back on her cot to look up at the wooden ceiling. She couldn't bear the way her heart ached whenever she saw the hurt in Alexander's eyes. It was as if a great piece of her had been cut from her chest and squeezed and she could still feel it.

"But you lied to me." The words were cutting, sharp

and Crow narrowed her eyes to prevent the tears from falling then balked when she realised that she was not able to cry. The pain, guilt, had numbed her, numbed everything but that sharp ache in her chest.

"No. You never asked," she whispered. "You only assumed, just like everyone else." She heard a snort from where Alexander was and felt herself bite her lip in response, to prevent her wincing.

"Fine," Alexander conceded, tone stinging. "But you actively deceived me. Without giving a second thought as to how I would react."

"That's not true," Crow said, pushing herself up onto her elbows and ignoring the flaming pain from her midsection. She fixed Alexander in her sights and forced upon him the truth of her words. He met her gaze evenly but the coldness there cut into Crow. "I thought nearly every day about what you would say, what you would do. Fine, I actively deceived you, but do you know how much I wanted to tell you? How much I wanted you to know what it was doing to me that I was keeping something so great from my best friend?"

"If you hated the deception so much, why did you keep it from me? It's not like I don't already know your great secrets. Oh, look at me, I'm Crow, the self-determined mystery of Kyper palace. I pretend that all is cheery with the world but I love it when people fawn over me, demanding to know my secrets. Because I've got a horrible past and people will only respect me more when they know it. Oh, by the way, I'm a woman." Alexander rose of the stool in his anger and glared down at Crow. He saw hurt in her eyes and guilt, remorse, but none of the anger he had expected. The anger that had made Crow so dangerous and frightening and so exhilarating was gone. Now, he saw only truth. And that scared him even more.

"If you really thought that, you wouldn't have stood by me for so long," Crow said softly.

"Why?" Alexander asked, pulling his hands through his hair to prevent himself from falling to his knees and pleading with Crow. "Why didn't you tell me?"

Crow looked at the Prince and sighed, voice surprisingly gently as she spoke, "Would you have thought of me differently?"

"Of course," Alexander said desperately, swinging his hands through the air, as if to prove a point. His emphatic response made Crow close her eyes and take a shuddering breath before looking away.

"That's why," she said. Licking her lips, a movement that Alexander found both distracting and infuriating, Crow turned back to the Prince, feeling shaky and exhausted and more than a bit guilty. "Whatever you may think of me now," she continued, sinking back down and gasping slightly in relief from the pain in her stomach, "you were my greatest friend and I was yours."

"That may have been. But now I know who you really are," Alexander hissed, voice low. Crow gave a breathy sort of chuckle and shook her head slightly.

"No," she bit back. "You knew me the first day we met. You knew me in all the conversations we had. You knew me the day I told you about my past and the day that I defended my honour. You knew me when we went riding. You may have believed my gender to be different, but you knew me. The real me. Now that you know the only secret I had left to guard, you think everything has changed. You think that I have changed. But I haven't. Only your perception of me has changed."

Alexander said nothing to this, only turned away from Crow and stood in the door, shoulders hunched slightly as he took in all that had been said. Without looking at her, he said clearly, in his most noble, regal voice, "Goodbye, Crow." Then, he was gone.

Crow did not see Alexander again through all the time she was in bed healing. The fair ended on the day she had awoken and she couldn't decide if she were relieved or annoyed that the distractions and noises of the fair were gone, allowing her peace in which to think. Jek came and tended to her every day, patiently dressing her wound and asking nothing of what had happened. He only told her what Matharus had told him.

"The arrow missed yer vitals an' got caught in the very last layer of muscle ye had on your stomach. Yer bandages slowed the arrow down and ye'll be a'right. It'll take some time to get yer muscle back, but Matharus says ye'll be on yer feet in a week. Doin' work in a week and a half." The news was delivered in the hopes that Crow would be cheerful, but she said nothing. In fact, she said nothing at all from the time Alexander left to nearly two weeks later when she emerged from the house one morning, pack and chest in hand. Jek looked at Crow, confused and she met the smith's eye.

"I'm leaving," she announced and her words were like a blow to her former master. He had suspected she would not stay long after she got her master's certificate, but he loved Crow like a daughter and didn't want to lose her. Crow saw all this in Jek's eyes and walked forwards, enveloping the smith in a powerful hug. She no longer wore the bandages and when Jek held her back to look at her, he saw a beautiful young woman, a Lady if he had ever known one.

"Ye'll be missed," Jek said and smiled waveringly at Crow. She smiled in return, the edges not quite reaching her eyes. Crow shouldered her pack and carried the chest against one skinny hip, walking through the forge one last time. She had her Scheren at her side and carried what few tools she had to her name, a few other projects and pieces in her bag. Her fingers tightened over the necklace that she had made for the day when she would no longer have to hide. It hurt too much to think about. Crow ran her fingers over the silver and gems, swallowing a lump in her throat. She turned her back on the piece, looking to a pile of tools instead. When she had been through the forge once more, she looked at Jek and smiled again.

"Goodbye, Jek. I love you," she said. She didn't wait for a response, just walked away to the stables, vanishing into the building before returning outside with the sorrel horse, her pack and the chest of money tucked away into the horse's saddle bags.

"I love you, too, my daughter," Jek said as he watched Crow ride out of the empty courtyard, her countenance grave and yet, somehow, hopeful. He didn't know where she was going and he doubted he would ever see her again. But he would keep that image and all the images of Crow in his head, to remember her by.

Jek turned and walked back into the house, not up to working anymore. He took a shuddering breath, surprised to find tears at the corner of his eyes and shook his head, "Yer a stupid, sentimental ol' man, Jek." He walked into Crow's old room and nearly choked when he saw that it was pristine, looking like it had never been lived in. She was gone, her only remaining legacy at Kyper the pieces she had made and the memories she had forged. Jek blinked as he saw a wrapped bundle on the bed and picked it up. The piece was heavy and there was a single piece of paper that fluttered down to the bed. For Alexander. Congratulations on coming of age, you old man. Your friend, Crow.

Jek unwrapped the cloth around the bundle and saw the sword that Crow had made for Alexander, taking in the elaborate decorative work, the beautifully honed blade, perfectly balanced and made just for Alexander. It was, by far, her finest piece of work and Jek tightened his grip on the sword, determined. He marched from the small house and up to the Palace, moving through the great wooden doors as if he had been born there and it was his right. Servants saw his expression and did not protest. Guards did not question him as he moved through the palace. Even the guards near Alexander's door, pacing up and down the hallway, did not move to stop him as he burst through the Prince's door, expression passionate and blazing.

"Jek," Alexander said dryly, his expression curious but disinterested. He had always liked the smith and still liked him, though he was hurt by the refusal to speak of Crow's secret.

"Yer Royal Highness," Jek said, bowing mockingly at the Prince, taking in the unkempt look of Alexander, the slightly haunted expression in his eye.

"Jek," Alexander said, voice suddenly revealing his exhaustion. "What is it? I don't want to speak to..her."

"Ye won't have to," Jek grumbled. "She's gone."

"What?" Alexander said, half rising out of his seat, shock written on his face. Jek snorted as Alexander remembered himself and sat back down, trying to affect a disinterested look. "What do you mean?"

"I mean, she's gone. Left this mornin'. Took her pack an' money an' jus' rode off. Left this for ye, though," Jek said, thrusting the package at Alexander, note and all. The Prince looked startled and reached for the package, ignoring the note as it fell to the ground, and carefully unwrapping it. He stared in admiration at the sword, taking in each detail as he turned it over and over in his hands. The hilt, which fit his hand perfectly, the crossguard delicately designed. The blade, etched with beautiful designs, perfectly balanced and razor sharp. It was beautiful and made Alexander's heart ache.

"Where did she go?" Alexander whispered, turning to Jek in a moment of desperation as Crow had done so many times before. Jek saw all that was going on within the man before him and felt his countenance soften slightly.

"I don' know, lad," Jek said, shaking his head at Alexander. "Pro'lly to claim her birthright, whatever that may be." Alexander said nothing to that, only turned away and hunched over his desk. Jek wondered if he should go comfort the Prince but decided against it and turned away, leaving quietly. Alexander leaned over his desk, shoulders shaking as he cried for the loss of his greatest friend and the departure of Crow, whom he barely knew at all. He saw the note that had come with the gift of the sword and picked it up, reading the words.

With a wordless cry of anger, Alexander hurled the note as far away from him as he could and watched in disappointment as the paper simply fluttered through the air and floated gently to the ground. He looked at the sword, again taking in the great details. Growling, he turned away, stalking towards the door before turning back and sliding the sword into the sheath at his side. A perfect fit, as he knew it would be.

Alexander walked through the palace, not really sure of where he was going, thinking over everything. Every word, every gesture, looking for some sort of hint that Crow had given to her true identity. Something, anything, that would make him look the fool for ignoring it or make her a liar for not giving it. In both cases, he was dissatisfied. The hints were there, he decided, but far too subtle for him to have noticed before.

To his surprise, Alexander found himself in the throne room where the Court sessions were conducted, the chairs empty, the table deserted. Except for one man, stately in his finery and regal in stature. The King fixed Alexander in his gaze and beckoned his son come closer. "What sword is that?" he asked, gesturing to the intricate blade at Alexander's side. "I do not know it."

"It was a gift," Alexander found himself saying, adding on, "from Crow." His voice betrayed no bitterness and that alone was shocking to the Prince.

"Ah, yes. It was reported to me that she had gone," the King smirked, hiding the look behind steepled fingers.

Suddenly, Alexander was furious, "You knew? You knew and you didn't tell me?"

"Relax," the King said, raising his hand lazily as if to bat away Alexander's anger. "I did not know until she revealed that she was a child of the Jackal. The Jackal had only one child and that was a daughter."

"And you didn't feel that it was important to tell me?" Alexander hissed, narrowing his eyes at his father. The King had never been an affectionate man and that Alexander's anger was directed at him was somewhat unnerving, but he simply waved it off with a smile of self-determined wisdom.

"What good would that have done? You have to find a queen and you don't have time to be distracted by daughters of thieves, no matter how good of friends you were with her. As long as you thought she was a boy, it was better for your future. You could search among the nobles for a queen without distraction," Alexander's father explained, as if it were the most obvious thing in the world.

"Why would knowing Crow's gender have been a distraction?" Alexander asked, moving forwards as if to entreat his father. The King fixed him with a hard look and the Prince moved no further. Realisation dawned on his face and he scoffed openly, "You think I would have fallen in love with Crow? Crow was my best friend. I couldn't have..."

"Couldn't have done that? Couldn't have taken a single, simple step to further the relationship with the person that you were closest to? It would have been so easy; you two were already so close. Knew each other's secrets, knew your likes and dislikes, how to cheer you up, make you laugh. Trust me, boy, it would have been so easy for you to fall in love with her, had you known. Things are better this way." The King settled back into his throne, folding his hands across his chest. Alexander stood, stunned.

"Even if I felt that way," he muttered, barely loud enough for the King to hear. "Crow wouldn't have done anything."

At this, the King simply laughed, causing Alexander to stumble backwards as if the laughter were a physical blow. "Boy, she was already desperately in love with you."

CHAPTER 20

The journey from Kyper palace to the lands that were Crow's by heritage took little more than two weeks. In that time, she travelled alone and said very little when she did come in contact with people. She stayed at a few inns in villages when she came across them, but spent more time on the ground, wrapped in a bedroll. In the quiet moments when the fire was dying and the night encroached on Crow's campground, she thought of the hunting trips with Alexander and all of their conversations, all of the exchanged words and looks, ideas and feelings. She remembered her shock when he walked naked in front of her and chuckled to herself.

"I've gone, Alexander," she said softly, staring up at the stars that twinkled coldly above her. "I wonder if you even notice or if you've forgotten all of the good times we've had for the fact that there was one thing I couldn't tell you." It was the quiet moments that Crow took for herself, mourning her loss and sacrifice with tears that slipped silently down her face.

When she rode into Hotun, at the end of two weeks time, Crow had grown skinny, losing all the weight that was not muscle on her body. But she still sat proudly on her sorrel horse, her pale face looking at the people she passed with curiosity and wonder. They likely didn't even remember her, Crow, the cheery lad that was Sythfeld's apprentice. At the local inn, Crow dismounted and walked inside, eyes searching.

She spotted the man she wanted leaning against the bar, talking with a woman wearing a revealing dress, her cheeks rosy from lust, her smile wide. The man, however, had a leering look about him and his silver and brown hair was slicked back at his temple, giving him a slimy countenance. He was gaunt and wore clothing that was far finer than anything the other towns people wore. Crow walked up to the man, pushing her way past people who milled about for a mid-day meal, and stood behind him, her height a couple inches more than his.

"Robert Nesmith," Crow said, voice catching the attention of all in the room. The man, Robert, straightened and turned, moving backwards involuntarily as he realised Crow's height and proximity as well as the blank and beautiful expression on her face.

"Do I know you?" he asked, narrowing his eyes at Crow. She simply lifted her chin slightly and smirked.

"I am the Duchess Tyra Gabbon, daughter of Kamal Gabbon, Duke of Shadow Lake, known as the Jackal," she said. Complete silence filled the room, pregnant with shock and disbelief. Crow simply kept her eyes fixated on Robert Nesmith's face, watching as his eyes widened.

"You cannot be," he decided after examining her face. Crow raised her eyebrows and folded her arms, revealing the thin sword she had at her side.

"And why not? You know me," she replied evenly, a knowing smile on her face. "I told you I would return to claim my birthright."

"I was told by the Duchess when she was young that she would return," Robert said carefully. "But that child was taken and killed by the Mazemaker. A boy from Hotun was captured as well and killed the monster. The Duchess never returned."

"You fool," Crow said, curling her lip in disgust at the man. "I am that boy. I was apprenticed to Sythfeld from the time I returned to just over a year ago, at which point I left and went to Kyper, finishing my apprenticeship to Jek, the royal smith, and making enough money to rebuild my father's estate."

"The Duchess," Robert insisted, "is dead."

Crow narrowed her eyes, "Then I shall have to prove it to you." She pulled out her Scheren and brandished it before Robert's eyes, making sure he saw the blade and her obvious skill. "I was taught the art of Mak'tal by the Jackal, a near master at the age of six. If you want me to prove that, then I would be happy to run you through. But perhaps it would be easier if you saw my scars." At that, Crow raised the lower part of her shirt, receiving gasps from the people in the room, some turning away at the impropriety. Others were drawn in, staring at the thousands of scars traced there, at the hard muscle that was prominent through Crow's skin, at the hip bones that were apparent. She lowered her shirt again and narrowed her eyes at Robert.

The man stared at Crow and lowered his head at last, acknowledging Crow's position. "Forgive me, great Lady, I knew not to whom I spoke," he said, the words obviously paining him.

"I have come to claim what is rightfully mine. I have come to rebuild my home and to preside over Shadow Lake," Crow announced. "Robert Nesmith, you were given leadership of Hotun and its surrounding regions in my absence. I now call upon you to send word to all in the region of Shadow Lake that I am returned. Once my home is rebuilt and I am established, I shall survey my lands."

"Yes, your Grace," the man said, bowing his head lower. Crow grumbled inwardly, unused to the formal words and attitudes that usually surrounded them. She sighed and slackened her posture slightly.

"And for goodness' sake, don't call me that," she snapped. "My name is Crow. That's what people call me and that is what I shall go by."

"Of course, Duch—Crow. Where will you stay while the estate is being rebuilt?" Robert asked, straightening. Crow took one look at him and snorted, shaking her head.

"I won't intrude on you, if that's what you mean," she said, walking out of the inn and moving to her horse, glaring at a young boy who was inching for the sorrel's reins. The boy squeaked and ran off, taking shelter behind a house. Crow turned her head to the forge, smiling cunningly at the sight of the shirtless man bent over an anvil, the distance far enough that she could only make out the barest of features; his brown hair, muscular physique. "I'll stay where my living says I should."

"What?" Robert asked, attempting to help Crow into her saddle. She managed alone, gracefully, and looked down at the gaunt man, mirth plain on her face.

"I'm a Master smith. Where else should a Master smith stay but by a forge?" she asked and rode towards the forge, leaving Robert to stare after her in confusion. Crow took the sorrel up to the forge and dismounted, leaving the horse outside. She walked in and smiled at the familiar heat that hit her face. The smith, bent over an anvil, had average features twisted by bitterness. He glared up at Crow.

"I don't want no women here," he snarled. Crow simply watched him and put her hand at her hip, just above the hilt of the Scheren.

"That's what you said to me when Sythfeld died. You had the advantage then. You'll find this time you won't be so lucky," Crow replied evenly, looking about the familiar forge. Not much had changed since Sythfeld's death and she felt a twinge of nostalgia being back there.

"You," the man spat, straightening and looking Crow full in the face. She allowed him to, letting him take in every feature, let him see the lack of her burning rage and the presence of much more dangerous emotions in her eyes.

"Me," Crow confirmed. "I'm back, Tyto. I left when you told me the last time, went to Kyper to be apprenticed to the royal smith, Master Jek. I made some money and now I'm here to stay."

"You don't belong here, whore," Tyto growled. Crow said nothing, having heard the argument before. "What did you do, spread your legs for that smith Master of yours so he would teach you?"

"No," Crow snarled, feeling annoyed. "I proved my worth. Something you have not mastered. In any case, I'm staying and it's not your place to refuse."

"And why not, Crow," Tyto sneered, making her name sound like a slur. Crow simple curled her lip in a wicked grin and laughed.

"That's right. You named me that before you left to be apprenticed. You thought that it would hurt to call me a scavenger, a thief, a whore. But even at eleven, Tyto, you had no power over me. Now Crow is my name and it is known to many people," Crow said mildly, fingering a hammer. She smiled over at Tyto and he raised his hammer as if to strike Crow down. She lunged and twisted the tool away from him, making sure not to break his wrist. Tyto backed up a pace, eyeing her warily. "Much harder to overpower now that I'm bigger, eh?"

"I can always bring you to your knees, whore. And you'll beg me to do it by the time I am done," Tyto snapped. Crow sighed and raised the hammer, bringing it down on the piece of metal that Tyto was working on, flattening it despite its barely glowing heat.

"Now, listen Tyto. And listen hard," Crow said, her

voice slipping towards coldness. "I'm a Master smith now and you cannot turn me away. I'm tired of useless displays because that is what everyone seems to expect of me. But if you insist, then I can make an exception. It would be far easier to let me in your house."

"No. The guild doesn't care whether or not I let you stay in my house. They won't care about some small village like Hotun," Tyto said, moving forwards as if to push Crow out of the forge. She stood her ground and frowned.

"They would because I was Master Jek's apprentice. They would because I am a silversmith as well as a blacksmith. But if that is not enough for you, then know that they would because I am your Duchess," Crow said. She let Tyto meet her gaze to ascertain the truth of her words and when he had, he glared and turned away. Crow sighed and put the hammer she had taken down, moving to where her horse stood. "I would be well within my rights to punish you for turning me away, with the guild and the Courts, but no one deserves that kind of inequality. Not even you. Tyto, I hope that you find out what exactly you're angry at and that you simply let it go. I don't hold a grudge against you. Not then, not now, not ever. Know that."

At the conclusion of her speech, Crow rode back to where Robert was still standing outside the inn, an expression of intense thinking on his face. Crow approached and the man looked up at her, "Is all well, Duche—Crow?"

"I will take a room at the inn," Crow announced and

dismounted, leading her horse to the stables and taking her pack and money, handing the horse to the stable boy who looked less than pleased until Crow flipped him a bronze bit.

"It isn't proper for someone of your status," Robert argued when Crow emerged again. "I know of a dozen houses which would be better suited. I could have them prepared for you by tomorrow."

"And displace the families there?" Crow snorted. "I don't think so. I don't care about what's proper for someone of my status, I will not push someone out of their home. I will take a room at the inn, just like everyone else, until the estate is finished."

"But most nobles—" Robert started.

"I'm not most nobles," Crow replied, hauling her pack on one shoulder and the bag of coins on the other, refusing the help Robert offered as well as the pleading look in a young street urchin's eyes.

"I can see that," Robert muttered under his breath before following Crow into the inn. Crow got a room, fairly small by the inn's standards, but she refused to make someone move rooms. Once she was unpacked and bathed, Crow went to work on rebuilding her father's estate, speaking with local builders and architects. She acclimated to her home as quickly as she had to Kyper. Soon, it was not strange to see Crow around the town, wearing simple breeches and a shirt, exchanging greetings with the people and doing her own work. She kept up forging, working next to a newly silent Tyto at least one day a week. The remainder of the time, Crow would confer with her builders, carpenters, stonemasons, riding up to the ruins of the estate nearly daily, helping in clearing the debris and helping to lay a foundation.

No matter how she insisted, people only called her Crow to her face and after much grumbling as to its being improper. When she was not around, they called her the Duchess or Lady Tyra, or even Her Grace. The people of Shadow Lake all grew to know Crow or know of her and she was never in want of company. Daily, it seemed, people came to her with their problems as they would any normal ruling noble, albeit on a more frequent basis since Crow allowed it. She listened as she worked and offered the best advice she could. But, as she had done on her journey, during the quiet parts of the night, Crow would sit on a small outcropping of rock and look at the stars, wishing for Alexander.

"Time heals all wounds," she muttered, wrapping her arms around her knees and holding back tears. "Yeah, right."

While Crow was rebuilding her home and becoming acclimated to her new position, her title, her life, Alexander was busier than ever, taking over most of the politics for his father who had become confined to his bed. He had eaten something or caught some cold and his condition had deteriorated. His triumph over Crow's disappearance was his last act as King. Alexander had, therefore, taken up the mantle of regent as well as Crown Prince, working to make certain his kingdom did not suffer. His father, though, seemed determined, even in his weakened state, to take care of the Shadow Lake region. He rifled through the papers, seemingly looking for something which he never found. After going through the papers, the King always seemed more cheerful, but it never lasted.

"Alexander," the King rasped one late evening when the Prince was sitting by his father's bed, working at the desk he had moved from its position by the window.

"Don't exert yourself, father. Rest. Everything will seem better in the morning," Alexander said, scratching out some letters on a proposal by the Court. He had one hand tangled in his hair and leant on it, frustrated. He turned his head as his father began to cough and abandoned the proposal immediately as he saw the King choking, face flushing then deepening into a blue colour. Alexander shouted for help but the guards who rushed in could do nothing. One ran to fetch Matharus but the King was gasping for breath, his hands flailing with what weak strength he had. Alexander held his father in an upright position, searching the man's face desperately. The King looked at Alexander and mouthed something which Alexander could not understand as his eyes filled with tears. He swallowed audibly as the King's hands dropped to his side and he stared up at the canopy above his bed. There was a sudden relaxation of muscles and the King stared unseeing beyond his son's head. He was dead.

Alexander screamed in anger and disappointment, clutching his father's head to his chest. He screamed again and again, trying to make sense of the pain in his chest. Matharus came in and saw the sight then put his hand on Alexander's shoulder. With a shuddering breath of sorrow, Alexander rose and walked out of his father's room, breaking into a run as he made his way through the halls of the extensive palace. He burst out of the great doors and into the empty courtyard, shrouded in darkness but for a patch of red. He ran for the light, tears blurring his vision and grief making him stumble as he ran. Finally, the Prince, regent, and soon-to-be-King entered the forge, swallowing back a wail. He saw Jek and a new, harsher grief filled his chest. Jek was not the one he wanted.

"Lad?" Jek asked, moving away from the fire towards the Prince. Alexander lunged forwards and wrapped his arms around the big man, crying visibly now. Jek said nothing, only returned the hug awkwardly. But it was returned.

"The King is dead," Alexander said softly. His voice was mangled with crying and he felt wrong for doing so. But when Jek simply tightened his grip on the Prince in a gesture of fatherly comfort, Alexander knew it was alright.

"Long live the King," Jek said, letting Alexander lean into him at the words. He kept his grip firm when the Prince began to pull away and let Alexander be weak when he had been strong for so long. He let Alexander cry, knowing that it was not for his father but for the loss of his one true friend, the person who would have known exactly what to say, what to do, to make the world right again. Who would have given Alexander sympathy for the death of his father but joked about it the next minute. Jek let Alexander cry for losing Crow and for not knowing what she meant to him. And when the tears finally stopped, Jek led Alexander into the house for a bowl of soup, in that moment making him more a father to the Prince than the King had ever been.

The funeral and coronation was two days hence, planned in a hurry and executed with precision despite the lack of planning. The King Byron Fenyr was buried in the royal tomb, a place below the dungeons where the royal family was laid to rest. Alexander led the procession and watched in stoic silence as his father was sealed inside a stone vault for the remainder of time, a sword at his breast, a circlet of gold around his head. He looked peaceful. He looked regal. He looked kind. Alexander knew better and turned away the moment the tomb was sealed, walking back up the great stairs to stand in the hall, preparing for his coronation.

Quiet strains of music began and the doors to the throne room opened, showing a completely changed room. Where once the throne had sat at the head of a table, it now sat alone, the chairs of the Court moved along the wall where they were filled by nobles. All but two had people in their greatest finery sitting in them. One belonged to the former Duke of Westmont and the other had been vacant for years, its owner a mystery to Alexander. The one person he wished were there was not. Alexander walked past the people standing along either side of the carpet rolled out and dotted with rose petals. The music grew to a trembling, sorrowful and yet joyous crescendo as Alexander reached the foot of the stairs where the royal steward stood in grand robes, a priest at his side.

"At the death of the Great King Byron Fenyr, we have gathered for the crowning of a new King," the steward called. He looked at Alexander, the handsome young man barely come of age, eyes claiming more wisdom than youth usually allowed. Alexander, in turn, watched the steward, a thin balding man with wisps of white hair around his temple. "Crown Prince Alexander Fenyr," the steward continued, "kneel."

Alexander did so, bending to one knee, his head bowed in respect to his duty. He felt all of the need, at that moment, of being made to kneel. To bend before the weight of his duty, before the people which were his. He was their King but also their guide. He was responsible for them and he answered to them. He was not above them, but equal to them, if not below them. At that, Alexander thought of Crow and how she had seemed to know the truth of justice between people, how no person should be greater.

"Alexander, by blood you are to be the next King. But you must answer to your people. Do you swear to be just and true, to do your best by your people, to protect them from enemies, to be good by them, to feed them in times of famine, to treat them fairly? Do you swear to defend the honour of your land, to preserve truth and push for righteousness? Do you swear before God to be a shepherd to your sheep, knowing that they are worth more than you?" the priest asked, stepping down to the same ground as Alexander.

The Prince, the man, clenched his fist, feeling the truth of the words, their power resonating through him. He lifted his head enough to meet the kind gaze of the priest and whispered clearly, his voice carrying over the people who stood in the throne room, holding a power he had previously not possessed, "I swear."

"Then so I name you, Alexander Fenyr, King of Iona," the priest called out. The steward took a crown from a stand next to him and lowered it to rest on Alexander's head. "Rise and may your reign thrive." Alexander stood and climbed the step to stand at the foot of his throne. He turned and faced the people in the room. The steward handed him the gold sceptre, a symbol of his power and Alexander sat in the throne, officially accepting his new role as King.

As one, the people in the room yelled, "Long live the King! Long live the King!" Alexander smiled slightly, feeling alone in his role and power. He would be treated with deference and respect, more so than before, and he had no one with whom to share his troubles. The one person he had decided would have been so suited for him, who would have been the best companion possible in his life was gone. And he wasn't sure that he would ever see her again.

CHAPTER 21

Time moved on, and while both Crow and Alexander longed for the other, they never sought the other out. Alexander was sure he would go find her, but his duties were heavy and he didn't have the time to scour the land. His father had neglected much of his royal education, waiting until after Alexander came of age. The former king had died too soon, leaving Alexander studying and alone in Kyper. He had no idea where Crow was and while he pestered Jek, the smith was unsure as to where Crow's land was, if it were even in Iona or the Eastern Lands. Alexander, though, planned and thought and went over maps in his spare time, thinking of all the places Crow could have possibly gone. He came up with nothing, and any knowledge that his father might have known was gone, taken with him to the grave.

As for Crow, she loved Alexander more than ever but was sure that he would despise her. After all, she hadn't trusted him with her greatest secret and it was plain that he took her truth as betrayal. So, no matter how much she wanted to simply ride back to Kyper Palace and congratulate him as well as offer her condolences, she could not. She was determined that she would give Alexander space and freedom from a relationship he did not want. Her duties also grew as time went on. The estate was slowly being built up and Crow was beginning to take control over the land. She rode through her land as the estate was in progress, making herself known to her people and spending time in each village, each township, that was under her title. To her surprise, she met with little resistance in taking back her lands. Mostly, that was to do with the people who had travelled to the Kyper fair and seen her fight to defend her honour.

Two years passed in this manner, with both Crow and Alexander caught up in the responsibilities belonging to them and each falling more in love with the other as each day passed. Alexander lost some of his boyish good looks and grew to become dangerously handsome, despite the sadness in his eyes, and Crow changed as well. She grew her hair out until it rested at her shoulders and, despite her exercising each day vigorously, she gained some figure. She would never be a curvaceous woman, with her small breasts and narrow hips, but it was nigh impossible to hide her gender under the guise of bandages any longer.

"Crow," her head builder said, watching her carefully after she had attacked the ground with a hoe. She grunted in response and the man sighed. He was shorter and bearded but with burly arms and a thick waist and he somehow managed to intimidate Crow. "People are beginning to talk."

Crow snorted and straightened, fixing her hair so that it was tied back in a horse-tail. "The moment people stop talking is when I'll be worried," she said, then caught the expression on the builder's face. "Malcolm, no need to be so worried. What are they saying about me?"

"Well," Malcolm said uneasily, driving the point of his shovel into the ground. "You're a pretty woman, Crow. Beautiful, in fact," he said. Crow raised her eyebrows in question and tilted her head, a few strands of her black hair framing her pale face. "But people are worried that with you spending all your time in breeches and a shirt, you'll never find a husband."

At this, Crow tilted her head backwards and laughed, her voice ringing out and making the other workers look at her in awe and worry. She shook her head and returned her attention to Malcolm, "And is it a problem that I don't have one?"

Malcolm lowered his head, fiddling with the hem of his shirt, "I don't think so, no. But most of the others think it is a serious problem. You see, we don't want the line to die out. You're a good person, Crow, and we just want to see you get settled into your home. We want you happy."

"Oh, Malcolm," Crow said, leaning her weight on the hoe and looking up at the sky. "You should know by now that I'm a terrible home-maker. I spend hours in the forge, exercise via hand to hand combat and Mak'tal, would rather be outside than in and I don't know the first thing about being lady like. Finding a husband that'll put up with me is going to be harder than you think."

Malcolm stuttered at this and his face flushed. Crow didn't see, her gaze fixed on the clouds slowly moving across the sky. "Maybe you don't need to know all the things about being a lady, right away, that is."

"Oh?" Crow asked, turning her head to look at the builder. He was recovered by now and gave Crow an encouraging smile and a nod. "Then what do I have to do to satisfy my people? Up and marry the first person who asks? Which," she said, pointing her finger at Malcolm, "has not happened yet, mind you." Crow's thoughts flew to Leon and she swallowed down a blush, still as capable of hiding her emotions as ever. She had been in an understanding with Leon and she knew that if she had loved him, he would have married her and she him. She hadn't loved him. But Crow wasn't going to tell Malcolm that.

"WELL," THE BUILDER SAID, KICKING AT A ROCK WITH his foot. Crow smiled; this conversation was obviously far more awkward for Malcolm than it was for her. "If you just wore a dress every now and again..."

Crow balked, waving her hands in front of her, "No, no. I haven't worn a dress since I was six. I wouldn't know the first thing about walking or moving or styles or fashions or anything. I like breeches. I can move in breeches."

"You wouldn't have to wear one all the time," Malcolm argued, voice becoming slightly stern, as if Crow were a child to be reprimanded. She looked at him sheepishly, wanting desperately to duck her head and hide. "Just every once in a while. It would make people happy and let them know that you're getting settled into your position."

Crow opened her mouth to reply and considered. Her people could be quite stubborn. And maybe they had a point. She sighed instead and put the hoe on the ground, "Fine. Lead me to the dress-maker." Malcolm grimaced but nodded as Crow glared at him. He abandoned his work and the two walked from the estate into town where Crow was greeted by all the people. As Malcolm extracted her from a conversation with a cow keeper, pulling her towards the dress-maker's shop, it was fairly obvious that people were whispering and talking.

Crow went into the shop and was struck immediately by how feminine it was and how out of place she felt. There were fabrics everywhere and a tall mirror on the far wall. A pedestal was positioned in front of the mirror and there were sewing implements of all sorts, which Crow was certain she would not know how to use. A plump woman with a starched apron blinked as she took in Crow and Malcolm then split into a grin, moving swiftly to snatch Crow's wrist. Malcolm moved to leave but Crow glared at him.

"You're not going anywhere," she said, voice low. "You got me into this mess and you're going to stay until it's done." Malcolm looked at Crow in horror but the dressmaker negated Crow's order.

"Tosh," the woman said, pulling Crow to the pedestal. "This is a woman's profession and a shop for women. Go back to your work, Malcolm. I'll send her to you when I'm done."

"Right," the builder said, relief on his features, "thanks, Miriam." The woman waved Malcolm away and Crow blinked as the builder left. Miriam looked at Crow and circled, her eye critical.

"Alright, I assume you are going to want dresses, since that's what I do and I know you don't own one. And you're going to need gowns in beautiful blues and greens. Yes, greens that will match your eyes. I'll stay away from reds for now, but how about purple? Purple would look wonderful! And besides gowns, you'll need clothes for every-day. Those don't have to be quite so fine, but since you are a Duchess, I think they should reflect your station. We'll make them easy to move in and breathe. And riding habits, yes. Perhaps more masculine than I would usually do, but I think we can come up with something for your riding," Miriam exclaimed over Crow and set to work, attacking the beautiful Duchess with pins and needles, commenting over the newest fashions and taking measurements.

As Crow was completely overwhelmed in the dressmaker's shop, Alexander was pacing his study, reports of taxes in his hand. They had already been checked by the collectors, but he liked to go over the final reports. Alexander muttered under his breath as he reviewed the numbers and holdings, noting with pleasure that the holdings of the former Duke of Westmont were doing exceptionally well now that the land was under the people's command. Thinking of the Duke of Westmont had Alexander thinking of Crow and he felt the all too familiar pang in his chest. Alexander sighed and his manservant was immediately at his side.

"Do you need anything, your Majesty?" the man asked, holding out a goblet of water.

"No, Geoff," Alexander growled, his pacing quickening as his mind turned over Crow. Geoff recognised the symptoms and leaned his weight against a wall, arms folded.

"Thinking of her, again? You're going to have to realise that you're not going to find her," the man said, voice gentle but the words cutting Alexander to the core.

"I know," the King whispered, looking at the sword at his side, running his hands over the metal as he had done a thousand times before. "But I love her."

"That's all well and good," Geoff replied carefully, thinking on how best to phrase his words. But where Geoff was a reliable manservant, he was not subtle nor cunning. "But your people are expecting you to marry and provide them with an heir. They think that you should have been married almost as soon as you became King. It's been two years since then, and you haven't heard hide nor tail of Crow."

"What would you have me do?" Alexander snarled. "Give up and marry the next noblewoman I see?" He picked up the tax reports again and resumed his pacing, ignoring the conversation that Geoff had brought up until he couldn't any longer. "I know that my duty to my people is to marry and give an heir, but Geoff, I can't marry someone unless I love her and the only person I could ever love like that is Crow."

"Of course, Sire," Geoff sighed and shook his head, drinking from the goblet he had offered to Alexander earlier. The King grumbled under his breath and ran his hands through his hair, returning his broken attention to the tax reports. He went through the papers silently, then paused and stared in disbelief.

"Amazing," Alexander said, a slight grin on his face. He leaned against his desk and looked at the paper, reading it through a second then third time.

"Sire?" Geoff asked. Alexander looked at his manservant and chuckled slightly, handing over the paper. Geoff looked at it then looked up, confused, "It's just a report on the Shadow Lake holdings. The Duchess Tyra Gabbon seems to be doing very well, though I haven't heard her name before."

"When Crow was still here and Sir Leon had just arrived, we travelled to the former Duke of Westmont's holdings. On the first night of camping, Leon told a story about the missing, mysterious Duke of Shadow Lake. The claim was that there was an heir who would return one day to claim his birthright. Neither Crow nor I believed him, though it was a good story. Apparently, though, it's true. But the heir is an heiress. The missing holders of Shadow Lake have returned," Alexander said, the memory strong. He smiled to himself as he thought of Crow and her blatant disbelief of the story. Then, the pain in his heart returned and the smile fell from his face.

Geoff watched all this in silence then, "Maybe you should pay this Duchess Tyra Gabbon a visit. It might be just the distraction you need."

Alexander paused and looked at his manservant with a question written on his face. He had never known Geoff to be clever, but the man had presented a rather good idea. "You may be right," Alexander said. "I'll depart in the morning."

"And who knows, you may fall in love with Lady Tyra and forget all about Crow," Geoff grinned and Alexander sighed, rolling his eyes. The tactless Geoff returned. Alexander moved from his study into his room and began preparing a pack.

"I doubt it," Alexander said in response. "But a distraction is a distraction and I'll take it. Besides, I've not taken time for myself in I don't know how long." The matter was settled and Alexander left in the morning, wearing simple clothes so as to be identified as anything other than the King. He had his finery to wear when he arrived at Shadow Lake and, wishing he had Crow with him, he rode off, alone.

A little over two weeks passed and Crow surveyed the completed estate, a grin on her face, "It's beautiful. Much better than it was."

"I think anything would have been better than it was," Malcolm said and Crow shot him a look. "And it isn't really done, yet. You have to get furniture and trappings. I don't think the single pack and chest will make it seem lived in, but you have a home."

Crow stood for a moment longer, staring at the grand stone edifice, the sun glittering on the glass. It was smaller than most estates, but Crow did not have a large family and she didn't want to be knocking about in the place alone. "Thank you," she said to Malcolm. "It's so much more than I ever imagined."

The builder, wearing his nicest shirt for the occasion looked at Crow. She, too, had dressed up for the unveiling of her new home and wore a green dress in a beautiful silk, the waist narrow and the skirt full. The top was square cut and fell off her shoulders, emphasising their curve and adding a femininity to her muscle. Crow had put her hair in an up-do, the most she could manage with the help of one of the maids at the inn, and a single strand of hair curled around her neck, making it graceful and slender. She was stunning, her beauty fully developed and her manner unassuming. With her black hair and pale skin, she shone like a faerie and, despite the fact that her origins were well known, Crow was believed by the townspeople to have been delivered to the Jackal by faeries.

Crow strode forwards, walking up the path to the house, still unused to the feel of the dress around her legs. But she found that she was slowly becoming accustomed to it and her movements were almost as graceful as ever. Malcolm let her walk to the house on her own and Crow opened the great wooden doors with a push, awe writing itself over her face. She stood in the entrance for many minutes, just taking in the building. It was beautiful and simple and, most importantly, it was hers.

So engrossed was she that Crow did not hear the sound of a horse approaching. The crunch of gravel under the rider's foot was missed as well and it wasn't until the person called out, "Duchess? Lady Tyra?" that Crow realised she was not alone.

Still staring at the entrance, the sun illuminating the grand room as well as her skin, Crow acknowledged her company, "Do you like it? It was just finished today." She turned, fully intending to continue and froze, shock the only thing preventing her legs from collapsing underneath her. "Alexander?"

The King had stumbled backwards as Crow had turned, leaning his weight against his horse for support. He took in her figure, her dress, her hair, her face and was struck by her beauty, but also by the familiarity in her eyes. "Crow," Alexander whispered, joy blooming within him. His love, his Crow, more beautiful than ever and yet still the same, somehow, was standing before him, stunned and wearing an expression of shock and love. Swallowing, Crow nodded in response to her name but did not move. Fear filled her, contrasting with the love she wanted so desperately to embrace.

Grinning suddenly, Alexander raced forwards, bounding up the steps to the great door where Crow was standing. He wrapped his arms around her waist and spun her around, blue eyes meeting green ones with no anger, no hurt or betrayal, just love. He laughed and set Crow down gently, touching his forehead with hers.

Crow smiled and her breath hitched slightly as she realised she was crying. Glittering tears dripped down her cheeks and Alexander gently reached out to touch her chin, tilting her head upwards and wiping the tears away. Crow laughed softly and smiled further. How long she had waited for this day, for the time when Alexander would touch her lovingly, willingly.

"So," Alexander said, pulling Crow to his chest and kissing her hair. Crow responded in kind, wrapping her arms around him and pressing her face to his chest, breathing in his scent. "Your birthright is Shadow Lake and you're a Duchess. And Crow isn't even your real name?"

Crow laughed and shook her head as much as she could without losing contact with Alexander, "Not even a father as cruel as Kamal Gabbon, the Jackal, would name his daughter Crow. I picked that up from some taunts thrown at me and it has been my name ever since. My father named me Tyra. It means war, which is much more appropriate, don't you think?"

Alexander scoffed and chuckled, the sound vibrating through his body. Crow closed her eyes as she felt it and sighed as she smiled. "Much more appropriate, though I think I like Crow better."

"Me, too. That's why I kept it," Crow said, looking up at Alexander and smiling. Alexander noticed how her features had changed subtly; her eyes were brighter, her lips fuller and more rosy. Or perhaps it was just because he was seeing her after so long.

"Crow," he murmured, lifting a hand to stroke the

skin on her cheek. Crow trembled involuntarily under his touch and closed her eyes, her breath coming out faster. Alexander smiled as he felt her breasts grow taught against him and he responded in kind, making Crow smile. "My Crow, a Duchess. Is there anything else I should know about you, just so I don't keep getting surprised by you?"

Crow huffed and gave a false pout, "You doubt me? After all this time? What's the fun if I can't surprise you?"

"None, love," Alexander said. Crow blinked in surprise as he uttered that last word then smiled fully, the corners of her eyes crinkling in pure delight. "But I would appreciate if you would let me know anything major. Just so I can stop doubling over in surprise every time we have a conversation."

Crow pressed her head against Alexander's chest again and said, barely loud enough for him to hear, "I'm desperately in love with you."

Alexander pulled Crow back, his hands on her shoulders and for a moment, Crow was afraid that he would push her away, just as they had found each other. But there was no anger in Alexander's blue eyes, only happiness and love and passion. "But I already knew that."

And he kissed her.

The End

ABOUT THE AUTHOR

E.G. Stone is an independent author who has been writing, quite literally, since the age of six. Since then, E.G. has improved rather a lot and has written several full-length novels, various short stories, a screenplay, snippets of poetry, and various blog entries that may or may not make sense. E.G. enjoys writing in many different genres. The favourites are science fiction, mystery (preferably of the murder variety), adventure, fantasy — basically anything where the world isn't quite what you would expect. When not writing, she is off musing about the workings of languages, both real and created, or wandering around and experiencing new people, places and things. E.G. reads voraciously, perhaps to the point of slight-insanity. Weird, nerdy, perhaps a little crazy, she is having a grand old time writing, reading, reviewing, interviewing, and causing trouble.

ALSO BY E.G. STONE

Speaker of Words

The Wing Cycle:

The One Who Could Not Fly

To Never Hear the Song

The Forsaking of the Blind

Pestilence and Plague: An Anthology of Stories about the Virus

www.ingramcontent.com/pod-product-compliance
Lightning Source LLC
Chambersburg PA
CBHW060548310726
48982CB00008B/1047/J

* 9 7 8 1 7 3 4 7 9 6 5 9 9 *